17 Days from Galveston

The final Journey

17 Days from Galveston

The final Journey

Deidre Whipple Lopez

3 dogs Publishing House
Hitchcock, Texas

ISBN 979-8-987-1516-2-4 ebook
ISBN 979-8-987-1516-3-1 paperback
ISBN 979-8-987-1516-4-8 hardback

Cover Picture by Deidre Whipple Lopez
Editing by Kimberly Beecher

Dedication

I would like to dedicate this book to my many friends and family, which supported my first book and encouraged me to keep going. I would like to also thank my friends and family that inspired the characters of this book.

And finally, I want to thank my mom Collene, and husband Josh, for putting up with me when I come to you for advice. Thanks for your love and support!

TABLE OF CONTENT

CHAPTER ONE

Day One at the Deer Lease

Day 1

We had been on this road a thousand times before, but it had been over a year since we had been back. The trees and the weeds in the ditches looked way overgrown. We had heard they had gotten a lot of rain this summer. The deer lease was our home away from home. It was deep in the woods of East Texas.

Doug and Barb, and their 2 teenage daughters, lived in a home Doug's grandfather had built many years ago. Where the county road and the driveway met, there was an enormous gate and an old iron sign that hung above it that read "The Strong's." Once you got through the gate, it had a long drive with tall pine trees on both sides. Sometimes the forest service would come through and thin out the pines. But it had been many years since they did it last. The forest along the drive was very dense. You couldn't see past the first row. The drive curved twice before you came to another smaller iron gate and a cattle guard you had to cross. Once you crossed the cattle guard, you were inside the 5-acre compound. There was no fence, but a dense forest surrounded the compound. The main house was in the middle, a garage and workshop were beside it. In the back was a large barn and five tiny cabins along the forest line. Doug and Jay, with the help of Jay's dad, Nate, had built each of the five tiny cabins. During deer season, they rented the cabins out to hunters and allowed them to hunt on the 700 plus acres surrounding the compound. The barn housed several 4-wheelers that the hunters could use. Once a year during memorial weekend we would have a family reunion, and the family would stay in the cabins and ride the 4-wheelers.

Along the west side of the compound were utility buildings that held the rainwater collecting system, the many batteries for the solar power, and generators. Next to the utility building was a metal door in the ground that led to an underground bunker. Although, it was mainly used to store food and other supplies.

On the east side were ten RV pads. Anytime we stayed, we always parked our RV in the 1st spot. Everyone knew that was our spot.

Outside the compound was over 700 acres of combination forest, pastureland, and a river that ran along the south side of the property. They could also find hundreds of ATV trails and hiking trails.

It had been 17 days since the entire world went dark, and everything stopped. The people that survived the first wave of car crashes and airplane crashes now had to survive the second wave of hunger, thirst, and vicious gangs of people that wanted what they had. It hadn't even been a day when people started looting and breaking into businesses and homes, taking what they wanted.

Ten days ago, we left our home in Las Vegas and made our way to East Texas. As we topped the hill and looked toward the gate. A huge chain was wrapped around the gate to keep it locked. Three large solar spotlights shined down from either corner of the Iron sign and two fire pits with a roaring fire on either side of the gates lit up the entire area. As the scene came into focus from the firelight, I screamed; "Oh my GOD." Hanging from the large iron sign were three bodies. The bodies were hanging by their feet and all three of them had hoods covering their heads.

Jay slammed on the brakes. The others came running out of the bunkroom. "What is going on?" Dre asked. But all Jay and I could do was stare. Vickie and Dre bent down and looked out the window. "Oh my God!" Vickie said. Jay opened the bus door and got out slowly. I followed him out of the bus. "Who is it?" I cried. "I don't know. It's too dark to tell," he replied. The bodies were too high to reach, but from the looks of the clothing, we could tell they were all men. Their clothing was dirty and torn. "Stay here. I'm going to see if I can open the gate. If not, I'm going to climb over it and run to the house," Jay commanded. I stood by the bus staring at the bodies, trying to see any familiarity that I could see in the dark. Vickie, Dre, and Casey joined me, standing and staring. "We don't know who it is yet," I said. "I just pray it's not any of our family," I said under my breath.

Jay couldn't get the chain off because of a heavy-duty lock joining the two chains. "I'm going to run up to the house," he yelled. "Be careful. You don't know what has happened in there," I yelled back.

Jay jumped over the fence, pulled his handgun out of the back of his pants and started jogging towards the compound. Not getting very far because of being out of shape and being too dark to see, he slowed down to a fast walk. Suddenly, rustling in the trees to his right caught his attention. He stopped. Not making any noise. He heard a rifle cock. Suddenly, a light appeared around a tree. All he could see was the beam of the light swaying back and forth as the person was walking towards him. Then, suddenly, the lights were pointed right in his eyes, blinding him. "Jay is that you?" a familiar voice came from behind the light. "Doug?" he replied, "Oh my God, I'm glad to see you," Jay said. Doug pointed the light away from Jay's eyes and ran to him as they hugged. "Who is that hanging from the gate?" Jay asked. "They were part of a gang of people that tried to force their way into the compound. I figured if I hung them there, others would think twice about trying anything," Doug responded. "Oh, Thank God it's not family," Jay said.

Doug shone his light towards the area Jay had come from. "Where's D'Ann?" Doug asked. "They are waiting on the bus. I couldn't get the gate open," he responded. "They?" Doug asked. "We have a couple of people with us from Las Vegas. We couldn't leave them. It was terrible back in Las Vegas," Jay replied. "Let's go get them and get them in here," as they walked towards the gate.

"Look, I see a light," I said. "Just in case, we should get on the other side of the bus, till we know who it is," I continued. Quickly, we all ran around the bus and got on. Sean and Andie were sitting on the sofa and were watching us. "What's going on?" Sean asked. "Jay went to see what's going on in the compound, and we saw a light coming this way. Not sure who it is, just to be safe, we thought we better get in here."

The light approached slowly. As it came closer, I could see it was Doug and Jay. "It's Jay!" I said, getting up and running out the door of the bus.

"Thank God, it's you!" as I hugged Doug. I pointed to the three hanging bodies. "No one we know," Jay replied as I let out a breath.

Doug walked to the chain on the gate, pulled a key from his pocket, and unlocked it. "Go ahead and drive in. I'll fill you in on everything once we get to the house," Doug said.

Jay and I got back on the bus as he drove through the gate. Doug locked it behind us and climbed onto the bus.

Pulling into the compound, it looked normal. There were lights on in the main house and lights on in the shop. I looked at Doug, "Lights?" I asked. "The solar is up and running," he answered. "Is there hot water?" I asked with a smile on my face. "In the shower house only," he replied. "That will work," I said. They built the shower house last summer when we were there. Jay and Doug installed 3 open air shower stalls, with 3 composting toilets.

"Is your family, okay?" I asked. "Yeah, I had to go get Barb and Ally at the Gun shop, in that old pickup truck, but we made it here." "I can't wait to see her," I replied. "Did my mom and brother make it here?" I asked. "Your mom is in one of the cabins," he said. Tears filled my eyes with excitement to see her. "What about any of our other family?" I asked. He shook his head no. "I'm sorry, no one else has made it," he replied. "But my brother and his family are here. They brought my mom?" I asked.

The bus came to a stop in front of the main house as Doug opened the door and got out. Waiting for an answer, I got up and followed him out the door. Barb came walking out the front door carrying a rifle. "We come in peace," I yelled at her as she put the rifle down and ran towards me. We ran into each other's arms, and both started crying. "You made it, you made it!" she whispered in my ear. "Yeah, it was touch and go for a while, but we made it," I said. "Are you guys, okay?" I asked. "We are safe," she replied.

"Doug said my mom and brother made it. Where's my mom at?" I asked her. "She's in cabin #1," she replied. "I'll be right back, and we will catch up, but I need to go see her, let her know we made it," as I hurried off towards the cabins.

I knocked on the door, and it slowly opened. She looked at me like she couldn't believe it was me. "We made it!" I said as we hugged. "Thank God, I've been praying and praying," she replied. "Are you okay?" I asked. "Just worried about your brothers," she replied. "My brothers? Isn't Jace here?" I asked. "No, him and Collin brought me, but Peggy and the girls were not at home when it happened. Peggy was in Dallas working, and the 3 girls were away at college. Jace went to look for them, but he has been gone for over two weeks. I'm so worried about them," she continued. "There is no way to communicate with anyone, so I have no idea about Mike and Sue, or anyone else in Kansas, she said. I bent down and snuggled with Gracie, her West Highland Terrier. "Well, let's go to the main house and talk with everyone and get filled in on what's going on," I said. She slipped on her shoes, and we walked down the stone path to the main house.

Everyone was sitting out on the porch. Jay got out of his chair and offered it to my mom. "So, what's going on?" I asked. "Did you introduce everyone?" I asked Jay. "No, was waiting for you."

I started down the line as they were sitting. "This is Sean and his wife Andie, mom you remember Sean, don't you?" I asked as she nodded her head. "Vickie, Sean's mom, and Dre, Sean's Brother. Sean and Jay worked together when we first got to Las Vegas. And this little girl here is the best dog watcher I've ever seen. Her name is Casey," I continued. "This is my mom, Kay, and that's Gracie," I said, pointing to her dog. "That is Doug and Barb, over there. They own the place, and their 2 teenage girls are somewhere?" as I shrugged my shoulders looking around. "They are in their room; we got a DVD player, and a TV hooked up to the solar. They are watching a movie," Barb said. "Casey, would you like to go watch it?" she asked. Casey looked at me. "It's okay. Do you want to?" I asked her. Casey shrugged her shoulders and slightly shook her head yes. "I'll go with you and introduce you to the girls. They are around your age," I said as I got out of my chair and grabbed her, putting my arm around her shoulders.

We walked into the house and down the hall to the girl's bedroom. I gently knocked on the door. "Come in," I heard a voice say. I slowly opened the door. "Anyone home?" I asked. "Aunt D'Ann," Abby and Ally yelled in unison. They both got off the floor where they were lying, ran to me, as we all embraced in a hug. "This is Casey. Casey, this is Ally and Abby. Is it alright for Casey to watch the movie with you guys?" I asked. "Sure," Abby said. "We were just getting ready to watch a different one," Ally commented. Abby reached and grabbed Casey's arm and tugged her to the beanbag chair. "Sit here," she said. "Casey, you okay here?" I asked. Casey looked at me and smiled and shook her head yes. I closed the door and went back to the group.

Doug was talking about how he had to rescue Barb and Ally in town. I sat down and Barb looked at me. "So, what's with the teenage girl? Jay said you would explain," she asked. "Well, we found her all alone, waiting for her parents to come home from work after the incident. Their work was on our way, so we took her to her parents, but when we got to where they worked, an airplane had crashed into the building, and they were dead. The only other relatives she had in the area were her grandparents, but they were on vacation in California. That is their bus out there. I couldn't leave her there by herself. She's very quiet and has grown very fond of dogs. Oh, crap, speaking of. I need to ask for a favor. We have Diamond's body on the roof of the bus. I'm sure it is ripe by now, but I just couldn't leave her. Some assholes killed her. Can we bury her over at RV site 1? You know that spot is our home away from home," I asked with tears in my eyes. "Of course," Doug said, looking at Barb for approval. "Thanks, I appreciate that," I said. "We'll get her down in the morning and bury her," Jay said, looking at me.

We finished telling them all the problems we had had since the incident. The people we lost along the way, and all the trouble we had.

Doug and Jay built a small bonfire. We continued talking about our trip from Las Vegas and laughed about old times. It was like the outside world had just melted away.

"I think I'm exhausted. I'm going to go lay down, we will catch up in the morning," I said. "Do you want me to walk you back to your cabin?" I asked my mom. "Yeah, that would be fine," as we both got out of our chairs. I walked her down the path and opened her door. "I'm so worried about your brothers," she said. "How are we going to know if they are, okay? And what about our family in Kansas? I just don't understand what is happening," she added. "It's bad out there. You wouldn't believe the things we saw," I replied. "But I know Mike and Sue will be okay. Mike is too ornery not to survive," I said. "Hopefully we can find out how to communicate with them," I said, trying to make her feel better and not worry. "Maybe when Jace gets back, he can run up to Kansas and get them, bring them back here." I said, "I'll talk with you in the morning," I said as I gave her a hug.

She closed the door behind me as I walked back up the path towards the house. Jay was moving the bus over to "Our Spot" as I walked back to the group. "Casey can stay in the house with the girls if she wants," Barb said. "Okay, just ask her. If she wants to come sleep in her bunk, the door will be unlocked. Just tell her to come on in," I said. "Goodnight," I said as I hugged Barb, then Doug. "Glad you guys are here," Barb whispered in my ear. "Me too," I replied.

Vickie, Dre, Sean, Andie, and I walked back to where Jay had parked the bus. "Should someone keep watch?" Sean yelled back to Doug. "No, I got it handled tonight. You guys get some rest, and we will figure out a watch schedule tomorrow," he replied. As we got to the bus, I let the dogs out to run and go potty. I sat at the picnic table we had bought a few years back. "It's so peaceful here. I feel safe," I said to Jay as he sat beside me and wrapped his arms around me. "I do too, but we still must keep alert. You just never know, people are dying out there and are desperate," he said. We sat and watched the dogs run around and play in the grass for a few more minutes before we went inside and went to bed.

CHAPTER TWO

Sneaking Out

Day Two

The sound of a gunshot made us jump out of bed. The dogs started barking and throwing a fit. It was still dark outside as I looked towards the window. Remembering there was no glass in the window, the gunshot sounded like it was right beside our bus.

Jay slipped on his shoes, grabbed his AR, and ran out the bedroom door. I tried to settle the dogs down so they would stop barking. But as we heard yelling outside, the dogs started up again. I rushed into the kitchen and grabbed some treats. That did the trick. They were too busy eating to pay any attention to the commotion going on outside.

Sean met me coming out of the bunk room with his rifle in hand. "What's going on?" he asked. "Not sure, heard a gunshot and Jay ran out the door with his AR. Are you going out there to see what is going on?" I asked. "Yeah, stay here till I check it out," he replied. The shouting had ended, and I could no longer hear anyone outside. I peeked out the windows but saw nothing. I sat on the sofa waiting for either Jay or Sean to come back in and tell me what was going on.

Jay had his AR and a flashlight ready to go when he went out the bus door. He saw Doug standing on his porch, looking towards the gate. Doug noticed Jay come out of the bus and motioned him to come over to him. "What's going on?" Jay asked as he approached. "I saw movement on the outside of the gate near the road, so I shot in the air to scare whoever was there. I yelled at them to get off our property," he said. "Do you want to walk out there and see if we can see anyone?"

Jay asked Doug. About that time, they saw Sean exit the bus with his rifle, walking towards them. "Everything okay?" Sean asked. Sean was still not one hundred percent after being shot but was feeling a lot better. "We are gonna walk out to the gate area. I saw some movement over there, not sure who or what it was." Doug said as they all started walking towards the gate.

They reached the cattle guard and stood there, looking and listening to anything that moved. They heard what sounded like something running in the woods. Jay and Doug ran towards the sound as Sean stood watch. Shining the flashlight all around, they saw nothing, just the bushes moving where someone, or something ran through it. They continued to follow the noise of running feet. They made it all the way to the county road when they stopped. "You see those men hanging? That will be you if you come back," Jay yelled out to the dark. Moving the light from side to side and up and down the road, they saw nothing more. Whoever or whatever it was, they were gone. They climbed over the barbwire fence and on to the road. Walking back towards the big gate. The smell of the rotting men was almost too much to handle. They both put their shirts up over their noses hoping it would help, but the smell was too bad. After climbing over the gate, Jay ran to the side of the road and vomited all over. Doug grinned and let out a little giggle as Jay stood up, wiping his face. "Fuck you," Jay said. They both took off running up the drive to get away from the smell. They got to the cattle guard where Sean was standing. "Nothing! Whoever or whatever is gone." Jay said. They all walked back towards the house. "You guys should go back to bed. I'll continue to keep watch," Doug said. "Nah, I'm up now. I can keep watch. Why don't you go get some rest?" Jay replied. Sean walked back to the bus, while Doug and Jay walked to the house. Jay sat down on the porch swing with his AR in his lap. "I'll go make you a cup of coffee," Doug said as he went inside.

Sean opened the door to the bus and stepped in. "So, what was it?" I asked. "They chased something into the woods, but never caught up to them. Jay is going to take watch now so Doug can get some rest," Sean replied. "I guess we can all go back to bed," I said as I got up and headed to the bedroom. "See ya in a couple hours," I continued.

I laid back in bed. I just kept replaying the evening in my head. Wondering how we would get communication with my family in Kansas, my mind kept replaying the evening until finally my eyes closed.

The dogs started stirring around, making the bed move. I opened my eyes and Tator was standing there staring at me. "What?" I spoke. "Do you guys gotta go potty?" I asked. I got up, and the three ran to the bedroom door, scratching and prancing around, eager to get outside. "Hold on!" I opened the door, and they all ran out to the bus door.

Vickie was sitting in the recliner drinking a cup of coffee. "Good morning!" she said. "What was all the racket last night?" she asked. "Guess they saw something, but Jay and Doug chased them away," I replied.

Dre and Andie walked out of the bunkroom. "Good morning!" I said to them. Dre waved his hand, and Andie smiled. "What are we going to do today?" Andie asked. "I guess we need to get with Doug and Barb to see what needs done," I replied. "I know since none of our family made it from Galveston, we need to make some plans to go after them," I said. The three of them looked at me with horror on their faces. "You mean go out there again?" Vickie said. "I can't sit here not knowing what happened to my kids and Jay's family." I replied. Vickie nodded her head like she understood.

Vickie and I stepped out of the bus and walked towards the house. Jay was still on the porch swing drinking a cup of coffee. "You tired?" I asked as I approached. "Yeah, but we have too much to do today. We need to secure the perimeter of the area in case those people come back." As I sat down beside him, I said, "we need to talk about going to get our family in Galveston." He turned and gave me the same look the others gave me when I said it earlier. "I'm not going to sit here and not know what has happened to them. I will go by myself if I have to, but I am going!" I demanded. Jay starred at me for the longest time. I could see him thinking but wasn't sure what he would do. "No, there is no way I'm letting you go by yourself. Give me a couple of days to get the fence up and help Doug," he said. I looked at him with tears in my eyes. "Don't worry, we will go. Just let me get things settled first. We just got here," Jay said.

I got up from the swing and pouted as I walked off towards my mom's cabin.

Knocking a little too hard on the door. Kay came and opened the door quickly, while Gracie was barking up a storm. "What? What is it?" she asked, all out of breath. "Can I come in?" I asked. "Jeez, don't scare me like that," she scolded opening the door wider to allow me to walk in. I could tell she hadn't been up long; she had a robe on and a cup of coffee sitting on the side table. "I just want you to know I'm going to Galveston to find Jordan and Ashlyn, and Jay's family." Again, for the third time, I got that look of horror. "Casey will take care of you and Gracie if you need anything. Will you help her take care of my dogs while I'm gone?" I asked. "Who is going with you?" she asked. "Well, I hope Jay and maybe Sean, but I'm willing to go by myself if they don't wanna go. I must find out if my kids are okay." Looking at me like I was crazy, she said, "you can't go by yourself, that's just crazy!" I looked at her with tears in my eyes. "Well, if Jay won't go, I have no choice but to go by myself," I said as I walked towards the door. "I'll talk to you about it later when I have my plans figured out." I said as I closed the door behind me and started walking towards the bus.

Wiping the tears from my cheek as I walked from the cabin, I started devising a plan. Getting on the bus, I grabbed the maps that were still on the table, shut and locked myself in the bedroom. I plopped down on the bed and buried my face in my pillow and cried. Several minutes went by as the anger welled up inside. "I'm going to do this, even if I have to do it alone," I said out loud. I spread the map out on the bed and grabbed the pen and paper lying on the floor and wrote out my route.

I heard a soft knock at the door. "D'Ann, are you in there?" came a soft voice. I stuffed the map and pad of paper under my pillow and got up to open the door. Casey was standing there. "Watcha doing?" she asked. "I was wondering if I could ask you for a favor?" I said. "Sure, what is it?" She replied. "I was hoping you would stay here and would take care of my mom and the dogs while we go get my kids and

Jay's family?" I asked. "Of course, I will," she agreed. "When are you going?" she asked. "Jay said a couple of days, but I can't wait. The longer we wait, the worse it will get," I said. "You can't go by yourself. It's too dangerous," she begged. I took Casey's hand and set her down on the bed. "Look Casey, I really need your help. I'm counting on you to take care of my mom and my dogs. If something happens to me, God forbid, I need you to be here for them. Can you do this for me?" I asked her. Casey had tears streaming down her face but shook her head yes slowly. "One other thing. You can't say anything to anyone I'm leaving. Not even Jay. Promise me, promise me." I begged. "Okay, I promise," as she hugged me. "Now, how did you get along with the twins?" I asked her. "I really like them. They are cool," she said. "Cool," I agreed with a smile. "Let's go see what's going on outside," as we got up and walked down the hall and out of the bus.

I could see Barb working in the garden on the side of the house. Casey and I walked over to see if she needed any help. "Good morning, well, almost noon," I said, looking at the placement of the sun. "Need any help?" I asked. "No, just picking out the weeds," she replied. "Let's go get a cold drink," she said, picking up her gloves and stretching her back while reaching towards the sun. We walked towards the house, as Jay and Doug were stretching out wire fencing on the ground. Dre and Sean were holding one end of the fence so they could pull it straight.

We walked into the house as Barb walked over to the refrigerator. "How long does the solar last to keep the electric on? I'm clueless about this stuff," I said. "We have several batteries, so it's been going 24/7 now since all this crap started." She added. Barb handed me a cold Diet Coke. "OMG, are you serious?" I said, so excited I couldn't stand myself. "Where did you get this?" Barb looked at me with the biggest smile. "I've been saving it for you," she said. "I love you; I love you; I love you," I replied. I popped the can open and took a drink. It had been over two weeks since I had a cold Diet Coke. I thought I was in heaven. I sipped it and savored every sip. Barb laughed at me. "Oh, you have no idea," I said. We both laughed and sat down at the kitchen table. "I'm going to go play with the dogs,"

Casey said as she walked back towards the door. "Yeah, I guess I need to go clean and organize the bus, unless you need help doing anything," I said. "No, I think I'm good. I have a big deer roast in the roaster oven for dinner tonight," she replied. "Sounds good, as I got up and went to the front door." I turned to Barb, "so Doug came and got you in that old truck out back when this all happened? I can't believe it started. He didn't have to do anything to it. You guys were lucky. You would have had to walk all the way home," I said. "Yeah, it's been a great truck. We've run to town in it a couple times now," she added. "How did you get diesel in it?" I asked. "We have some gas cans in the back of the bed. We filled them up the last time we went to town. Should last us quite a while," she added as she got up and headed to the bathroom. "Okay, then I'll see ya later. Holler if you need any help doing anything," I yelled as she shut the bathroom door. I noticed car keys handing by the front door and made a mental note of where they were.

Vickie and Andie were sitting on the porch. "Anything we can do to help?" Vickie asked. "No, I don't think so. If you guys want to move into the cabins so you have your own spaces, I'm sure it would be alright. "Yeah, I think Sean and I would like to get our own space," Andie replied. "Dre and I can share one," Vickie added.

"If I remember right, cabin 5 has two twin beds in there, it might work for you guys," I said.

We all headed to the bus. Vickie and Andie started packing their stuff as I went to the bedroom and shut and locked the door. I pulled out the map and pad of paper. Looking at the map, I figured it best to take highway 259 to Nacogdoches and then 59 down to Livingston. We usually always stayed on 59 all the way through Houston, but I wanted to avoid Houston if I could, so I decided to take 146 from Livingston all the way down. I hoped and prayed they had stayed at home and were not stuck on the road somewhere. It would be a nightmare trying to figure out which way they went. Highway 146 would take me to the outskirts of Houston and all the way to Galveston.

My plan was to pick up Nate and Veronica first, Jay's dad and stepmom. Nate would be able to help me if I needed fire power. Then

I would head to Jordan and Ashlyn's place. I figured they stayed at the dog rescue, not wanting to leave so they could take care of the dogs. After that, I would try my best to get to Jay's sisters and their families. I knew there wouldn't be enough room inside the truck, but I don't think they would mind riding in the back just to get out of there. That was the plan.

I closed my eyes and said a prayer that everyone was okay, and it would all work out according to my plan. "Now, how am I going to get out of here without anyone seeing me or stopping me?" I asked myself. "Oh crap, how am I going to get the lock on the gate off?" I spoke. "I wonder if the padlock key is on the truck keys," I thought to myself.

I grabbed a small backpack from the closet and threw a couple of items of clothing in. Then opened the bedroom door to see if anyone was still on the bus. Vickie and Andie were just coming out of the bunkroom. "We are going to go check out the cabins. We'll be right back," Vickie said as they went out the door.

I hurried to the pantry, grabbing granola bars and protein bars, shoving them into my bag. Then grabbing several bottles of water in the cupboard under the stove where we had stored the extra bottles of water we had gotten from the military base and shoved them into my bag. I stood there for a few seconds, thinking of anything else I might need along the way. I went back to the bedroom and grabbed Jay's backpack. Going back to the pantry, I grabbed several MREs, just in case. It was a 5-hour drive from the deer lease to Galveston, on a good day. No telling what I would run into this time. But I needed to be prepared.

Going back to the bedroom, I stuffed the bags in the bottom of the closet and laid my jacket over them. I went to the bedside table and pulled out 3 boxes of 38 Special bullets. "I'm going to need this, probably," I said as I stuffed them in the side of the bag. I sat down on the bed to think about what else I could possibly need.

I heard the bus door open. "D'Ann, you in here?" Jay asked. "Yeah, just cleaning up a little. What's up?" I asked as I heard him walking to the bedroom. I quickly shut the closet doors.

He sat down on the bed next to me and grabbed my hand. "Look, I must help Doug put up this fence around the perimeter of the property so we can be more secure. It will take us a couple days to finish, and then if our family hasn't shown up, then we can talk about going to find them. Okay? Are you good with that?" Jay asked. I looked down at the floor. "I guess I have to be," I said. Jay put his arm around me and gave me a hug. "It will be okay," he said. "I know," I replied. "If I take my gun with me, can I take the dogs on a walk down the road? I know there are some wild blackberries that grow out there. Doesn't a blackberry cobbler sound good for dinner?" I asked. "I don't know if you should," he replied. "I'll be careful, any problems and I head back right away," I said. Jay shrugged his shoulder and shook his head like he didn't care.

We got up and headed outside. Casey was sitting in the grass with Tator on her lap, while the other two dogs rolled around her. "Hey Casey, you want to go for a walk with me and the dogs?" I yelled at her. "Be careful!" Jay added and walked to where Doug and Sean were working on the fence.

"I need to run to the house for a second, be right back," I said as I walked to the house. I opened the front door and Vickie and Barb were in the kitchen getting dinner ready. I stepped inside the house but stood right in front of the keys. I watched Barb and Vickie and the second they both had their backs turned, I grabbed the car keys. "You all need any help?" I asked, knowing they would say no. "Nope, we got it," Barb said. "Okay, I see ya in a bit," I replied, walking back out the door.

Casey, I and the three dogs walked out the first gate and headed down the road. "Why are we walking out here?" she asked. "I need to see if this key works on that big lock on the gate," I replied. "I really don't like it that you are going," she said. "I know, but I planned the safest route, and I will be very careful," I said. "Remember, you promised not to say anything," she looked at me and shook her head. "I know I won't say anything."

We made it to the gate. The smell from the hanging bodies was almost unbearable. I hurried and checked the lock to see if the key would work and it unlocked. I locked it back and put the keys in my pocket. As fast as we could, we walked back to the compound. The dogs were exhausted and thirsty. I took them inside the bus and gave them water and a treat. Casey sat down on the sofa and pulled out her headphones to listen to her CDs. Looking at the battery-operated clock on the counter, it was nearing 3pm. "I'm going to go take a little nap," I said to Casey. "Okay, I'll be right here," she replied.

I laid on the bed trying to sleep, but my mind would not stop thinking about my trip tonight. I finally decided to quit fighting sleep and go check on my mom.

Casey had fallen asleep with all three dogs on the sofa. Brooklyn looked up at me but paid no mind. I slipped out the door and walked towards the house. Kay and Vickie were sitting on the porch both with a glass of wine talking. "What's going on?" I asked as I sat down in the chair next to Vickie. "Nothing, just talking," my mom replied. "I guess I will go see if Barb needs help with dinner," Vickie said as she got up out of her chair.

My mom looked at me with a serious look on her face. "Are you still planning on going to Galveston to get Jordan?" she asked. I looked at her, then looked around to see if anyone was nearby. "I am, but I don't want anyone to know," I replied. "Promise me you won't say anything to anyone." I begged. "I don't think you should do it. What if you and Jay have trouble?" she asked. Remembering I didn't tell her I was going by myself. I didn't answer. I stared out towards the forest.

After several minutes, Vickie came out the door. "Dinners ready! Can you go tell the guys out back?" she asked while looking at me. "Yeah, I'll go tell them," I replied.

I walked towards the back of the property where Doug, Jay, Sean, and Dre were working on the fence. "Dinner's ready!" I yelled. Doug looked up. "Be right there," he yelled back. I walked to the bus and woke Casey up and told her to come and eat.

We all sat outside on the picnic tables we had built a few summers ago, where we had our big potlucks at the family reunions. It felt like old times, like nothing had happened in the world, like the world had not changed completely.

"This is a great dinner, Barb," I said as I picked around the deer meat. I didn't much care for deer meat, unless it was processed and cooked right, without that gamey taste. But knowing that was what I would be eating probably for the rest of my life, I knew I had to get used to it.

It was now getting close to dark. The men decided to call it a day and get to bed early so they could get an early start in the morning. "Who's on watch tonight?" I asked before everyone dispersed. "Well, we haven't made a schedule out yet. We need to do that," Doug replied. "I can take watch for a while; I had a nap today and was not tired. I'm sure you guys are exhausted after working on the fence all day," I said. Doug looked at Jay as if he was looking for his permission. Jay shrugged his shoulders and shook his head slightly, indicating a yes. "Okay, I guess you can take watch," Doug said.

"Wake me up around midnight or 1am unless you get tired before that, or if anything happens," Jay said as he got up to walk to the bus. I got up, took his plate and mine into the kitchen, rinsed them off and put them in the rack to dry. Then I followed him to the bus. "Which rifle do you want me to use?" I asked as we stepped on the bus. He grabbed the rifle sitting in the passenger seat, checked that it was loaded. "Where are the extra bullets for this?" I asked, "you know, just in case." Jay reached under the passenger seat and pulled out a big storage box that had several boxes of bullets. "Here, take one of these boxes, but you shouldn't need them. If you have any trouble or see anything, come wake me," he said. "Okay, I will. I'm sure things will be fine, especially since you guys got most of the fence up on the back side of the property." I replied.

I grabbed the box of shells he handed me and went out the door. Casey was walking up from my mom's cabin when I met her on the path. "I helped your mom to her cabin and got her settled," she said. "Thank you so much," I replied. "I really appreciate everything you're doing. I know it's tough for you right now. But just know we are your family now," I said with tears in my eyes. She reached out and hugged me as she whispered in my ear, "you're going tonight, aren't you?" she asked. "Yes, I'm leaving, and I'm trusting you to take care of my mom and my dogs," I said. "I will, I promise," she replied. We hugged tighter and then released each other as she turned to walk to the bus.

I walked over to the porch and sat down on the swing. "I will give everyone about 2 hours to fall into a deep sleep. Hopefully, they won't hear the truck start," I said to myself. The truck was parked on the other side of the barn, quite a way from the house and bus.

The night was still. The lights in the house had been out for over an hour now. I knew Jay would be in a deep sleep quickly after lying down. I walked around the side of the house to see if any of the cabins had lights on, but they were dark as well. "I'm gonna give it another hour, then I'm going," I said under my breath.

I walked to the bus, slowly and quietly opened the door. I could hear Jay snoring, so I knew he was in a deep sleep. I opened the door to the bedroom and saw that the dogs were nowhere in sight. I backed up and opened the door to the bunk room, and there they were, all snuggled up with Casey. I gently closed her door and tiptoed to the bedroom, opened the closed door, and grabbed both backpacks from under the jacket. "I better take this too," I thought to myself as I put the jacket over my shoulder. Then, quiet as I could, I went back out of the bedroom and shut the door. I reached down and grabbed a couple more boxes of rifle bullets and stuffed them in the already full bags and walked out the bus door.

I unlocked the truck, threw the bags in the seat, then shut the door. I looked in the bed of the truck and saw three large gas cans. I couldn't quite reach them to see how much diesel was in them, so I shoved them with my fingers. They didn't budge. "Must be full." I hoped. I was going to wait another 30 to 45 minutes before I left. I walked back to the porch and sat down on the swing. Staring out to the forest and planning my trip in my head.

Seemed like only 15 minutes went by and I could no longer contain myself. I had to leave. Making sure all the lights were still out in the cabins and the house, I walked around the barn and got in the truck. "Okay, here it goes. I'm going to start it and take off. Hopefully, no one will hear the engine. But I'm not going to stop if they do." I turned the key, and the truck started. I looked at the gas gauge. "FULL" it said. Put the truck in reverse and back up. At this point I could see the house and the bus. "No lights yet." I slowly drove out the gate, looking behind me to see if there was any movement. I got to the main gate, unlocked it, drove out, and locked it back, then headed towards the highway.

It was close to midnight when I reached the highway. No lights for as far as I could see. It was completely dark, not even the moon was out. The road would probably be clear till I got closer to Henderson, which was about 30 miles. Passing a few cars and 18-wheelers that were stranded on the highway, with no people around. They had burnt the only gas station between the deer lease and Henderson to the ground as I passed it. My stomach was still in my throat as I continued to drive. "I must calm down. I must keep a clear head," I said out loud. As I approached the outskirts of Henderson. Up ahead I could see torches burning. "Crap, a roadblock." I pulled over to the side of the road, reached down and grabbed the map out of the side pocket of my backpack. "Is there a back road to get to highway 259?" I asked myself. Looking at the map, "If I backtrack a couple miles, there is a county road I can take. Looks like I must take a couple, but it will get me there, eventually."

I turned the truck around and headed back the way I came for about 2 miles. Then turned off on the county road. This road seemed even darker with all the trees alongside. "This is scary," I thought.

The road was curvy and hilly. Too scared to drive any faster. I kept the speed around 40 mph. When there was a clearing of trees, I could see homes tucked in the open. Once I thought I saw some lights in a window.

It was going to be about 10 miles out of the way, but at least I didn't have to go through town and deal with the roadblocks and people. I knew this was only the beginning. Eventually, I would have no choice but to deal with it. But, for now, I was safe.

The highway was ahead of me. I slowly approached it and turned off my lights. I wanted to see if there was a roadblock and which side of it, I was on. Driving slowly, because I could hardly see the road, I pulled out onto the highway and stopped. Looking forward, then behind me, I saw nothing. "Hopefully, I'm past it," I said. I waited for a few more seconds, looking all around to make sure it was clear. I turned on my lights and proceeded south on Highway 259. The next big town I would come to would be Nacogdoches. I knew from past travels they had a loop that went around the town. "I'm sure it would be safer to take it, then go right down the center of town." On the south side, I would catch highway 59 down to Livingston. "Only problem is there are dozens of small towns I must go through before I get there. Man, I wish Diamond was with me," as I thought back to the night, they killed her. Tears filled my eyes. "I'm so sorry, my girl, I didn't protect you," as I looked to heaven.

Deep in thought and not paying much attention to the road. Headlights appeared over the next hill. "Crap, Crap!" I spoke. "What do I do? Do I stop and ask if the road ahead is clear, or do I just keep going?"

As the lights got closer, I couldn't tell what kind of car it was, or how many people were in it. My heart started beating faster. I felt like I was going to throw up. I pulled my handgun out of the side of my bag and sit it next to my leg on the seat.

The car stopped in the middle of the road. "Shit!" I approached slowly as a man got out of the car and stood in the middle of the road. I couldn't tell if he was armed or not, but he held up both arms, indicting for me to stop. "Okay, here we go!" I said, holding my breath.

I stopped the truck and rolled down my window just a little. The man was an older man, looked to be in his 70s. "Hello, I didn't mean to scare you, but I need to get my wife to a hospital," as he turned towards the car and pointed to his wife in the back seat. "Is there a hospital open in Henderson?" he asked. "I'm sorry I didn't go through town, but there are roadblocks there with people. They could probably help you," I replied. The man looked deflated. "I'm really sorry," I repeated. The man turned to get back in his car. "How far did you come? Is the highway clear?" I asked. "We only came from Mt. Enterprise a few more miles south, but it's clear all the way," he replied. "Thank you. I hope you get the help you need," I said as the man speed away.

I sat for a few more minutes, trying to catch my breath and calm my nerves. When I could breathe again, I put the truck in drive and continued my journey. I reached Mt Enterprise about 30 minutes later. Driving slowly through the town, looking at every little thing along the street, nothing moved. The tiny houses along the main street were dark. When I reached the edge of town, I let out my breath that I didn't know I was holding. Stepped on the gas and rolled down the windows to let the cool air in. I was getting sleepy, but I knew I had to keep going. I knew I couldn't stop to sleep. I had to get to Galveston.

I couldn't tell, but it felt like an hour had passed by the time I got to Nacogdoches. I exited on to the loop and started my way around the city. I had only gotten halfway around the city when a big pileup of cars and trucks blocked the highway. "Dammit!" I said. I had no choice but to turn the truck around and go back to the last exit. Take city streets to get around the block and back on to the loop.

I drove to the first exit I came to and exited. I stopped at the bottom of the exit and pulled out the map again. "Crap." This map doesn't have city streets. "I guess I'm going to have to drive and figure it out," I said under my breath. There wasn't a frontage road that ran along the highway like in most towns. I took the street that ran the same direction the loop was going. It was a residential area, the streets lined with houses. Trying to see them in the dark, some I could tell most of them were boarded up, others just stood dark. I tried to keep on major streets to keep close to the loop. It seemed to be a quiet little town. As I drove, I wondered where all the people were that lived in these houses, if they were in there, if they were dead. It had been over three weeks now since this all started.

I saw street signs pointing to the on ramp of the loop, so I turned towards it, but the minute I turned I could see a couple of blocks ahead were a group of people in the street. I slowed down, wondering what I should do, when I noticed in my rearview mirror, coming up behind me, what seemed to be several ATVs. As they got closer, I could tell there were at least 2 people on each one, and what looked to be baseball bats that they were waving in the air. "Oh, my God! I got to get out of here." I screamed. There was no place to go; forward was a group of people with no outlet to turn except the on-ramp. Behind me were the men on ATVs. "Forward, it's the only way out," I said as I hit the gas and speed toward the group of people. As I got closer to the group of people, I realized they also had bats and sticks. I scoured the crowd to see if they pointed anything at me, like a gun. I took my chance.

I didn't slow down. I was focused on the on ramp. I drove up onto the sidewalk to go around the crowd. But as I shifted to the sidewalk, the crowd shifted with me, coming straight for me. "Please God, protect me," I said, glancing up to heaven.

The first strike of a bat hit the passenger side head light. The bang was so loud I jumped. The second bang was the passenger side window. I screamed but kept going. A couple of people were running toward me on the sidewalk. "It's me or you," I said. I didn't slow down as they tried to jump out of the way. Hitting both, I looked in my side-view mirror as they both went flying. The last bang was near the bed of the truck. I reached the on-ramp, screeching around the corner. I never slowed down, finally back on the loop. I had to slam on my brakes to avoid hitting cars several times. I had driven like a maniac for about a mile till I realized I had a grip on the steering wheel so tight my knuckles had turned white. Sweat was dripping from my forehead, and I was shaking uncontrollably. I stopped the truck, put my head on the steering wheel, and sobbed.

After several minutes, I wiped my tears and put the truck in drive. Now it was even darker, with only one headlight. I saw the exit to highway 59 up ahead. I slowed down to see if there was any movement. So far, I saw nothing. I started shaking again, just wondering what was waiting for me at the exit.

As I exited the loop, I looked around. So far, so good, no one was there. I continued driving south on highway 59. "The next town is Lufkin. I don't know if I can do this," I said to myself. But thoughts of Jordan and Ashlyn and Jay's family crept in. "I got to keep going. I have no choice," I said.

The sky was turning brighter, the dark night was over. I had been driving for what seemed forever. Normally, the trip would have only taken 5 hours to get to Galveston. But these were not normal times. We would never have "Normal" again.

I was really getting drowsy now, dozing off as I drove. "Maybe I can pull over on a dirt road and take just a little nap," I thought.

I had made it through Lufkin with no problems. Taking the loop around the city again, but this time I was able to get all the way through it. Livingston was still several miles up the road. "I've made it over halfway. Surely, I can rest for a bit," I told myself.

The next dirt road I saw, I turned off. I drove about a mile when I found a pasture with a small drive that I assumed the farmer used to take hay to their animal. I pulled into the pasture and parked behind some trees where I would be hidden from the road.

I locked the doors, although with a missing passenger window, it wouldn't help much. Used my backpack as a pillow and dozed off.

CHAPTER THREE

She's gone

Day 3

Jay woke up with the sun shining on his face. He jumped out of bed, slipped on his shoes, and went out the door. Doug was standing on the porch. "Where's D'Ann?" Jay asked, as he approached Doug. "She was supposed to wake me at around midnight so I could take watch. She's not in bed." he said, looking around with a worried look on his face. "I don't know. She wasn't out here when I came out a few minutes ago. Maybe she is in the bathroom back there," as he pointed towards the shower house.

Jay walked quickly towards the shower house, knocked on the door, but no answer. He opened the door and yelled, "D'Ann, you in there?" Nothing. He walked towards Kay's cabin. Knocked on the door, but no answer. The door was locked. "It's early. She is probably still asleep," he thought. Doug met him halfway back. "Did you find her?" he asked. "NO!" Jay answered. He was now really worried. "Well, you go that way, and I will go this way. Look in the barns and the sheds," Doug commanded.

Jay looked all around, never noticing the truck was gone. He met Doug in front of the house. "Nothing!" Jay said. "Let's go wake up Sean and Dre and take the 4-wheelers and look in the forest," Doug said. "Okay," as Jay jogged to Sean's cabin.

After getting dressed, Sean and Dre joined them in the barn. Doug was filling up the ATVs with gas. "Go get those other gas cans out of the back of the truck on the other side of the barn," Doug said to Dre.

Dre walked out of the barn and towards the area Doug told him to go. He stood them dumbfounded as not seeing a truck on that side of the barn. Confused, he walked to the other side, and then the back side. "There is no truck," he said to himself. He walked back inside the barn and over to Doug. "I don't know where you're talking about. I didn't see any truck back there," he said. Doug looked up from what he was doing, looked at Jay and they both ran out the barn door. "Dammit, the truck is gone," Doug said. "No, NO WAY! She wouldn't be dumb enough to take the truck and go by herself," Jay exclaimed. "The truck is gone!" Doug repeated. "Oh, my God!" Jay said. "Where would she go?" Dre asked. "I'm pretty sure she headed to Galveston to get her son," Jay said as he headed towards the bus. "What are you going to do?" Sean said, trying to catch up with Jay. "I got to go after her. You know how dangerous it is out there," he replied. "Well, hold on, I'm going with you," Sean yelled. "NO! I need you to stay here and help Doug finish the fence and keep everyone safe." Jay demanded. Sean stopped in his tracks. "It's just as dangerous for you to go by yourself as it was for her to go," he yelled at Jay. "Then I will take Dre, while you guys stay here," Jay yelled back looking at Dre. "Dre go get some stuff ready we are leaving in 15 minutes," Jay said still looking at Dre.

Dre turned and ran to his cabin. Jay walked back to the bus as Doug walked into the house. "What's going on?" as Barb met Doug at the door. "D'Ann is gone, she took the truck," as they both looked to the hook by the front door and saw that the keys were gone. "Jay thinks she went to Galveston to get Jordan," he continued. "By herself?" Barb asked. "Are you going with him to find her?" she continued. "No, Sean and I are gonna continue building the fence. Dre and Jay will go look for her."

Jay knocked on the bunk room door and then opened it. The dogs, excited to see him, jumped down off the bed and ran to him. Casey opened her eyes and looked at him. Although she knew what was going on, she asked, "What's wrong?" "D'Ann is gone. She took the truck. I need you to stay here with the dogs. You can move in to one of the cabins till we get back. I'm going to go look for her." Jay answered.

Casey immediately got up and packed her backpack with her stuff and headed to the door. She didn't want to have any conversations with Jay in case he asked her if she knew D'Ann was planning this. She hurried out the door, yelled at the dogs to follow her, and walked down the path to the last cabin available.

Jay, frantic, not knowing what to do next. He looked through the pantry and the refrigerator to make sure he had enough supplies for him and Dre.

Barb knocked on the bus door. "Jay, you in there?" she yelled. "Yeah, come on in," he replied. "Sit and calm down a minute. You can't go off looking for her in this state of mind. You will get yourself killed," she said. "I can't sit down. I got to go," he demanded. "First, sit down, take some deep breaths. I'm not getting off this bus till you do," she replied.

Against Jay's better judgement, he sat down. Barb could see the anger welling up inside him. "Why? Why would she do this? I told her we would go in a couple of days," he said, looking out the window. "It's her kid, and it's your kid, and family," she answered. "I would probably have done the same thing," she added. "But you don't know how dangerous it is out there. We all just about didn't make it here," he replied.

The anger was leaving his face, now it was concern that covered his face. "She will be fine. You know she is a scrapper, just like me. I taught her well. She isn't got a big dick like me, but she is growing one," as they both laughed.

Barb put her hand on Jay's shoulder. "She will be fine. Go get your family," she said as she headed to the door. "Thanks Barb, you're right," Jay replied. Dre met Barb as she was getting off the bus. "Take care of him, don't let him go off half-cocked, you guys be careful," she said.

Dre climbed the stairs to the bus and threw his backpack on the sofa. "I'm ready," he said. Jay looked up at him and shook his head. "I need to unhook the electric and water on here, and I'll be right back. Check that we still have rifles and ammo in that hall closet."

Doug followed the bus to the big gate on his ATV to unlock it. "You really need to take those decaying bodies down now," Jay said with a smile as they passed.

Jay and Dre didn't get far in the bus when the steam came rolling out from under the hood. "Shit, shit!" Jay yelled as he hit his fist against the steering wheel. He jumped out and lifted the hood. Steamed rolled out of the bottom of the radiator. Dre met him at the front of the bus. "What is it?" he asked. "Not sure, gonna have to walk back to the deer lease, get some tools and see if we can fix it." He responded. "Either you walk back and get Doug and an ATV, and I'll stay here to secure it. Or you stay here, and I'll walk back. I have too much stuff in here for someone to steal," he said, thinking of all the marijuana he had hidden. "I can jog back. It would probably take me less time than you," Dre said. "Okay, let Doug know it's the radiator, could be a hose, bring something to fix it," Jay replied.

Dre took off jogging the 5 miles back to the county road, then it was another 3 miles to the deer lease. Jay climbed back onto the bus and sat on the sofa. "Dammit D'Ann," Jay growled.

Dre reached the gate, soaked in sweat. Breathing hard from jogging, and the stench of the bodies still hanging there, hurt his lungs and his stomach. He hopped the gate and ran faster to get away from the smell. The other gate was just around the corner. He stopped and bent over, holding his side. He started walking the rest of the way, breathing hard with his arms above his head.

"Dad!" Abby yelled as she saw Dre climbing the gate. Doug walked out of the house with his rifle. "It's Dre," as he started to walk towards him. "What's wrong?" Doug yelled. Dre stopped to catch his breath. "The radiator, radiator hose, we don't know, we need help," breathing heavily. Again, bending over, holding his side. "Jay said to bring ATV and stuff to fix hose or radiator," Dre said, standing up.

Doug headed towards the workshop, "I got some tape that will fix it if it's a hole in a hose, and some leaks stop, but it will have to sit and cure for a bit. Let's go get it and get over there."

Doug drove his ATV out of the shop with the supplies in the front basket. "Hop on, let's go fix it," he said to Dre.

It only took them 20 minutes to get to the bus. Jay was sitting in the driver's seat and could see them driving up in the side-view mirror. "That didn't take long to get help," Jay said, looking at Dre. "Let's see what's going on," Doug said as he got off his ATV.

Doug crawled under the bus to get a look at the bottom of the radiator. After a few minutes, he crawled out. "Well, what is it?" Jay asked. "I'm afraid this bus is not going anywhere. You blew a hole in the bottom of the radiator," Doug said. "Fuck!" Jay said as he punched the side of the hood. They all stood looking at the bus. "We could take the radiator off. There is an auto salvage about 10 miles towards Henderson. We can take it over there to see if we can find anything comparable, or maybe another vehicle on the way." Dale said. "Crap, I got so many things on this bus, I'm afraid it will get stolen," Jay said. Dale, knowing what Jay was talking about, spoke up, "I can take the stuff back to deer lease, grab Sean and the other ATV. While you stay here, keep watch. The three of us can go find a radiator. Barb can watch the lease while we are gone." Jay looked at Doug. "I guess we have no other choice," he said.

Jay went inside and grabbed the 3 bags of marijuana and strapped them on to Doug's ATV. Doug sped off towards the deer lease. Jay and Dre sat back down on the sofa, not saying a word.

Looking at the clock on the counter by the kitchen sink, it was now 11am. Jay just shook his head, knowing D'Ann had been gone for over 12 hours. Doug and Sean pulled up on the ATVs. "We will be back in a bit," Doug said as Dre hoped on the back of Sean's ATV.

A couple of hours later and they got back with the new radiator. They worked on the bus for hours trying to get the old radiator out and put the new one on. They didn't find the exact one, but it was close enough.

They worked through the night, and by morning light, it was finished, and they were all exhausted.

"Okay, put the antifreeze I brought and fill up the radiator. I think it's ready," Doug said. Jay poured the antifreeze in with a jug of non-drinkable water. "Let's see if it holds the fluid," Doug said. They waited for several minutes, and the water level didn't move. "Start it up. Let's see what happens," Sean said. Jay turned the key, and the engine roared to life. They ran it for several minutes, then turned it off and checked it over. "I think you will be good," Doug said. "If I were you, I would drive back to the lease, empty this thing out. Leave everything there. That way, if it breaks down again or on your way, you can find something better to drive," Doug said. "Your probably right," Jay replied.

Doug jumped on his ATV while Sean hopped on the bus. Dre had taken the other ATV back to the deer lease earlier that night to stand guard. They drove to the lease. Pointing up to the dead bodies, "Let me help you take them down and dispose of them," Jay said, stopping the bus right inside the gate. He and Sean jumped out as Doug took out a knife and cut the rope that had been tied around the fence and, one by one, the bodies crashed to the ground. The smell was still unbelievable; choking and gagging them all. Doug took the rope that was still tied to the bodies; hooked it around the hitch of the ATV and drug them about a mile down the road. Got off his ATV and rolled them with his feet into the ditch.

"Let's go," Doug said as he rode back to the gate. "I'll leave it unlocked for now. Just lock it back when you leave," he said.

The three of them cleaned out the bus with Casey, Ally and Abby's help in just under 30 minutes.

"Jay, why don't you and Dre take a quick nap? You've been up all night long. It's too dangerous for you to be drowsy. I'll wake you up around 5pm and have Barb fix you some dinner." Doug said. "Maybe you're right, I'm exhausted," Jay replied.

Jay and Dre climbed back on the bus and laid down. Jay tossed and turned and couldn't get to sleep worrying about what all could happen to D'Ann. Finally, after about an hour he got up, "this is useless, I can't sleep" Jay said as he walked towards the house. "I couldn't sleep. You got any coffee?" he said, walking in the door. Barb and Doug looked up at him. "Yeah, let me make you some," Barb said, getting up out of the kitchen table chair. "So, what's the plan?" Doug asked Jay. "I'm gonna find her, tell her how much she pissed me off by doing this, then probably hug her, and then go get our family," Jay replied, rolling his eyes. "Don't be too rough on her, she was only concerned about her kid," Barb comment. "I know, but this was not the way to go about it. I'm worried about my family too," Jay replied. He took the cup of coffee from Barb. "I'm gonna take off," Jay said. "You want something to eat before you go?" Barb asked. "I can make you a sandwich if you would like," she continued. "Nah, I'm good. I'll grab a protein bar from my bag if I get hungry." Jay replied as he walked out the door. "Be careful!" Barb and Doug said in unison.

It was late afternoon, he could tell by the sun, when he drove out of the drive.

Day 3 D'Ann

Barking off in the distance woke me up. "OMG, what time is it?" I sat up in the seat. I looked at the position of the sun, not quite overhead. "It's still not quite noon yet," I said. The barking was getting closer. For a second my drowsy mind thought it was Diamond, oh how I missed that dog.

I had to go pee, so I got out of the truck, grabbing some paper towels that were on the floor. As I finished and stood up, staring at me by the truck door was a gigantic dog dragging a chain. He was really skinny and looked like he had been dragging the chain for weeks. "Hello boy," I said cautiously. I drifted towards the passenger side door. He didn't move but watched me very intensely.

I reached for the broken window and pulled out my bag with the MREs. Opened one that said, "Salisbury Steak" and put it on the grass in front of him. Still looking me up and down, he walked with his head down, but the smell overtook him, and he pounced on the food. He ate the whole thing in one bite. I had another MRE, so I opened it and dumped it out also, closer to me. He scarfed it down just as fast.

I opened a bottle of water and poured a little on the bag of the MRE, making a makeshift bowl. He lapped it up. I continued to pour the water as he drank it all. I sat down on the ground, so I was at his height. I grabbed a couple of cookies out of the bag and held them out to him.

He walked slowly over to me and grabbed one out of my hand and backed away from me. I held out another one. This time he grabbed it but didn't back away. I held out my hand for him to smell it. To my surprise, he licked me.

I took my other hand, showed it to him, and placed it on his head. Then stroked his head and neck. He came closer to me and started wagging his tail. I opened another bottle of water and poured it out for him to drink. Still petting him on the neck, I slowly unlatched the chain and let it drop to the ground. He shook his head, like he knew he was free from dragging that heavy thing around.

I slowly got to my feet and headed around to the driver's side door. Opened the door to throw my backpack in, but before I could, the dog jumped in the cab. "So, you wanna go with me, huh?" I asked him. "Well, I could use a companion," I said. I took an old shirt that looked like a rag that Doug had used on the floor and wiped the glass from the window off the seat.

Back on the dirt road, I headed to the highway. The dog stuck his head out the passenger side window and settled in. I looked over at him. He looked like a younger dog and probably a pit mix. His fur was short brown with a white muzzle, around his neck where the chain was, the fur was worn off. It wasn't bleeding, but a few more days of dragging that chain around, and it would have become an open sore. After a few miles he lay down next to me and went to sleep. It felt natural to have a big dog lying next to me. I kind of felt like a hole in my heart was being filled. I looked to heaven. "Diamond, did you send this big boy to me?" I said.

We continued driving towards Livingston. "Maybe we can find you some dog food," I said. I knew from going through Livingston many times before there was a Family Dollar along the way. Chances are it had already been ransacked. But maybe dog food was the last thing people would think of.

By the time we got to Livingston, the sun was going down in the west. I really couldn't tell what time it was, but I figured I only had a couple more hours of sunlight.

Right before we hit the city limits, we turned off on to Highway 146, which would take us all the way down to Galveston. The streets were quiet so far. Several cars clogged the roads, weaving in and out. Some were burnt, most had their windows broken out. The dog was awake now and had his head out the window again. I could see the Family Dollar sign up ahead a few blocks.

Thinking I wouldn't be able to contain him in the truck because of the window being broken out, I figured if he ran off, so be it. At least he was in town now and could find more food. But we would stop anyway, and I would grab some dog food, maybe a collar and a leash, unless he ran away.

I pulled into the drive. Just as I thought; the glass doors lay on the ground. I sat staring for a few minutes to make sure no one was around. I slowly got out of the truck as the dog jumped out. "Okay, boy, but I can't wait for you if you run off," I said to him, petting him on the head.

To my surprise, he stayed right by my side. We crawled through the door, not bothering to open it. The store was a disaster; shelves thrown everywhere, what little product on the shelves were lying all over the floor. We made it to the pet section. Just what I thought, several bags of dog food, treats and accessories were still here, all over the floor but still here. I grabbed a XL collar that had spikes on it, showed to him, "You like this one?" I asked. He sniffed it and then walked over to a busted bag of dog food on the floor and started eating it. "Okay, we will get this kind," I told him.

While he was eating, I put the collar around his neck, "Dang, this barely fits. You're a big boy." I then grabbed the thickest leash I could find on the floor. Picked up a toy, stuffed it in my pocket and grabbed a couple bags of treats. Then tried to pick up the 25lb bag of food. "Oh, my God," this is too heavy. I'm going to have to get a smaller bag. "Let me get that for you," a voice came from behind me. I whipped around to see who it was. A young boy, maybe Casey's age, I thought, was standing there. At about that time, the dog turned and started growling. Thank God I had put that collar on him, I thought as I grabbed it. "I would appreciate that; can you get the big bag and carry it to my truck?" Still leery of his motives, I clipped the leash on the dog's collar, and we followed the kid out the door.

He threw the bag of dog food in the back of the truck and said, "Let me go get you another one. That's a big dog, he's gonna eat a lot," as he turned and walked back into the store. I watched as he came back with another 25 pounds of dog food and threw it in the back of the truck. "Thank you so much, I couldn't have done that without you." I said. "Are you alone here? Where do you live?" I asked. "My parents are dead. A gang of people shot them for their supplies. I got away and have been hiding here in this store." he said. "Do you live close?" I asked. "No, we were traveling to my grandparents in Baytown when the car stopped. We started walking, and that's when it happened," he replied.

I walked around to the driver's side door; opened it and the dog jumped in. "Crap!" I whispered to myself, thinking again, I can't leave this kid here alone. "I'm going through Baytown. Do you want to ride to your grandparents?" I asked, not sure I should be doing this. "Are you sure?" he asked with excitement in his eyes. "Let's see how the dog likes you and see if he will share his seat with you," I smiled. "I'm D'Ann, and this is, well, I don't have a name for him yet. I picked him up back a few miles, or I should say, he picked me up. He just jumped in the truck, didn't give me a choice," I said, smiling. "I'm Luke" he said. "Let Dog smell your hand. If he doesn't bite you, then you can get in," I said, smiling as Luke looked at me like I was crazy. Luke opened the passenger side door slowly and stuck his hand out to the dog so he could smell it.

The dog smelled it and then laid down next to me. "I guess you can come. Do you have any clothes or anything to bring?" I asked. "Can I run get my backpack? It's in the back of the store," he asked. "Yeah, just hurry. We need to get on the road," I replied. "What have I gotten myself into?" I asked the dog while petting his head. I reached down to the floor and grabbed a bag of bones. Opened the package and gave him one. He looked up at me like I was his favorite person and snatched it right out of my hand. I giggled to myself as I watched Luke come running out of the store. "We better get going. I see a group of people down the street coming this way," he said as he jumped into the truck. I looked in the rear-view mirror; started the truck and took off.

From this point I knew it would take about 2 hours to get to Baytown normally, but we still had several small towns to go through. I felt a little better knowing I had Dog and Luke to help me in case we got in trouble. "Luke, we need to think of a name for this dog," as I pet him on the head. "I used to have a dog named Jax," Luke replied. "Jax, huh?" as I looked down at the dog still chewing his bone. "Jax it is!" I said as Luke smiled and pet Jax.

"Where do you live?" I asked. "We live in Marshall. We were just going to my grandparents for the weekend," he said. "Do you have any brothers or sisters?" I asked. "Nope, just me," he replied. "Just let me know if I'm getting too personal or you don't want to talk about it," I said. "How many kids do you have?" he asked. "I have a son that lives in the mountains of Colorado. He's married and has two kids. He lives off grid anyway with no electricity, so he is used to this," I smiled. "Then I have my son in Galveston and his wife. All of my husband's family is down there also," I said. "Where is your husband?" he asked. "Well, he didn't want to come yet, so I left without him knowing, because he would have stopped me. We drove from Las Vegas to Texas, and it was dangerous. I had another dog like this. Her name was Diamond, and a man shot and killed her on our way here. It was bad," I said. "wow" is all he said.

I didn't want to ask Luke too many questions. I didn't know how painful his parents' death would still be. So, we rode in silence until he spoke. "Are you sure they are, okay?" he asked, looking out the window. "I hope so. Of course, there is no way of knowing since we have no phones," I replied. "Yeah, my grandparents are older. I don't know if they are okay either," he said, as his voice cracked. "Well, let's pray they are," I said.

We rode in silence after that. The sun was starting to set and because of the slow pace, I had to drive to avoid hitting stalled cars; I knew it would be dark by the time we got to Baytown. We went through a couple of small towns, but there seemed to be no one around. The towns were so small they only had gas stations, no other stores.

Off in the distance, we could see a bright light. "I wonder what that is?" I said as I pointed out the windshield. We watched it for a few miles and realized it was on fire. "Oh my God!" I said. "I think it's one of the refineries in Baytown. Where does your grandparents live?" I asked with concern on my face. "They live on the other side of town. Close to that big bridge that goes over the water. I don't know what the name of the streets are, but I can tell you how to get there." I just hope we can get there, I thought. As we got closer to the city and the water, the fire looked to be fairly close, but not quite at the bridge. It lit up the entire sky. "I bet it's been burning since all this started," I said as we got close to the bridge.

I approached the bridge hoping and praying we would be able to pass over it with no trouble. Going slow, I had to maneuver around a lot of cars, some pile ups and a few big trucks overturned. We saw a few bodies that were decomposing, and the smell was horrendous. We finally got to the other side. The two of us breathed a sigh of relief. "The next exit and then turn left," he said, pointing out the window.

I followed his instructions and weaved through the city streets. With one headlight, it was difficult to see all the obstacles before I came up on them. This neighborhood looked just like all the others I had been through since this whole thing started. Some houses are boarded up, and some just sitting there. "There," he pointed to a small house on the corner. "That's it," he said.

I pulled into the driveway. The house was dark. "Let me go up before you in case things are not good," I said. Jake looked at me with shock in his eyes. "Look, I'm just being honest, it's been over 3 weeks and things go wrong. Many people have died." I continued as I opened the truck door. Jax got up and started to jump out, "NO! you stay here." I told him as I shut the door. I pulled the handgun out of the back of my pants, which suddenly made my back feel better. "Dang, I shouldn't drive with that there," rubbing my back.

I knocked on the front door. Not really thinking anyone would come to the door. I started to head to the back when I saw the curtain move in what I thought was the living room. "Jake, come here," I yelled. Jake opened the truck door and walked toward the front of the house. Suddenly, the front door opened. An elderly man came walking out, "JAKE!" he yelled. "Grandpa!" as Jake ran to the man. Behind the door was an elderly woman holding the door open. "Grandma!" Jake yelled, running to the woman. I stepped back on to the sidewalk and walked towards the man. "You must be Jake's grandparents? I'm D'Ann," I said, walking beside the elderly man towards the door where Jake and his grandma were standing. "I'm Kenneth and this is my wife Leona," Grandpa said. "Jake, where are your parents?" Grandpa asked. Jake started crying and held his grandma. "They didn't make it," I said. "Jake hasn't really talked about it, but I found him hiding in a store on my way and gave him a ride," I replied. "Come in, come in," Grandma said, holding the door wide open. "Oh, I can't I have a dog with me. He's probably not too friendly." I said. "Nonsense, go get him and come in," Grandma insisted.

I walked to the truck and grabbed my two backpacks and Jax' leash. "Come on, you better be good," I said as we walked back to the house.

Grandpa locked the door and told us to follow him. We walked towards the kitchen, but before we entered, he opened a door that went down to a basement. "Wow, I didn't think people had basements in this part of the country," I said, following Grandma down the stairs. "This is not any ordinary basement," Grandpa said.

When we got to the bottom of the stairs, there was another door. It looked like it was made of steel. "I've been preparing for something like this for years," he said. "I've created a large walk-in faraway cage," as he swung open the heavy door.

We walked in and it was an entire house, a kitchen, living room and what looked to be a couple of bedrooms and a bathroom. Over in the corner was a ham radio station. "Wow!" was all I could say.

We sat down on the sofa and talked about the trip and what we saw. I told them I was heading to Galveston to get my family. "It's too late for you to be out there. It's too dark. You are staying right here tonight," Grandma insisted. You and your dog can stay in that room at the end of the hall. Luke can sleep on the sofa," Grandma said.

"I need to go get some food for Jax," I said. "I'll go get it," Jake said as he ran out the door and up the stairs. "He seems to be a great kid," I said. Grandma and Grandpa looked at each other, shook their heads, and smiled.

"Let me show you to your room, then come out and I'll make you something to eat," Grandma said. We walked down the hall with Jax right beside me. I put my bags on the floor and sat on the bed. "Oh, I wonder if they have water. I would love a shower," I thought to myself. I walked out just as Luke was sitting one of the 25lb bags of food down.

He reached up in the cupboard and pulled down two bowls. Filled one with the kibble and went to the sink and turned the faucet on and filled the bowl up with water. He sat both bowls on the floor as Jax went over and started eating. "Water!" I thought. "So how do you have water, and how have you survived over 3 weeks with no groceries?" I asked.

Grandpa walked over to another steel door on the opposite side of the room and opened the door. It was a vast room. Over to one side was an indoor garden. There were several rows of plants. There was even an apple tree with apples on it in a big pot over in the corner. To the left of that was a water tower, "that recycles and cleans the water," he said, pointing to it. "We have solar on the house, but I have generators that didn't get fried because they were protected. I told you I've been preparing for years." Grandpa continued. "Wow," again was all I could say.

We walked down a hallway that led to a big room with row after row of shelves fully stocked with canned goods, dried goods, and other food. Near the back of the room was a row of 3 huge deep freezers. He opened the first one. It was full of all kinds of meat. It reminded me of Nadia and Benny's room.

We walked back out as I turned to Grandpa. "So, you have water?" I asked. "I would absolutely love to be able to take a shower. Do you think that is possible?" I asked. Grandpa smiled. "We even have hot water." My eyes got big. It had been over 3 weeks since I had a hot shower. "Towels are in the cupboard, honey. "You go right ahead," Grandma said, smiling.

I tried to hurry so I wouldn't use all their water, but the hot shower felt so good, and who knows when the next time I would ever get a hot shower. I put a clean pair of pants and shirt on from my bag and walked back out to the living room. "I really hate to ask this, but would you have a brush or comb? I don't think I've brushed my hair in days," I asked. "In the top drawer in the bathroom, help you self to anything you need," Grandma replied.

I brushed my hair and could smell something wonderful cooking. It smelled like a hamburger. It had been weeks since I had a burger. I walked out of the bathroom and into the kitchen. Grandma had made hamburgers. She pulled down a bag of chips from her pantry.

The first bit into the hamburger was so good, I took tiny bits to savor the moment and flavor. Grandma and Grandpa just looked at me and laughed. "It's been a long, long time," I said with my mouth full.

After dinner, I helped Grandma with the dishes, and then we sat in the living room talking more about our trip and my trip from Las Vegas. When I could hardly keep my eyes open, I excused myself and Jax and I headed to bed.

I hit the pillow, and I was out. Jax right beside me. Mine and his tummy were full, and I was so relaxed from the hot shower. I would have the best sleep I had had in 3 weeks.

CHAPTER FOUR

Grandma and Grandpa

Day 4 D'Ann

I woke up to the smell of fresh bacon cooking. "You sleep here all night? Good boy," I said, petting Jax on his head. "You gotta go potty?" I asked as I got up, slipped my shoes on, and opened the bedroom door.

"Good morning!" Grandma said as she saw us walk out. "Good morning," I replied. Luke came out of the bathroom and asked, "do you want me to take Jax out?" I looked at him and grabbed his leash off the floor by the door. "That would be great. Thank you!" I replied.

Jake and Jax went up the stairs as I sat down at the kitchen table. "Can I help you with anything?" I asked. "No dear, I have it all ready," Grandma replied. Looking around, I didn't see Grandpa. "I'm so glad you guys are doing great. I've seen a lot of bad stuff on our way from Las Vegas to Texas. There is a lot of death and destruction out there." I spoke. "I've heard that on the ham radio," Grandpa said, coming out of the storage area. "Will you guys be, okay?" I asked. "I think so. We have over 3 years' worth of supplies in case this goes on for a long time." He replied.

"Have you heard anything on the radio about what happened?" I asked. "Bits and pieces. It almost sounds like our government provoked it and allowed it. What I mean is. For years, our government has been importing all the computer chips that everything we buy runs on. I belong to a lot of conspiracy groups and some of them think our own government has had the capabilities of incapacitating the entire world with one flip of the switch," he said. "Well, if they can switch it off, can't they switch it back on?" I asked. "From my research, I believe they have that capability as well. But they are probably waiting for people to weed themselves out, kind of like a purge, so only the strongest survive before they turn it back on. Even if they turn it back on, it's not like the electricity will just come back on immediately. I'm sure some components were fried. This is just speculation at this point. If this had happened, then we could be in for a fight. It could be the start of a civil war," he said. "That is so scary to think about," I replied. "Not to scare you more, but I have heard a few reports of militia groups that our own government has put together, taking over the United States, and it's not the military. Even though they hit our computers, guess they have ways of protecting their own," he explained. "WOW!" I replied. "I need to go get my family and get back to our deer lease before the shit hits the fan," I said.

"No more of this talk now. Eat before it gets cold," Grandma demanded. Jake and Jax walked back through the door. "My truck still out there?" I asked. "Yeah, it looks okay," Jake replied. Jake gave Jax some food as we all sat down to eat. "I want you and your family to stop here on your way back. I have a lot of supplies that I want to give you. They will go bad before we ever eat it," Grandpa said. I nodded my head in agreement.

Day 4 Jay

Jay didn't want to push the bus too hard because the radiator basically being put together with baling wire and duct tape. He took his time and drove about 40 mph. Approaching Henderson, he saw the roadblock up ahead. "Okay, well here we go," he commented as Dre moved up to the passenger side seat. Jay slowed down and approached the man as he held up his hand to stop. "Good afternoon where are you traveling to?" the man asked. "We are trying to find my wife. She was headed to Houston, so she probably took highway 259. We are just trying to get through town. You didn't happen to see an old white dodge truck come through here two nights ago. She would have been by herself.?" Jay asked. "No, but I usually work the day shift. If you are just passing through, I will let you go. Just go straight to Highway 259," the man said as he motioned the other men standing by the barricades to open them so they could pass. "Thank you, sir," Jay said as he drove off. "Well, that was easier than I thought," Jay said. "Hopefully they all are like that," he continued.

Jay turned off on highway 256 and headed south. Coming to the other roadblock, he didn't have to stop. They moved the barricades before he got there. He waved as he passed them by. "How long will it take us to get there?" Dre asked. "At this speed, it's gonna take us probably over 8 hours. It's only 5 hours on a good day," he replied. "There aren't too many towns between here and Nacogdoches. Hopefully, it will be smooth sailing," he said just as steam started rolling out from under the hood again. "NO, NO, NO! Dammit," Jay said, hitting his fist on the steering wheel. They had only gotten about a mile out of town. He pulled the bus over to the side of the road. "That's it! I'm going to walk back to town and find something else to drive. I'm done with this piece of crap," he yelled. "Come on, get your bag and we will have to carry our food supplies with us. I don't trust that they will still be here when we get back," Jay said, discussed. Dre grabbed his backpack and two of the other packs and swung them on his shoulder. Jay picked up his backpack and the backpack with the ammo and handed Dre a rifle. He swung his AR over his shoulder, and they locked the bus and started walking back towards town.

Carrying the load, they were carrying, it took them almost an hour to get to the outskirts of town. They passed several houses, most boarded up, a couple burned down, but no older model cars anywhere to be seen. "Maybe we should check down that dirt road up there. Maybe there is an old farm truck." Dre said, pointing up ahead. "Yeah, Okay, can't hurt," as they approached the dirt road. "This shit is getting heavy. You think we could hide it here in the trees and come back for it when we find a ride?" Dre asked, having trouble managing 3 backpacks.

Jay thought about it and looked around. "I think we can hide it down here in the culvert. We will get it when we get back. The two of them climbed down the embankment and threw their backpacks inside the culvert. They were getting ready to climb back out when they heard an engine coming down the road and turned off on to the dirt road. Jay grabbed Dre's arm and they crotched down so the people in the truck wouldn't see them. As the vehicle passed by, they could tell it was an old conversion van. They watched the van go down the dirt road and turn several hundred feet into a farmhouse driveway. "Are you thinking what I'm thinking?" Dre asked Jay. "Yeah, but we might have to wait till dark, I say let's walk past it and see if we can find anything else. If that doesn't work, then we come back for the van," Jay replied as they walked out of the ditch and toward the other farmhouses.

Jay was getting tired and sleepy. They passed a couple of houses and then spotted a house sitting alone with a barn in the back with several old vehicles around it. "That looks like an old auto shop," Dre pointed out. "Look, they have some cars out front for sale. They look old. What do you think?" Dre continued. "I think we need to check it out," Jay replied as they continued walking.

They got to the edge of the driveway and climbed down into the ditch beside the driveway. "Let's watch for some movement for a minute," Jay said, squatting down. Dre squat down beside him as they watch for movement. After about 30 minutes, and almost dozing off, Jay finally stood up. "I think we should go," he said.

They both climbed out of the ditch. Sticking to the shadows of the trees, they snuck up to the row of cars and trucks by the road. Trying the locked door handles, they peeked in the windows. "No keys," Jay said. "Look, it looks like there is a shed over there that they made into an office. Maybe there are keys in there," Dre said. "I'm going to go look in the windows of the house. I don't want anyone coming out with a gun and shoot us as we steal their car," Jay said. "Go ahead and see if you can get into the office and find some keys," Jay told Dre as they both moved in opposite directions.

Jay continued to stay in the shadows up to the house window. The blinds were open as he peeked inside. He crouched down and watched and waited. No movement inside the house. "Jay," he heard Dre yelling as quiet as he could across the yard. Jay turned and looked where Dre said his name. Dre was holding up some keys. Jay looked back into the house and still saw nothing. So, he turned and ran back to Dre. "I think these keys are for that old ford truck," Dre said, handing them to Jay. "Let's go see."

They both ran to the truck. Jay unlocked the door, got in, reached over and pulled the lock so Dre could get in. He put the key in the ignition and turned the key, but not all the way on. "Great, we have a full tank," he said. Then turned the key over. The truck started right away. "He must be a talented mechanic," Jay said. "Oh my God, GO, GO!" Dre yelled as Jay looked out the passenger side mirror. A man with a rifle came running out of the barn/shop building. Jay put it in gear and stepped on the gas. He watched the rear-view mirror as the man took aim. "Shit! Duck!" Jay yelled. Jay could see the smoke puff come off the gun but didn't hear any hit. They sped down the dirt road till they got to the highway. Jay pulled over as they both got out and ran down the ditch; grabbed their bags and threw them in the truck and took off. They both looked at each other and let out a deep breath. "Close one. "We need to put some distance between us and him in case he comes after us," Jay said.

It only took them a little over a minute to reach where they had parked the bus. "Do we need to stop to get anything out, or did we get everything?" Jay asked. "I think we got everything," Dre replied. "Oh wait, the gas cans, they are in the basement, we should grab those." Dre said.

Jay stopped as they got out and grabbed the gas cans. The cans were almost empty. "I guess we better find some diesel sometime. I think we can make it to Houston on the diesel we got. But we will need more. Just keep your eyes open for another diesel vehicle." Jay said. "It was a great bus that got us this far," Jay said as they drove away. "I think if we keep driving, we should get to Galveston in about 4 hours. I can go a lot faster in this," Jay said.

The day was slipping away from them. It would soon be dark. In late September, the sun sets earlier. He rolled down the window and let the cool breeze hit his face. But as he drove on, his eyelids were getting heavy. "I need to just pull over for a few minutes of shut eye," he said to himself. A couple more miles and he saw a road with trees all around. He pulled off and drove a little way up the road. He saw a barn up a way and pulled into the driveway. The barn was falling, so he knew no one would be around it. He pulled behind the barn; shut off the truck, leaned his head back, and fell asleep.

Day 4 D'Ann

Jake put Jax in the truck and put the rest of his bag of food in the truck's bed. "Thank you for everything," I said as I hugged Jake. Grandma handed me a sack, "for your trip, just some sandwiches and bottles of water," she said. "Thank you," I said as I gave her then Grandpa a hug. "You be careful, and we will expect you soon on your way back. We owe you everything for bringing our grandson home," Grandpa said. "Thank you, I may take you up on that," I replied as I got in the truck. "I checked the radio this morning about the road conditions to Galveston. They said most of it is clear, just be careful of some people that have formed gangs. They are attaching vehicles on the highway and taking their stuff." Grandpa said. "I will be careful," I said as I waved and backed out of the driveway. "Just you and me, boy," I said to Jax as his head went out the window.

Along the water to the east, you could see several refineries on fire. Still burning after over 3 weeks. "I guess they have a lot of products that will burn for a long time," I thought.

As I reached Kemah, things looked familiar, but different. There were more older cars on the road. As I passed several, we all just stared at each other like it was something new to see a car on the road. As I approached Bacliff, I knew the next road was the way to one of my best friend's houses. As bad as I wanted to get to my son, I knew I had to check on her and her family. Still battling my conscience about whether to take the chance. I slammed on the brakes and turned. "I got to check. I would never forgive myself," I said.

When the EMP went off, it was about 6am am Pacific Time, so it would have been 8am here in Texas. She might have already left for work, I thought. I turned down her road and could see her driveway. Her car was there, and her husband's truck was still in the driveway.

I slowly pulled in, put the truck in park. "Stay here boy, I'll be right back," I said to Jax as I put his leash on and tied it to the steering wheel.

I walked up her stairs to her front door. I knocked. "Amy?" "Bryan?" I yelled, but not too loud. I tried the door handle. It was locked. I walked around to the sliding glass doors. They were unlocked. I slid it open. "Amy, Bryan?" I yelled again. I stood still to listen. I walked over to her dining room table, which was right outside their bedroom. Then I noticed a note on the refrigerator.

Emma,
We took the side-by-side to Mira's house. If you get this, take the ATV and come.
Love,
Mom

I let out a sign of relief. I headed out the door and went to the garage to see if the ATV was gone, in hopes Emma had made it. Opening the garage door, I saw nothing left but a jet ski that I knew Bryan was working on. Walking back to the truck, I felt relief, but also sadness. I didn't know where Mira lived. She had gotten married a couple of years ago and she and her new husband bought a house, but I didn't know where. But at least I hoped Amy and her family were safe now.

I jumped back in the truck, untied Jax, and went back out of the driveway. Didn't take long till I was back on the road. The road would take me really close to where Nate and Veronica lived. I drove into their little fishing village and turned into their street. "Crap, it's been so long I don't remember their address," I said. I knew he drove a white pickup, and she drove a little mini cooper, so I looked for that. "I think this is it," I said.

Both vehicles were in the drive, but their little motor home was gone. "Dang it, I bet they are gone," I said. I parked and got out of the truck. Because they lived right on the Bayou, their house was on stilts. I climbed the stairs as fast as my knees would carry me. I knocked on the door and turned the knob.

I walked in. The scene was shocking. The furniture had been turned over; glass was broken all over the floor. Desk drawers were laying on the floor. I ran to the bedroom. "Nate?" I yelled. I didn't see anything, then I heard a noise coming from the bathroom. "Nate?" I yelled again. "Help, I'm here," came a voice from the bathroom.

I ran to the bathroom, stepping over clothes that were scattered across the room. I opened the door, and the smell hit me like a ton of bricks. That smell was familiar to me. The first thing I saw was Nate. His hands and feet were tied together with duct tape and tied to the plumbing under the pedestal sink. Blood was all over the floor. His pant legs were covered in blood. He had dried blood all over his face. A laceration across his forehead had already dried and scabbed over.

"Oh my God!" I screamed as I ran to him. "Are you okay?" I asked, bending down. "Get me out of here," he said as tears filled his eyes and the tears mixed with dry blood and became wet again. I tried to pull the tape, but there was too much of it and it was too strong. "Let me go get a knife so I can cut it off," as I ran out the door to the kitchen. I grabbed a big knife, went back and cut his hands free from the plumbing, and cut the tape on his legs.

He was clearly sobbing now as he crawled over by the bathtub. I hadn't even noticed till now. In a puddle of dried blood was Veronica. My hand covered the scream that wanted to come out. "Aww, NO," I cried. Nate reached his wife, laid over her and sobbed uncontrollably. Her body was already stiff. "What happened?" I asked Nate. Between cries he said, "Some guys came in looking for the motorhome keys. When I wouldn't give the keys to them, they tied us up. They took her to the bathroom. They tied me up and held a gun at me. I could hear her screaming. They were in there for a long time. She was screaming and screaming, and I couldn't get to her." As he continued to sob. "Come on, we need to get out of here. There is nothing we can do for her. I'm so sorry, I loved Veronica," I said, trying to pull him up. "Are you shot?" I asked, looking at the dried blood on his legs. "I'm not shot. They sliced my legs with a knife," he replied. "How long ago did this happen?" I asked. "I don't know, I was out of it for a couple days, maybe 2 days ago," he said, trying to get up. I helped him up and into the bedroom. Sat him down on the bed. I ran to the kitchen and grabbed a bottle of water off the counter and took it to him. I picked up some of his clothes and set them on the bed. "Change out of these clothes. I'll step out and try to get some of your stuff together. You can't stay here." I said as I walked out the bedroom door.

I went to the kitchen and looked through the cupboards to find any food or anything we could take with us. Throwing several canned goods in a plastic bag and all the bottles of water. I wrote a note to Jay in case he showed up there, that I had his dad, and we were headed to Jordan's. I put it on the front of the fridge in hopes he would find it. I knocked on the bedroom door. "You, okay?" I said "Yeah, you can come in." he had put on a pair of shorts which exposed the cuts on his legs. I went back to the kitchen and got a towel; opened a bottle of water and poured it in the towel and poured the rest on his legs. The cuts had already scabbed. I cleaned them up the best I could. "Can you walk?" I asked. "I think so," I helped him up, and we walked into the living room. He looked around at the mess. Tears filled his eyes. "I know, I'm so sorry," I said. "Sit here and let me get some of your clothes together and then we will go," I said, sitting him in a chair. "Will you grab that picture? It was next to the bed. I think it's on the floor now?" he asked. "Okay," I replied.

"Okay, I'm going to take this to my truck. I will be right back," I said as I carried the food and his clothes out the door. I threw them behind the seat and pet Jax on the head. "I'll be right back," I said as I went back up the stairs. When I went back inside, Nate was no longer in the chair. I could hear talking coming from the bedroom. "Nate? Are you ready?" I asked, walking into the bedroom towards the bathroom. "Goodbye, my love," he said as he turned towards me, and we walked out.

Jax wasn't too sure about Nate. But after a few smells of his hand, Jax decided to let Nate in the truck. Jax still kept his eye on Nate. But sniffing his leg, as most dogs do, knew he was hurt, and warmed up to him.

"Where are we going?" Nate asked as we drove out of the drive. "I'm headed to Alvin to get Jordan and Ashlyn," I replied. "After we get them, I'm going to try to get to Estelle and Megan. I wonder if Gale was home from college," I said. "I don't think she went this semester. She should be home, at least from college. She may have been at work, not sure," he replied.

From Nate's house to Jordan and Ashlyn's dog rescue was about 20 minutes. Only two small towns along the way. Jay had grown-up in one of those small towns and it can be a rough town, especially if there was no law enforcement.

My stomach was in my throat as I thought about Jordan and Ashlyn. Even though they were in their 30s. They were still kids. My kids. Sometimes they don't think ahead, and I really don't think they were prepared for this. I looked over at Nate and he had fallen asleep. I'm sure he is exhausted, I thought to myself.

We reached the city limits of Hitchcock. I could see right away I needed to be on alert. The houses along the highway; if they weren't burned down, there had graffiti written all over them. I think gangs have taken over this town.

When Jay and I were dating, we would go to his grandpa's house here in town. We would often take a drive around town, as he smoked his weed. Driving down by the school, and then back around to grandpa Wello's house, stopping at the Jack-in-the-box, we would order "10 tacos and a shitload of hot sauce" every time. So, I knew the back roads around the town. I slowed down to try to get a look ahead. I was scared. I really hadn't felt this feeling before, not the entire trip from Las Vegas to Texas, but something didn't feel right as we crept into town. "Nate," I whispered, not to startle him. He slowly opened his eyes. "I need you to help me keep an eye out for things. I just got a weird feeling about coming into town." I said. Nate sat up and looked out the window.

We passed the Jack-in-the-box, which was at the first stoplight in town. The town wasn't anything but a couple of miles long. We had 3 more stop lights and then we were out of town. As we got closer to the second stoplight, that's when I noticed. In the rear-view mirror I saw movement, but I couldn't quite tell what it was. I kept looking back. "D'ANN!" Nate yelled. I looked in front of us and a bunch of ATVs came screeching out of the fire station and blocked the road. I slammed on my brakes as Jax hit the floor. "Fuck! Now what?" I said under my breath. "Just do whatever they say. No stupid moves, you hear me?" Nate said. I watched as 5 ATVS and several other men with bandannas covering their face blocked the road. I then looked up in my rear-view mirror at several more ATVs coming up behind us. "Oh jeez," I said as I shook.

Jax was growling now as he saw what we were looking at. "Quiet, boy, I don't want you to end up like Diamond," I said, looking at him. We watched for several minutes as no one made a move. "Let me go talk to them and see what they want." Nate said as he opened his door.

Nate limped up to the closest ATV but still stood about 30 feet from it. The guy on the ATV got off and walked up to Nate. I couldn't hear what was being said. Suddenly, a man was knocking on my window with the butt of a flashlight. Jax started barking and growling hysterically. "Jax, calm down," as I held on to his collar.

I rolled the window down halfway, mainly for my protection but for his protection from Jax. "Get out of the truck," the man said, in a threating tone. "Tie the dog to the steering wheel if you want to keep him alive," he continued. I did what he said and told Jax to be good and opened the door.

The second I did, the man grabbed me. I tried pulling my arm away, but he tightened his grip. I looked over my shoulder and noticed they had also grabbed Nate. Nate was fighting with all he had. Another man came up behind me, pulled my gun out of the back of my pants. He grabbed my other arm, and they walked me towards the fire station. I couldn't turn my head enough to see what was happening to Nate. But I could hear him yelling and screaming to let us go. Then suddenly, the screaming stopped. I tried with all my might to turn to see what happened, but they were just too strong for me.

The fire station was at the back of the police department. I had only been here once when Jay had been arrested for possession of marijuana. I kept fighting them until I was completely exhausted. They walked me into the back of the police station and directly into a room with holding cells, pushed me in and locked the door behind them. I grabbed the door, which was made of chain-link fence. "What do you guys want?" I asked. "We don't have anything but a few bottles of water and some cans of food. You are welcome to them." I yelled as the men walked out of the room. "NATE," I screamed, hoping he would hear me and yell back, so I knew he was okay. "NATE," I yelled again. "Shut the fuck up in there or we will make you shut up just like your friend," a man yelled back. I sat down on the bench and started to cry.

I didn't know how much time went by, but it seemed like over an hour. The door opened. A man came through the door with a muzzle around Jax's mouth. He opened the cell door and let Jax come in. The man said nothing, just nodded his head. I reached down and took the muzzle off Jax. "Are you okay, boy?" I asked him as I snuggled around his neck. He sat down next to me and didn't make a sound. Not even growling when a man walked in the door. He handed me a bottle of water. "Thank you! You wouldn't happen to have a bowl or a cup so I can put water in it from my dog," I asked in a shy, timid voice. The man walked out the door and a few minutes later came back with a plastic bowl. "Thank you!" I said. "Can I ask what you guys are going to do with us?" But the man didn't answer. He just turned and walked out the door. There were no windows in the room. I could see there were two more cells, but they were empty.

I laid down on the cold concrete floor and started to cry. Jax lying beside me kept me warm as I cried myself to sleep.

CHAPTER FIVE

Hitchcock, Texas

Day 5 Jay

Jay woke up in a panic. "Wholly crap, we slept through the night," he yelled. Dre jumped awake. "Crap, you scared me," he said. Jay jumped out of the truck, went to the side, and peed. Dre did the same. "We gotta get going," Jay said. They jumped in the truck and sped off towards the highway. "We still need to keep an eye out for diesel," Jay said as Dre shook his head.

They reached Nacogdoches in about 30 minutes. Jay knew this road well, so he hoped on the loop that went around. Halfway round he came to a stop. In front of him was a huge pileup of cars, trucks, and some 18-wheelers. "I'm going to have to turn around and go around," he said as he backed up, turned and went to the entrance and got off the loop. He drove under the bridge and went up the exit to the northbound lanes and drove south. The road was clear all the way to the exit of Highway 59.

Occasionally, they would pass another car, traveling in the opposite direction. Before they got into Lufkin, Jay took the loop around the city. Everything was quiet.

Back on highway 59, they headed to Livingston. It took just over an hour to reach Livingston. Just as they were almost to town, they noticed a vehicle on the side of the road with its hood up and a man standing in front, looking at the engine. Jay approached slowly and rolled down his window. Dre held his rifle out of sight as Jay pulled his pistol out and put it between his legs.

"Problems?" Jay asked. "I think I got some bad gas; it's choking and coughing," the man said as he walked towards Jay. Jay felt the hair on the back of his neck stand. The man was looking around, making Jay feel extremely uncomfortable. "I don't like this," Dre whispered. "Me either," Jay replied. "Sorry dude can't help you," as Jay stepped on the gas and rolled up the window. He watched the man in the rear-view mirror as he saw another man come out from behind some trees and out of the ditch. "I knew it didn't feel right," Jay said, as Dre turned and looked out the back window. "Follow your gut every time," Dre said. "Yip," as they drove on in silence.

After about an hour, Jay asked if there were any more protein bars. "I'm starving," Jay said. Dre dug out a couple and gave one to Jay. "You think we should find some more food? I mean, we didn't pack very much," Dre asked. "I just don't know how much we would be able to find by now. It's not like when we left Vegas. People are getting desperate. Killing for a snicker's bar." Jay laughed. "I guess you're right. What about one of these 18-Wheelers that doesn't look like it has been broken into?" Dre asked. "Yeah, we can sure stop and see," Jay answered.

Several miles from Baytown, they could see smoke from the burning refineries. "Man, I bet they exploded," Jay said, watch all the smoke in the air. "There," Dre pointed. On the highway up ahead was a Grocery Store truck and trailer. "Let's see if it's been opened," Dre said.

Jay pulled the truck up to the back of the trailer. They both got out and Jay grabbed the crowbar in the back seat of the truck. They took turns hitting the heavy-duty lock with the crowbar until it finally gave way. Jay opened the door, but the smell of rotten fruit and vegetables hit him right in the face. "Oh, yuck!" he said, putting his shirt over his nose. It didn't seem to bother Dre, but he had worked in the produce department of a grocery store. Jay held the doors open while Dre crawled up in the truck. Moving boxes of decaying and spoiled fruit to the side, he saw several pallets of canned goods. He carried several cases to the end of the trailer as Jay put them in the back of the truck. After loading about 30 cases of varies things, Dre jumped down and handed Jay a case of Slim Jim's. "Oh, my favorite," Jay said as he opened one.

"What about the diesel from this truck?" Dre said. "Did we bring the syphon kit?" Jay asked. "I think it's in my bag," as Dre opened it and brought it back. Jay took a gas can to the truck, and they syphoned the diesel out. Jay poured the first two cans into the truck. Filled up the three cans and put them in the truck's bed. "Okay, I think we can make it the rest of the way," Jay said as they got back on the road and headed towards Baytown.

"Where do you think D'Ann went? To her kid's first?" Dre asked. We talked about this a few days before she left. We were going to my dad's house first, pick him and his wife up and then head to her son's. After that to my daughter's and then my sisters. I'm hoping she kept the same plan. I'm sure we will catch up with her soon," Jay replied.

They drove by the refineries, still burning. Mesmerized by the flames that still shot up into the air as the product in the pipes escaped. "Almost there," Jay said.

They passed through Kemah and then arrived on the outskirts of Texas City. "This was my old stomping grounds," Jay said as they passed the Texas City exit. Texas City also had several refineries. The smoke could be seen for miles. "I have several friends that worked there. I hope they got out safe," he said as they passed by.

They reached Interstate 45, that went on south/east into Galveston. Entering the interstate, Jay noticed movement ahead before his exit. An old 1950s tow truck that he recognized; one that used to be in the Mardi Gras parades. They were moving vehicles out of the way.

Jay pulled over next to the tow truck. Immediately recognized his old boss and his wife, Manny, and Ms. Ada. At the same time, they recognized him. Jay stopped the truck, got out, and ran over to them as they jumped out of the tow truck. "What are you doing here?" Ms. Ada asked. "Coming to get my dad and family," Jay replied, as he gave her a big hug. "Is your family, okay?" Jay asked. "Yeah, we are all good. We are just moving this pile up so people can get through with supplies to Galveston. Then the entire family is heading south to our ranch," Manny replied. "Yeah, I'm trying to pick up my family and take them to our deer lease in east Texas," Jay said. "I'm so glad you made it," Jay continued as he hugged Ms. Ada and Manny again. "We better get going," Jay said. "Be careful and good luck to you and your family," Ms. Ada said. "You are too!" Jay replied as he turned back to the truck.

Jay waved as he went by. "They are great people," he said to Dre as they drove towards Nate's exit.

Day 5 D'Ann

The door banging woke me up. My body hurt from sleeping on the cold floor. With no windows in the room, I had no idea what time it was, still night or day. I sat up moaning and groaning, as a woman and man walked in the door. The woman was carrying a tray of food, and the man had a bowl of dog food and a bowl of water. As they got closer, they both stopped dead in their tracks. "D'Ann Zepola?" the man asked. "OMG, D'Ann," the woman said. "What are you doing in here?" she continued. They both pulled down the bandanas they had on over their faces. "Lil' L? Vincent? Is that you?" I asked. "What is going on?" I asked. "We thought you guys were a part of the gang that came into town last week and looted and burned several homes with people in them. They were driving a truck just like yours. That's why they stopped you." Vincent said. "Where's Nate, Jay's dad?" I asked. "Oh my God, that's Jay's dad. I thought he looked kinda familiar." Lil L replied. "What are you doing in Texas? Last time I knew you were in Las Vegas," Lil L asked. "We escaped right after the event. We are staying at the deer lease in east Texas, but I came down here to get my kids and Jay's family to take them back up there," I replied. "We gotta get her out of here," Lil' L said to Vincent. "I don't have the keys," Vincent said. "Let's go tell "T" the boys have made a terrible mistake," Vincent said. "We will be right back and get you out of here," he continued. "I'll find out what they did with Nate," Lil' L said as she sat the tray of food and slid it under the gate. "Here though, I'm sure you're starving," she said as they hurried out the door.

"Yummy, eggs!" I said, as I gave them to Jax. I ate the piece of toast as Jax scarfed the eggs down. A few minutes later, the door opened, and Vincent unlocked the cage. I put Jax' leash on him and we followed Vincent out the door. The sun was bright. "Was I here all night?" I asked as we walked towards the City Hall building next door.

I followed Vincent to the door, with Jax by my side. He pushed open the double doors to the courtroom. In the middle of the room was "T" and sitting next to him was Nate. Nate seemed fine, just looked a little tired.

"D'Ann, I'm so sorry my boys did this to you guys. They mistook you for someone else," T said. "They came to me last night and told me they caught part of the gang that terrorized the town. But I didn't look to see who it was," he continued. "Nate, are you okay?" I asked, looking at him. "Yeah, I'm okay," he replied. "Again, I'm so sorry," T apologized. "Where is Jay?" Vincent asked. "I'm sure he is on his way to find me. I kinda left without his consent or telling him I was coming. I am here to get my kids and his family back to the deer lease," I replied. "Jay might come through town anytime soon. I don't know what he will be driving. We drove a big bus from Las Vegas, but it was on its last leg," I said. "We'll keep an eye out for him and make sure he gets through town safe and sound," T said. "Thank you! Oh, can I get my gun back, and I'm sure they took our rifle?" I asked. "Definitely," T responded, looking at one of the guys by the door, and nodded his head. A few minutes later, he came back with my pistol and the rifle I had hidden under the truck seat. "Your truck is out back," T said. "Let me help you to your truck," T said as he helped Nate stand and walk him out.

"We will probably come back this way, either today or tomorrow. Depends on what I find at my kid's house," I said. "No problem, we will keep an eye out and know it's you," T said. "If you need a place to stay, we have several houses we can put you up for the night," Lil' L said. "Thanks, I'm hoping to get them and get back on the road," I replied as we got in the truck.

"Oh my God! Wow! What the actual Hell!" I said. "Where did they take you?" I asked Nate. They held me in the fire station, sat me in a chair, and kept asking me where the rest of my gang was most of the night. I kept telling them I had no idea what they were talking about. But they just kept on. After about an hour, they left me alone.

I slept in that chair," he said. "Damn, and I thought sleeping on the hard floor was bad," I replied. "Let's get to Jordan's and get some good sleep, hopefully," I said as the pit in my stomach came back, not knowing what we were walking into once we got to Jordan's place.

Day 5 Jay

Jay pulled into the drive. He noticed the truck and the car but noticed the motorhome was gone. "I bet they're not here," he said. "Their motorhome is gone. They hopefully went to pick up the family. But I'm gonna run up and see, just in case one of them went somewhere and the other is home. I'll be right back," Jay said as he ran up the stairs. He opened the door, and the familiar smell of death hit his nose. "Oh, my God! No! Pop?" Jay yelled.

The house was small, with only two bedrooms. The kitchen and living room were one big room. He ran to the bedroom and threw open the door. The smell was worse. He hesitated and then walked slowly to the bathroom. At first, he saw all the blood all over the floor. His stomach went to his throat. He pushed the bathroom door open wider. The sight was more than he could handle. He gagged and ran out of the house. "What? What is it?" Dre said, concerned, as Jay ran down the stairs gagging and puked at the bottom. Once he caught his breath, he looked at Dre. "My stepmom," he hesitated. "She's dead! My dad is not in there," he said, grabbing a bottle of water to rinse his mouth out. "I wonder where he is," Jay said. "I need to go back up there and see if there are any clues as to where he went," Jay said as he climbed the stairs. He opened the door, and this time took his time and looked around. He noticed the house had been ransacked. Things thrown everywhere. He stood looking at the destruction. He then went to the kitchen to find another bottle of water when he saw the note on the refrigerator. "Thank God!" he said as he ran back out the door and down the stairs. "Now what?" Dre asked. "D'Ann was here. She has my dad. They are headed to her son's house," he said as he ran and got in the driver's seat.

Jay knew the road well to Jordan's house. Except for a couple of stalled vehicles, he opened it up and stepped on the gas. It didn't take long till they were in Hitchcock, his home "town. Jay knew he didn't have time to reminisce. He had to get to his dad. Driving faster than the speed limit would have been terrible back before the event. The police were very much on top of speeding in their town. But now, he knew there wouldn't be any police. He passed the Jack-in-the-box and saw a roadblock up ahead. "Crap, not again," he complained. He came to a stop and men in bandanas approached his truck. "Jay?" the man said as he pulled down his bandana. "Vincent!" Jay said as he got out of the truck and hugged him. "We've been expecting you," he said. Jay looked at him crazy. "What?" Jay asked, with a puzzled look on his face. "Long story. I'm sure D'Ann will fill you in," he said. "You saw D'Ann? And my dad? Are they okay?" Jay asked with worry in his voice. "Yes, they are fine. D'Ann said you might come through here," Vincent said. "Someone wants to see you if you came through town. Come on, I'll take you to him." Jay hesitated. He really wanted to get to his dad, but he and Dre got out of the truck and followed Vincent into the City Hall.

Opening the doors to the courtroom, he saw T and Lil' L. "Wow, it's great to see you guys," as he hugged Lil' L and pounded a fist with T. "Are you guys good? Vincent said D'Ann and my dad came through here," Jay said, looking over at Vincent. "Yeah, they left here a few hours ago, said they were headed to her son's house and that you would probably come through." T said. "Yeah, I really need to get going, but it was so great to see you guys and know you made it through all this," Jay said. "You too and stop and stay a night with us on your way out," T said as they hugged. "I will, promise," Jay replied as he and Dre headed out the door. "Be careful, and tell D'Ann we are so sorry again," Lil' L yelled back at Jay. Jay gave Dre a look like "what in the world is she talking about?" as they got in the truck and took off towards Alvin.

Day 5 D'Ann

D'Ann rounded the corner to the dog rescue. Jordan and Ashlyn had lived on the property for about 5 years now. Jordan has started as the Kennel Tech, then in a brief time became the manager. When the owner of the property mysteriously died, her family didn't want anything to do with the property, so they let Jordan and Ashlyn buy it. The rescue was a place for senior dogs to go to live out their best lives in the last few months of their life. It was hard on Jordan and Ashlyn when a dog died. But they took pride in making the dog as comfortable as they could during its transition over the rainbow bridge.

My heart started beating fast and my stomach was still in my throat as we pulled into the drive. It was a long drive that led up to their small house and the multi-building kennels. I could see that some dogs were in their kennels in the outside runs. I slammed it into park, opened the door and ran as well as I could to their front door. I knocked hard on the door and then opened it without waiting for anyone to answer. I ran through the house yelling Jordan's name. No answer. I noticed the back door was open and the screen door was shut. I flew out the back door and stumbled on my way to the kennel office.

The dogs in the outside kennels started throwing a fit, barking and carrying on. I had only made it halfway up the walkway to the office when I saw Jordan come yelling out at the dogs to be quiet. Then he looked up and our eyes met. He ran back inside and in a few second came busting out the door. He threw his arms around me, and we hugged for the longest time.

Tears were flowing down my cheeks. I looked up and Ashlyn was standing in the doorway. She ran over to us and embraced us both. "I didn't think I would ever see you again," he said. "I knew you wouldn't leave the dogs to come to the deer lease, so I came to get you," I said. "When did you guys get to the deer lease, and where is Jay?" he asked. "It's been about a week, and I'm sure he will be here soon. I kinda left without him knowing. I had to get here to make sure you guys were okay," I replied. "We are doing great. Some of the dog parents have brought us food and water, even dog treats and food," he said. "Wow, I can't believe you are here?" Ashlyn said as she hugged me again.

Nate came limping up the walk. "Nate!" Jordan said as he ran up to Nate. "Here, come sit down," as we all walked over to the picnic table under a tree. "You, okay?" Jordan said, looking at Nate. "Yeah,

I'll be fine. Just didn't get a lot of sleep last night," he replied. "We have a few family rooms with beds in the kennel for the dog parents to visit and stay with their dogs. You're more than welcome to lay down," Ashlyn said. "Come on, I'll show you." Nate got up and limped behind her as they disappeared inside the office.

"I came here to take you guys back to the deer lease. Things are gonna get worse every day," I said, looking at Jordan. "You know I can't leave. We have 7 dogs right now. Two will probably pass tonight sometime. Three in the next day or two, but the other two probably will be a while," Jordan said, looking at me. "Well, I'm not leaving without you. I guess we will have to wait until they have all passed, then we can take the other two back with us. Oh, crap speaking of, I almost forgot," as I got and walked around the house to the truck. I grabbed Jax' leash, and we walked back to where Jordan was sitting. "This is Jax. He found me a few days ago," I said. We lost Diamond. She was killed on our way here from Vegas," I continued. "Aww my Doe Doe," Jordan said with sadness in his voice. "He's pretty, though," Jordan said as he took a treat out of his pocket and handed it to Jax. He was scared at first, but Jordan was a dog whisperer, and when he talked, the dogs listened. Jax took the treat and laid down on the ground and chewed on it.

Ashlyn joined us as we sat for over an hour talking about what had happened to each of us since the whole thing started. I told them what I had found at Nate's house and that he was still in shock. Ashlyn told us how the community rallied around the kennel to make sure the dogs and them were good and had everything they needed.

Jordan looked at his watch. "Do you know how to tell time on that, since it's not a digital?" I asked, joking with him. Jordan and I had a relationship that most didn't understand. We could joke around with each other, call each other names, and we always knew we were just kidding around. "Yes, mother," he said. "Yeah, after I showed him," Ashlyn laughed. "It's time for supper and meds for the dogs," he said, getting up. "I think we should move Ginger and Isabelle to the rainbow room tonight. I think it's close," Jordan said as we all walked towards the office.

I didn't think Jax would enjoy staying in the kennel, and I truthfully wanted him next to me anyway, so he walked on his leash everywhere I went. We watch Jordan and Ashley move the two elderly dogs to the rainbow room. The dogs were small dogs, Ginger was a mean little poodle and Isabelle was a beautiful min pin. Jordan had to carry Isabelle. She was too weak to walk very far. While Ashlyn led Ginger slowly to her little room.

In the room there was soft relaxing music playing. It was unlike any kennel I had ever seen. A big soft fluffy dog bed lay in the middle of the room. They dimmed the lights a little. Jordan laid Isabelle on the dog bed. Ashlyn handed her a syringe as Jordan caressed and talked to Isabelle. She didn't even make a move when Jordan gave her the shot. "I don't think it will be very much longer," Jordan said. I couldn't watch. Tears flowed down my cheeks. I thought of Diamond and the way her life ended. "I'm gonna step out. It's too much for me," I said as I walked out of the room. Ashlyn followed me out and went into the next room where Ginger was. I watched Ashlyn as she sat next to Ginger, petting her and talking to her, telling her it was okay for her to go play on the other side of the bridge.

I shut the door, and Jax and I walked outside. I was sobbing now. I walked to the house and opened the back door. Jax followed me in, and suddenly we heard barking come running out of a room. Waffles, their chiweenie, came right at us, barking up a storm. I didn't know how Jax was around other dogs, so I stayed in between them. But it seemed like Jax wanted to play. Waffles was more interested in me than in Jax. Waffles never liked me, even when he was a baby. Maybe because I always called him "Pancake" instead of Waffles. I looked around to see what they used for lights.

The kennel ran off solar and a generator, but the house was not connected. I saw a few candles on the table. It was now getting dark, and hard too hard to see. A lighter was lying beside the candles. I light all 5 of them as shadows danced on the walls. Then I heard the low deep growl of Jax and then Waffles started to growl. He came over by me and stood there as Waffles ran to the bedroom. I could see well enough with the candles to see the hair on the back of his neck stand up. He was looking towards the front door, which I had left open when

I came through earlier. I grabbed his collar as I saw a shadow appear at the front door.

Day 5 Jay

It only took 30 minutes for Jay to get to Alvin, then Jordan and Ashlyn lived about 15 minutes north, in between Alvin and Pearland. It was getting dark now, as Jay had to look hard not to miss Jordan's road. In the country around Alvin, the roads were not marked very well. Jay had only been to Jordan and Ashlyn's house a handful of times. But he thought he remembered the way. He drove slowly trying to see what looked familiar. "I think this is the road," he said, turning off the highway onto a blacktop road. He drove about three more miles, then he could see on the hilltop the outline of the kennels. "We are here," he said as he turned down their long drive. Jay pulled up behind Doug's truck. "Let's check it out," Jay said as they both got out of the truck. Dre stood by the door and watched as Jay disappeared in the dark.

Jay looked through the front door of the small house. But all he could see were lit candles sitting on the table as shadows danced on the walls. He opened the screen door. Then he heard it. A low, deep growl. "Who's there?" He heard the familiar voice coming from the dark. "D'Ann, it's me Jay," he said. "Jeez," I said as I ran over to Jay and threw my arms around him. I was so excited to hear his voice I had let go of Jax and forgotten all about him. The deep growl turned into snarling. "Jax, Jax, it's okay," as I ran back to him and grabbed his collar. I had taken his leash off and laid it on the table when we first came into the house. I reached for it and put it on him and held him as he growled and barked.

"This is Jax," I said as I made Jax sit down. Jay held out his hand, but Jax continued to growl. He'll get used to you," I said as I lead him to the chair and made him lie down underneath it. I sat down and motioned Jay to come sit down at the table as well.

"Where is my dad?" Jay asked. "He's asleep. We had a bad day and night yesterday," I replied. I was stopped by T and Lil' L in Hitchcock. They indicated something but didn't tell me what it was.

Lil' L said to tell you she was very sorry again about what happened. What happened?" he asked. "It was just a case of mistaken identity. They got pretty rough with us until Lil'L, and Vincent recognized me and your dad. Then they let us go," I replied. I said little about what they had done to his dad. "But we are fine," I said. "I can't believe you took off in the middle of the night like you did," Jay said with a touch of anger in his voice. Here it comes, I thought to myself. "Look, I know you're mad at me, but I am exhausted. Can we talk about this in the morning?" I asked. "Did you make the trip by yourself?" I asked. "Crap, no, Dre is outside waiting for me to let him know it's okay," Jay said with a slight smile. Jay got up and walked to the door. "It's okay Dre, you can come in," Jay yelled.

Dre walked in the door. "We found you," he said, looking at me through the candles. "Yes, I'm fine, tired as hell, but I'm good," I replied. Jordan and Ashlyn are out in the kennels. They have two dogs that are getting ready to pass away tonight. They have several family rooms when the families come to spend time with their dogs before they pass. I guess we can stay in one of them. That's where your dad is," I said as we got up and headed toward the back door. Jax walked beside me but kept a very close eye on the two guys.

We walked in through the office and towards the rainbow rooms. Jordan was just coming out. "Jay!" he ran up and hugged him. "Mom told me you would probably be here soon," as he looked at me. I rolled my eyes and gave him a look that said, "Why you tell him I said that?" Jordan grinned and gave me a look back. It was like we could read each other's mind sometimes.

"How are things in there?" I asked. "They both are gone now. We move their bodies to the freezer and if the family is involved, they can either have them buried in our pet cemetery or we can cremate them. If the families aren't involved, we cremate them and put their ashes in a special place at the cemetery." He explained. The two, unfortunately, we don't know what happened to their parents, so we will have to cremate them tomorrow." He added.

"This is Dre," I said as I pointed him out to Jordan. "This is Jordan, my youngest son," I said as Ashlyn came out of the other room. "This is my daughter-in-law, Ashlyn. This is Dre." I said. You guys remember Sean, don't you from Vegas, the tow truck driver Jay worked with?" I asked. "Yeah, yeah, I remember him," Jordon shook his head yes. "Well, this is his brother," I replied. "Nice to meet you," Ashlyn said.

"You guys can follow me, and I will show you where you can stay." Ashlyn said. "We turned the generator that runs everything but the freezer off at night. So, there won't be any lights. The bathroom is the 3rd door down the hallway. But we are also trying to conserve water, so if you can, guys, just step outside." Ashlyn continued. "Good night, yawl," Jordan and Ashlyn said as they walked towards the office and out the door to their house.

Jay and I shut the door to our tiny room. It had a full-size bed and a dog bed. "Jax, this is your bed tonight," I said as he looked up at me with a question in his eyes. I giggled. "He has been sleeping with me. I guess he thinks you should sleep in the dog bed and him and I on the bed," I said with a smile. "Ha Ha," Jay responded.

CHAPTER SIX

It's a boy

DAY 6

"Good morning!" I said as I walked in the back door. Jordan and Ashlyn were sitting at the kitchen table drinking coffee. "Good morning. How did you sleep?" Ashlyn asked. "Good," I responded. "So, we need to figure out what we are going to do," I said. "Well, we checked on the other 3 dogs and we think it will be soon." "Maybe we should go see if Gale and Jay's sisters are okay, and then come back here," I said, looking up as we heard the back door open. "Good morning," Jay said, walking in the door. "You got coffee?" he asked. "It's instant coffee, that okay?" Ashlyn asked. "Yeah, sure, I can get it just point where things are," he said as he walked over to the kitchen counter. "The water on the stove is already hot. Cups are up there," as Ashlyn pointed to the cupboard. "Got any more for me?" Nate said, walking in the back door. "Pop," Jay said, walking over to his dad and giving him a bear hug. "I was so scared after seeing what your house looked like," Jay said. Nate said nothing, just shook his head.

Nate and Jay sat down at the table after making their cups of coffee. "So, I guess Jordan and Ashlyn have 5 dogs left here at the kennels. Three are probably going to die in the next few hours, they can't leave until then. I think we should go get Gail and Lynn and see if your sisters want to come with us. What do you think?" I said as I looked at Jay. "I don't even know where they live now," Jay said. "Well, Estelle and Ron bought a beach house out by Jamaica Beach.

Megan still lives in Texas City, and Gale lives in the same apartment complex. So, they should be together, I'm assuming," Nate said.

"Should we split up and I'll go get Estelle and her family and you go get Megan and Gale?" I looked at Jay. "I don't think we should split up again," Jay said. "I don't think they will all fit in the truck," I said. "I will just go get them and be right back. You go get Megan, Gail and the kids and we will meet back here," I said. "We need to get the food and water out of the back of my truck first," Jay said. "We can help you do that," Ashlyn said. "Okay, I guess we could do that. Are you sure you will be, okay?" Jay asked me. "Dre you can stay and help with the dogs. Pop, you can go with me. The truck I got is a quad cab," Jay said. "When are you going to leave? It looks like it's going to storm. The sky is really dark off to the east," he asked.

"I guess I should get going, then maybe beat the storm. Do you have Estelle's address?" I asked, looking at Nate. "Her address is in my phone, which doesn't work, but it's pretty easy to find. You know the water tower as you get into Jamaica Beach? The next road, it says Public Beach, turn there and go all the way to the beach. The street runs along the beach, she is the 3rd house on the right. It's the only sea green house, can't miss it," Nate said.

"Okay then, do you need help carrying the food in?" I asked Jay. "We can help," Jordan said as he got up. "Let's do it then, before it starts raining," Jay said as he and Nate walked towards the door.

"Hey! Jordan, can I leave Jax here? There just won't be enough room in the truck?" I yelled before he went out the door. "Yeah, he can stay here in the house with Waffles," he responded. "Alright, I'm gonna go. I will be back as soon as I can," I said, giving Jordan and Ashlyn a hug.

I walked out to Jay's truck. "I'm going so I can get there before the rain comes," I said, reaching out to hug him. "Please be careful. I saw Manny and Ms. Ada are clearing the interstate so people could get into Galveston," Jay said. "Oh, I'm glad to hear they are okay," I replied. "It was great to see them," Jay replied.

"I'll see you all soon," I said as I waved at everyone and walked to the truck. I turned the truck on and looked at the gas gauge. "I should be able to make it there and back," I said to myself as I put it in drive and drove out of the driveway.

I didn't dare go through Hitchcock again by myself just in case T and Lil' L weren't around. So, I took highway 517 to Dickinson and caught the Interstate to Galveston. Alvin had a lot of farms around the area, so it did not surprise me to see a few older model trucks on the road. The 517 highway was mostly clear, with a few cars still sitting in the middle of the road. Some houses along the way were boarded up. Some even looked like there might be people in them.

I reached the city limits of Dickinson and noticed at the CVS on the corner of 517 and Interstate 45 was a big white tent in the parking lot and a trailer that said "RED CROSS" with a long line of people getting water and meals. "That's great, this city has got it together," I thought as I entered the interstate and headed South towards Galveston.

On this stretch of interstate, there was big truck after big truck stranded along both sides of the interstate. It looked like all the truck trailers had been opened and whatever was in them was gone now.

Up ahead I knew was my most favorite store in the world, BUCEES. I so wished it was open. I loved the Beaver Nuggets and the Candied Cashews. As I passed it, I saw several old trucks and the doors to the store open. "What, are they open?" I said about wreaking the truck into a stalled car. "I'm gonna have to check that out when I get back," I said, all excited.

The rain started falling down. I turned on the windshield wipers as they screeched across the glass, and a piece of rubber flew off. "Jeez, I better hurry," I thought. The rain was coming down hard now and with the windshield wiper it was hard to see out the windshield, so I had to go slow. Water was pouring in the broken passenger side window. "Oh, Lawd, whose idea was it to go to Galveston?" I shook my head.

Going over the causeway into Galveston, I looked to see if I could see the water. I always loved seeing the water in the bay. But the rain was too hard. Occasionally, it would let up a little and I would get a glimpse of the gulf. I turned on the 61st Street exit and headed towards the Gulf. The sky was black. Reaching the Seawall, I could see through the bands of rain the waves kicking up in the Gulf. The tide was high. It was covering most of the beach. I drove along the seawall and towards Jamaica Beach. At least the rain was hitting my window and not coming in the passenger side anymore. The wind was making the rain seem like it was falling sideways. By the time I got to Jamaica Beach, the surge had reached the seawall. "Oh my God!" I realized. "This could be a tropical storm or a fricken hurricane,"

I started to get really nervous, "what if I get stranded here? The water is known to cover the road in this area during storms." I said. I could barely see the water tower and looked intensely to the road signs Nate told me to watch for. "There it is," as I turned towards the Gulf. I slammed on my brakes. "Crap, what if the water comes up to her house and floods the truck? Then we defiantly won't get out of here. I backed the truck up back on to the highway. Across from the road was a house that was all boarded up. It looked to be on higher ground. I will leave it here and walk. It's not that far.

I got out of the truck and locked it. Again, not that it helped with a broken window, but it made me feel better. The rain was freezing and coming down hard. It stung my skin as I walked towards Estelle's house. The wind was making it difficult to walk. It seemed to be getting stronger. Through the wind and the rain, I finally could see the green house. I was shivering, and the cold was making it more difficult to walk. My joints were killing me.

I reached her house and climbed the stairs one step at a time, hurting with each step. I banged on her door. Soaking wet, Nick opened the door just a crack. "It's me D'Ann," I said. Nick opened the door wider to let me in. "Wholly shit, MOM! He yelled. Estelle came out of her bedroom, her pregnant belly so big. Stacie came running out behind her. "D'Ann, Oh, my God, what are you doing here?" she cried, grabbing the throw blanket off the couch and wrapping it around me. "Let's get you out of these wet clothes," she said as she helped me to the bedroom. "I'm sorry I'm getting your floor all wet," I said, with my teeth chattering. "It's all good we can mop it up," she said. She went to her closet and pulled out a robe. Me being quite bigger than her, I looked at it and said, "I don't know if that will fit." "Here, just wrap it around you. "We will hang your clothes in the shower and hopefully they will dry soon," she said.

Estelle stepped out of the room and closed the door. I got undressed and hung my clothes over the shower doors. Put the robe on and then took a blanket off the bed and wrapped it around me. I walked out to the living room. Estelle and Nick were standing at the French doors, looking out at the black sky and the Gulf bubbling. "I think it's a hurricane," Nick said. "With no way to get warnings, we have no clue how bad it can get or when it's going to hit," he continued. "I know the water was almost up to the highway when I was on my way here," I said as they turned to look at me.

Stacie ran up to me and hugged me. "I'm glad to see you, Tia D'Ann," she said. Stacie was 9 years old now, and one of the most beautiful little girls you would ever see. We knew someday she would be a model. Jay and I lived in the area when she was born. When Estelle had to work, we would watch her. As she got older, she would spend the weekends with us. She loved her Uncle Jay, and he spoiled her rotten. Nick was no longer a boy. He was around 7 years old when I came into Jay's life. Now a grown man at almost 21. He had just finished welding classes at the college and was looking for his first actual job working in the refineries.

"Is Ron not here?" I asked. Estelle turned and looked back out the window. "No, he was on a trip to the east coast, and never made it back," she said with sadness in her voice. "When is the baby due?" I asked. "About two weeks. I'm so scared. We had no way to get to the hospital. I was afraid I would have him here at home. But you have a vehicle, right?" she asked with hope in her voice. "Yes, I parked it up by the highway on high ground, so hopefully it won't get flooded if the water rises more," I replied. "It looks like cities at least in this area are starting to organize and help people. I saw the Red Cross in Dickinson and it looked like they had the buses open and doing something there.

I'm hoping you guys will come with me to meet up with Jay and your dad and go to the deer lease. Jay is out checking on Megan and Gale right now," I said. "you said my dad? Then he and Veronica are, okay?" I looked down and then back up and met her eyes. "What?"

she asked. "Your dad is fine. He is at Jordan's place, but I'm sorry to say Veronica didn't make it. She was gone when I got to your dad's place," I said as I looked at Stacie. "We will talk about it later," I whispered.

The wind started blowing harder. "Do you think we should put boards on the windows?" I asked, watching the wind whip the rain around. "We have hurricane shutters on these windows and door, I can go out and latch them shut," Nick said. "I think it's time, it's getting bad out there," Estelle said. "Be careful," she said.

Nick went out the front door so the wind and rain wouldn't come in the doors facing the gulf. He walked around on the deck, closed the shutters and latched them tight. Picked up the deck chairs one by one and took them downstairs underneath the house and tied them to the pillar so they wouldn't blow away. The trash can had already blown in the street, so he went to retrieve it. The wind was getting so strong now; he had to wrestle the dumpster all the way back to the house.

"Man, it's really getting bad," he said as he came in soaked. You could feel the house sway with the wind. "Have you seen any of your neighbors since this all happened? I asked. "Yeah, we've seen them out walking on the beach a few times," Estelle replied. "They are probably just as surprised about this storm as we are," I commented. Estelle lit a couple of candles as the shutters cut off what little light there was coming from the doors and big windows. "Are you hungry? It should be close to noon?" she asked. "We have quite a bit of food left. When they said this season was going to be bad for hurricanes, I went out and stocked up. We have a generator that had been running the refrigerator, but we ran out of gas last week, and the neighbors ran out as well." She continued.

She opened a bag of chips and a bottle of salsa and sat them on the table. "Oh, that would hit the spot. I haven't had chips and salsa for weeks," I said, walking over to the table and sitting down. "I guess we just sit and wait it out," I said, looking out the kitchen window.

"I think I'm going to go lie down for a while. "My back has been hurting today," Estelle said as she walked to her bedroom. Stacie was in her bedroom, playing with her dollhouse. I got up and went to sit on her bed. She handed me a barbie and asked me to brush her hair. It was getting dark in her room, so I asked her if she wanted to move some things into the living room and play there. We played Barbies and colored for hours. Even Nick colored with us, as the storm raged on outside.

Day 6 Jay

Jay and his dad headed towards Texas City. The rain was coming down now, and the sky was getting dark. "So, what's been going on with Megan? Didn't you say she was getting divorced?" Jay asked Nate as they drove. "Yeah, I guess Landon found a girlfriend, so Megan kicked him to the curb," Nate said.

Megan was Jay's youngest sister. She was about 8 years younger than Jay. When I met Jay, he told me, "If my sister Megan doesn't like you, then I can't be with you." Fortunately, for me I think she liked me. Megan's oldest daughter, Celia, was a teenager now. Her father was Megan's first husband, Isaiah. He worked in construction. Then with her second husband, Landon, she had twins, a boy Jonny and a girl, Tally. They had just turned 8 in the summer. We had heard from Nate several times that she was having problems in her marriage, and when Isaiah would pick up Celia for a visit, he would take the twins as well.

"Isaiah has really stepped in and taken care of the kids. He's a great father," Nate said. "Yeah, D'Ann and I always loved Isaiah. Even today, we still consider him our brother-in-law," Jay replied. "I think Isaiah was working out of town when it happened, not sure if he will be there. "Hope he's okay," Jay responded.

Jay turned in to the apartment complex. "That way," Nate pointed. "Park right here, I'll run up there and see if they are okay," Nate said, getting out at the exact time a bolt of lightning struck a tree on the other side of the street. The thunder shook the truck. "Shit," Jay yelled, covering his head.

Nate got to the overhang where he was out of the rain. Walked over to the door but noticed a note of the front of the door. "We are at the shelter at the high school. Gail and baby with us," it read. Nate ran as best he could back to the truck and quickly jumped in as thunder rattled the truck again. "Wow, it's getting bad. They are at the high school; guess there is a shelter there," Nate said, all out of breath.

Jay backed out of the parking place and proceeded out of the drive. Slowly they traveled to the high school. Dodging stalled vehicles and blowing debris in the streets. The high school entrance had an awning that covered the front of the building and covered the driveway. Several people were standing outside, watching the weather. Jay pulled right up under the awning. They both jumped out and Jay locked the door. He didn't want to take the chance that someone would take off with the truck as they all looked at him.

They walked into the building and followed the noise to the gymnasium. It looked like hundreds of people were in there. Sleeping bags, blankets and pillows covered the gym floor. Kids played in the bleachers. Jay spotted Gale right away sitting on one of the benches with a book in her hands. Sitting beside her on the floor was Lynn, playing with another little girl around the same age.

Gale was Jay's only child. She was only 6 years old when I met Jay. She was a precocious little girl and grew into an exceptional woman. At 18, after high school, Gale had gotten into a very abusive relationship, but being the strong woman she was, removed herself from the situation. Even though she found out she was pregnant. She went on to college and now she was in her last semester of Medical School. She was going to be a doctor soon. Her little girl, Jay's granddaughter, was now 5 years old and had just started school. With the help from Gale's mom, Mindy. Gale and Lynn both thrived.

Jay and Nate walked across the gym floor, stepping around makeshift beds. Gale had looked up, and looked right at them, but didn't comprehend who she was seeing. Taking a second look, she got up and started sobbing as she ran towards them. "Daddy," she cried. The two embraced in a hug. Lynn saw her mom get up and run crying. She got up and chased after her crying. Then Lynn saw Pawpaw. She ran straight to Nate. He scooped her up in his arms.

"Are you guys, okay?" Jay asked Gale as they walked over to the bench to sit down. "Yeah, Megan and I came here when we ran out of food. Our neighbor came and got us and told us the Red Cross was setting up a shelter. We've been here for over a week. I'm so glad you're here." She said as she hugged him again. "Where's Megan and the kids?" Nate asked. "The older kids are in one of the classrooms, down the hall. Megan is probably in the kitchen helping prepare food for everyone. The food here sucks, but it's better than starving at home," she said. "Well, we are here to take you to the deer lease with us, where we have plenty of food," Jay said with a smile. "But we are gonna have to wait till this storm passes, trees are being blown over and debris all over the roads," Jay said.

Nate got up "Where's the kitchen at?" he asked, looking back at Gale. "It's just through those double doors and down the hallway, can't miss it," she said. He walked in the direction she said. Through the double doors and down the hallway, just as he was reaching the door, Megan came around the corner. "Pop, is that you?" Megan said as she jogged over to him, and they embraced. "What are you doing here?" she asked. "We came to get you guys and take you to the deer lease, where it's safe," he replied. "Where is Veronica? Did she see the kids?" Megan asked. She saw the sad look in her dad's eyes. "Megan, Veronica is dead. Some men attacked us, and they shot her right in front of me," he said as tears filled his eyes.

Nate and Megan walked out into the gym and towards Gale and Jay. "Jay!" Megan screamed and ran to Jay. Jay got up and hugged his sister. "We came to take you to the deer lease," he said. "But we are gonna have to wait till this storm passes. It's too dangerous right now to drive in it." "That's okay, I need to help get lunch ready for all these people," she said. "I gotta get back to the kitchen, but I'll be back later," she said as she ran off toward the double doors.

Occasionally, the lights would flicker, as the generator would begin to stall. Lynn would start crying because it scared her, and she would run to her mom to be held. Nate and Jay sat back down on the bench. The lights in the gym were the emergency lights run by the generators. It was still a little dim. They sat in silence, listening to the storm outside, and watched the little one's play. They knew this was where they would have to spend the night.

Day 6 D'Ann

After playing hard with Stacie all afternoon, I laid down on the sofa and dozed off. Stacie had fallen asleep on the floor, and Nick was in his room. One shutter outside had shaken loose and was blowing in the wind and banging against the window.

I sat up and looked at the window that the shutter was banging against. At about the same time, it came loose from the wall and flew off to the side of the house. "Damn," I said, watching the lightning and felt the thunder rattle the house.

Stacie was still asleep on the floor. I got up and took the blanket off the end of the sofa and covered her up. I walked to the kitchen and opened a bottle of water. I heard a soft muffled noise, not knowing if it was coming from outside Nick's room or Estelle's room. I walked closer to the bedrooms. I heard it again. I knocked softly on Estelle's door. "Come in," she said, gritting her teeth. The minute I walked into the bedroom; I knew she was having labor pains. She was sitting up in bed holding her stomach. "Oh, no, you can't be going into labor now. There's no way we can get out of here. The storm is bad," I said, hurrying over to her bedside. "How long have you been having contractions?" I asked her. "A while, I think when I woke up with a backache this morning it was the start of them," she said. "Crap," was all I could say. "They are about 5 minutes apart," she said. "WHAT!" I yelled at her, "Why didn't you holler at me sooner?" I said with a nervousness to my voice. "I don't know nothing' bout birthin babies," I said quoting a line from my favorite movie. "Ron and I took Lamaze classes, but it's been 9 years since I had a baby," she said. "YOU! I said, "it's been 33 years since I had a baby," looking at her all crazy. "What do I do? All I know is what I see on TV. Boil water, get clean towels and sheets," trying to interject some humor into the seriousness of our situation.

"I have the urge to push," she said as a contraction hit. "No, Nope, you keep that baby right up inside of you till I figure this out," I said. Her moans were getting a little louder with each one. "HOLD ON, stay here," as I got up and ran to Nick's bedroom. Pounding on the door, "Nick, Nick," I yelled. He came to the door and opened it, his eyes as big as saucers. "What?" he said. "Your mom's in labor. She gonna have this baby right here and pretty damn quick," I half screamed. "Wholly crap," he said. "What do we do?" he asked. "I don't know. I was hoping you knew," I said, hiding my smile. He looked at me crazy. "Umm, that's the same look I gave your mom when she said the baby is coming," I said as the scream got louder, coming from Estelle's bedroom. "Is there any way to boil water?" I asked him, "Yeah, it's a gas stove and we still have some," he answered. "Okay, go put a big pot of water on to boil, even if it is rainwater, try not to use our drinking water. We are gonna need that," I commanded. "Okay," as he ran to the kitchen.

I went back into the bedroom, and Stacie was standing there crying. "What's wrong, little girl?" I said to her. "Why is mama screaming like that?" she asked with tears running down her checks. "Your mama is going to have her baby in a little bit. She is fine. It just hurts, but it's a good hurt. Now she is going to scream a little more and a little louder, but it's nothing to fear. Once the baby comes, it will all be over with. Are you ready to see your baby brother?" I asked her. She smiled and shook her head. "Okay, I need you to be my helper. Can you go get all the clean towels from mama's bathroom and your bathroom and bring them in here?" I asked. "Yes," as she ran out the room.

Nick came into the room. "The water is on to boil. What else can I do?" he asked. "Do you have a watch or a clock with a second hand that is working?" I asked. "I think so. Let me go find it," he said as he left the room.

"Estelle, we need to get you in to a long t-shirt or night gown, so I have access to your coochie. Aww Lawd, I'm going to see my sister-in-law's coochie," I said, smiling. Estelle again didn't think my humor was funny, as she let out another loud moan. Nick and Stacie came running back into the room at the same time. "Here," Nick said, handing me a watch. "Good, good," I said, let me have you take your sister out of the room so I can help your mama get into a nightgown," I said as Nick shoed Stacie out. Stacie didn't want to go, she started crying "I wanna stay with mama," she cried. "Okay Nick, she can stay," I said as Nick went out the door and closed it.

I helped Estelle get out of her sweatpants and put on one of Ron's big t-shirts. While I got her out of bed, I grabbed several towels and laid them on the bed where she would be sitting. I tore off all the top sheets and blankets. She crawled back into bed, and I covered her with just a sheet. "Nick, you can come in now," I yelled.

Nick opened the door. "The water is about to boil," he said. "Okay, just keep it hot. I don't know what we need it for, but who knows?" I shrugged my shoulder and gave him a smirky smile.

Estelle started moaning and panting as the pain intensified. "Okay, Nick, this is what I want you to do. Sit here beside your mom and when she has a contraction, the minute she starts to relax. I want you to time it till the next one starts, Okay?" I asked, "Yeah, Okay," he said as he sat beside her. "What can I do?" Stacie asked, looking up at me. "Here as I lifted her up on the other side of the bed. "When mama moans and scream, I want you to tell her Breathe Breathe and just keep repeating it, okay? Can you do that?" I asked "Yes, Breathe Breathe, like that?" she looked up at me and asked. "Yes, see another one is coming," as Estelle started moaning. "Breathe, Breathe, Breathe," Stacie and I said together. "Okay, Nick, time it," I said as her contraction subsided.

I left the room and went to the laundry room, got a clothes basket and brought it into the room. Took several of the towels and lined the basket. Then went over to the changing table and dresser Estelle had in her bedroom and found the suction bulb that every new mother has and put it in the basket. "Scissors?" I looked at Nick.

He got up and went to the kitchen and came back with a pair of scissors. "Do me a favor. I'll take the watch, take these scissors and hold them over the flame on the stove. I want to get them good and sterilized, then go into your mom's bathroom and look for some rubbing alcohol. Pour it all over the scissors. Don't touch the blades after that, then place them in the basket right there." I said. Nick got up and handed me the watch. "I timed it, and it was like 3 minutes and 30 seconds." I took the watch. "We are getting close," I said, looking at Estelle.

"Stacie and you go get me one of your rubber bands for your hair," I said as she got off the bed. "I better hurry. She's gonna start screaming again," she said, running out of the room. Estelle and I both giggled.

"Can you think of anything else we might need when the baby gets here? I got scissors to cut the cord, she is getting a rubber band to put around the cord. Towels and warm water to clean him up. Crap, I can't think of what else we might need," I said, thinking.

"I don't know if the kids should be in here when he's born. The blood and afterbirth might scare them," Estelle said as another contraction started. I started the timer and timed the contraction. "45 seconds," I said. "I know we are close, but when my dog had puppies, it took forever," I said, smiling at her while she gave me a dirty look. "I know, I know, you're not having puppies. It probably would have been easier. Brooklyn ate the afterbirth," I giggled. Finally, a giggle came out of Estelle and then right into another contraction.

"Should I look at your coochie now to see if I see anything?" I asked. "I don't know. I guess you could. Lord, this is embarrassing," she said. "YOU! You're not the one looking at it," I said.

I got up and shut the door, "wait a minute guys before coming in, I'm gonna look at yo mom's coochie," I said with a serious face, but laughing on the inside. "Really, Tia," Nick said, rolling his eyes. I giggled and shut the door.

"Okay, here it goes. I just want you to know I've never seen a woman's coochie up close like this," I said, looking at Estelle as she rolled her eyes. I lifted the sheet and moved her legs apart. "Oh, Lawd girl, least you could have done was shave that thing, I thought there was a bear down there," I said, "Shut up and get it done," she said going into another contraction. I waited till she was done and spread her legs apart again. "I'm going in," I said. "I don't see anything, except you have a trickle of blood, but I think that is normal. My dog did that before she had her babies. Should I stick my finger in there to see if I feel anything?" I asked her. "Yeah, sure, why not just violate me while I'm giving birth!" she said. "Oh, YES! she does have a sense of humor," I said, smiling at her. "Just do it already," she demanded. "Okay if you insist," I felt around without looking and inserted two fingers and pulled them out quickly. "Nope, Nope, don't feel anything," I said, as I grabbed a towel and wiped my fingers and hand off. "So gross," I said. "I guess that is what the hot water is for washing your hands," I said, covering her legs back up and opening the door to the bedroom. "You guys can come in now," I said.

The contractions continued about the same for hours. It was now dark outside, and the wind and rain were not letting up. We had moved all the candles we could find in the house and had a couple flashlights giving us as much light as possible.

Between contractions, Stacie wiped her mom's forehead with a wet cloth. Estelle tried her best to relax between contractions. The last hour, though, they were getting stronger and longer. The last one she had was a little over 2 minutes. "I'm getting the urge to push," she said. Well, I guess let me look and feel again. The kids left the room as I washed my hands in the bathroom sink with a pot of water we had moved in there. Lifting the sheet and spreading her legs, I stuck my 2 fingers in. "Oh, my God! I feel something. I think it's his head," I said, pulling out my fingers and going to the bathroom to wash. "I don't know, but I guess if you have the urge to push, do it. What do you think?" I asked, looking at her.

She was exhausted. "I wish I had ice chips, like when I was in labor with Stacie," she said. "I know," I said. The next contraction came so very hard. She screamed so loud; Stacie came busting through the door. "Mama?" she said with concern in her voice. "Remember, Stacie, I told you when it gets really close mama is gonna scream really loud and even cry, but she is okay, she will be okay," I said, holding Stacie against me as Estelle let out a bloodcurdling scream. Stacie turned her face to my side. "Do you want to wait outside?" I asked. She peeked out, and in a small mousey voice said, "No."

I helped her crawl back on the bed and next to her mom. I handed her a wet cloth, and she began wiping her forehead again. Estelle started panting. "Okay, here comes another one," I said, looking at Stacie. "Come on, let's all scream with her. Maybe it will make us feel better," I said as Estelle streamed and grabbed the sheets. In unison, we all screamed at the top of our lungs. Stacie smiled. "See, that felt better, Huh?" I asked her. "Here comes another one. They are coming quick now, it's almost time, girl if you gotta push then push. Let me lift the sheet so I can see what is going on," I said as I lifted the sheets over her legs. "Aww, man," Nick said as he moved to the top of the bed, "That's a sight you can't unsee," he said. "I know what you mean. I thought there was a bear down there the first time I looked," We laughed.

Estelle grabbed the sheets and screamed as she pushed. "Okay, Okay, you got it." Then another one and another one. She pushed and pushed and screamed and screamed. "Scream all you want. No one is going to hear you in this storm. What a tale to tell, being born in a hurricane, at home!" I said. I grabbed a towel and put it at the end of her bottom to catch the baby with. "It's coming, I can feel it," as she let out a big scream and pushed. "I see it, I see his head, push, push," I screamed. Another big push and his head was out. "Okay, now the shoulders," I said. I placed my hand on his head and supported his neck as Estelle gave it one more big push, and out he came. He was covered in goo. I grabbed the towel and placed him in the towel. "Hand me that sucker bulb," I said to Nick standing there looking with aww at his baby brother. I sucked the gunk out of his mouth as he began to cry. I took the scissors and cut the cord and immediately put the rubber band around the end that stuck out from his belly button. I wrapped him in the towel and handed him to Estelle.

Mama, sister and big brother looked in amazement at their new addition to their family. Then about 30 minutes later Estelle moaned again. "Here comes the afterbirth. You need to push. Make sure to get it all out," I said to her as I handed Nick the baby. I got it all in a towel and took the towel out of the bedroom and put it in a trash bag and tied it up, walked over to the front door and sat it outside.

I went back into the room and Nick had handed the baby to Estelle as she was examining his face and little fingers. "I don't know how long after you have a baby will he start breast feeding?" I said. "It was pretty quick within an hour after I had her," she said, pointing her head to Stacie. "Shoot, what time was it?" I asked. "It was about 45 minutes ago," Estelle said. I looked at the watch. 3:10am on September 30th, 2022. Write that down somewhere. I'm sure you need that for the birth certificate. Damn! With everything down, I wonder how you're gonna get a birth certificate." I said. Estelle just looked at me. "I'll go write it on the calendar hanging in your kitchen. Keep it for proof in the future." I said.

The baby had fallen asleep. "Let's put him in this bassinet. I made him and you need to get some sleep. I will check on you and him in a little while," I said as she handed him to me. I placed him in the basket and sat it next to her. We took the candles and the flashlight; I left the door open in case she needed anything. "Stacie why don't you get in bed now, you can see your baby brother in the morning," I said as she was falling sleep just walking to her bed. "I'll tuck her in," Nick said. "Thanks, I'm exhausted." As I plopped down on the sofa.

CHAPTER SEVEN

Hurricane Aftermath

Day 7 Jay

Jay woke up as the sun was shining through the skylights in the gym. Several people were up and moving around. "Pop, get up. Let's go outside and see what it looks like after the storm," Jay said, standing up and stretching. Jay helped his dad off the floor. Nate didn't move too well after a night on the hard floor. They walked out the front door.

The sun was shining, but off in the far distance north, you could see the tail end of the storm that had pounded them all night. Jay and Nate walked around the grounds and out onto the street. They saw a lot of tree limbs down, power poles knocked over and power lines laying on the ground. "Well, at least the power lines aren't hot," Jay said. "We can drive over them. It's the big power poles might be difficult to get around," he said. "Yeah, but it's not like anyone's going to come and clean it up," Nate said. "You're right let's just pack up and see what we find on the way," Jay said as they turned and walked back into the school.

Megan and her three kids were packing up their beds. Gale took Lynn to go potty. Jay and Nate walked over to Megan. "You guys ready to go?" Jay said, looking down at Jonny. "My mom said where we are going you have 4-wheelers you can take us on a ride," Jonny asked looking up at his Uncle Jay. "Yip, as soon as we get there, we will take you on a ride," Jay replied. "Cool," he said with a smile on his face. "Do you need to go by your apartment and get some clothes or anything? We might not be back here for a long time," Nate asked.

"Do we have room? I would like to get a few more things," Megan replied. "How about you Gale? Do you need to get some stuff out of your apartment?" Nate asked, as Gale and Lynn walked up. "Yes, that would be great," she replied. "Ready?" Jay asked, as he headed to the door.

They weaved in and out of tree limbs, power poles and other debris in the roadway, a couple of times having to drive up on the sidewalk to get past. They had almost made it when the street was completely blocked by a power pole that hit a couple of trees and were all lying in the street.

Jay stopped the truck, looking at the mess. Movement out the driver's side window caught his eye. He turned and saw an elderly woman waving her arms and screaming at them. "Stay here, keep the doors locked," he said as he got out. He walked up to the woman. She was screaming so much Jay couldn't understand what she was saying. "Ma'am, calm down. I can't understand you," he said to her. "My husband, please come help. A tree fell on the back of the house. My husband is trapped," she cried. "Hold on, let me get my dad," he said, running to the truck.

Nate jumped out, and they followed the woman into the house. When they got to the back bedroom, they could see where the trunk of the tree had smashed down on the corner of the house, landing on the bed where her husband had been sleeping. The tree covered the upper part of the man's chest, his face was completely under the tree. Jay knew just by looking there was no way he or his dad could get this tree off the man. Jay could tell the man was not breathing by no movement of his chest. The woman was crying and screaming hysterically. "Ma'am, I'm pretty sure he is gone," Jay said. The woman started screaming more and fell to the ground. "Let me go get Gail. She is a doctor," Jay said as he ran out the door. Jay explained to Gail and Megan what was going on. "Can you come?" Jay said to Gail. They walked into the house. Gail felt for a pulse. She shook her head. "Let me go see if someone from the shelter can come down and remove the tree," Jay said. "I will be right back," he added. "I'll stay with her," Nate said, helping the woman into the living room. Gail went to her kitchen and found a bottle of water and brought it back to her.

Jay ran to the truck, turned it around, and headed back to the shelter. "What happened Jay?" Megan asked. "A tree has fallen on her husband. "We need to run back to the shelter and see if they can get someone out here to remove the tree," Jay said, getting in the truck. It took Jay about 20 minutes to make it back to the house. "There are some men coming. Do you have any relatives here in town we can take you to?" Jay asked. "My daughter lives over by the dog shelter, but she stopped by here and said they were going to the shelter. We were supposed to join her later today," she said, crying again. "I can stay here, take her to the shelter. I'll wait for the men to come," Nate said.

Gale and Jay walked the woman to the truck, helped her in, and took her to the shelter. We walked into the shelter with her and found her daughter. They both broke down and cried when we told her what was going on. "Thank you so much," the daughter said. Jay and Gail walked back out.

The men were at the house by the time Jay had gotten back. They had chainsaws and axes. Nate came out and got in the truck. They turned around and headed to a different block to get through to Gale and Megan's apartment complex.

They finally reach the apartment complex. They parked in front of Megan's apartment. "Go get your stuff together and I will carry it to the truck for you," Jay said to Gail. "I'll watch Lynn for you," he continued. "That will help a lot," she said as she ran across the parking lot to her apartment.

Megan and her kids went into her apartment. "Grab your back packs and stuff them with all your clothes, then get a trash bag and put the toys you wanna take," she said as she went to her own room.

After about an hour and several trips to the truck, Jay finally asked, "are we done yet?" Megan took a last look around, "I think so. Is Gail done?" she asked. "Yip, I think we are ready to go." Jay said. On the drive out of the drive, Jay was thinking he really needed to find a motor home again. Something they would all fit in and be able to live in it when they got to the deer lease.

"Hey, Pop. You know anyone in this area that has an older motor home that possible would run?" Jay asked as he opened the back door for the kids and Gail to climb in. "I know we passed an RV dealership outside of Dickinson. We could stop there on the way to Jordan's house and look," Nate said. "Other than that, let me think as we go. I will keep my eye out for one also," as he opened his door and Megan climbed in the front seat.

"Looks like we all fit," Jay said, looking in the back seat, where the twins kept arguing they didn't have enough room. "Hey, quiet. We don't have that far to go, so sit there and be quiet," Jay said in a mean voice, but with a smile on his face, the twins couldn't see.

They took the expressway to I45, where they went north. As they passed an RV dealership, Nate and Jay both looked at the lot. "I forgot this one was here," Nate said. "I might see a couple in the back, couldn't really tell we were going too fast," Nate continued.

Jay took the exit and turned down the frontage road, going the wrong way. Megan looked at him. "There are no other cars on the road. I think we will be fine," he said, reading her thoughts.

They pulled into the drive and drove to the back lot. A couple looked promising. But they had to find the keys first. "You all stay in the truck, DO NOT get out until I get back, do you understand?" Jay said sternly. "Megan, there is a gun in the glove compartment. Use it if you must," Jay whispered. "WHAT!" Megan yelped. "Trust me, we saw all kinds of stuff on our way from Las Vegas. "People are desperate," Jay said as he and Nate got out of the truck.

They walked around to the back of the building, where they figured, they would have to break in the door or a window. But the back door was standing wide open. They quietly walked in. Jay pulled his pistol out of the back of his pants. They searched the office and found it had been ransacked. But the keys were still hanging on the board. "Wonder why people didn't take the keys or the RV's, he said, pulling down several," Jay said. "I know, weird. Maybe they know they won't run, or at least assumed they won't." Nate replied.

Jay took a handful of keys and gave Nate a few sets of keys. "let's try them," Jay said. The first RV Jay tried. Nothing happened. So, he went to the next one. "I think these are too new," as he turned the key on the next one. "Nothing," he said. He tried the third and the fourth one with no luck. Nate was a little slower, so Jay went over to help him with the last set. "Nothing," Jay said, "Let's go," he said, defeated. "I'm sure we will find something," Nate said.

They came back around and got in the truck. "None of them would start. I think they are too new," Jay said. "We need to find an older one, or" he thought, I bet this truck would pull a small travel trailer. People would have to ride in the trailer, and we would have to be very careful, but it could get us all home," Jay said, thinking about the idea he had just had.

He stopped the truck before going out of the driveway, got out, and went to the back to see if there was a hitch. Sure enough, there was. The truck was a Ford F250, yes; it was old, but it could pull a big trailer; he thought. They left the dealership, which only had motorhomes. But knew the dealership outside of Dickinson had both.

As they approached the exit to Dickinson, they could see that Dickinson had been hit a little harder by the winds last night. "Or they just had weaker trees," he thought.

Dodging tree limbs, and debris like garbage cans and boxes, trash all over the place, and the several power poles, they finally got through the neighborhoods and reached the edge of town. It was a lot clearer here. The trees were further away from the road.

After driving several miles, they reached the RV dealership. "Oh jeez," Jay said as he saw several trees laying on top of some RVs. He couldn't pull very far into the drive because of a gigantic tree lying in the middle. "I'm gonna have to move that tree to get an RV out," he said, looking at the tree. "I saw a chain under the back seat earlier. We can hook it up and pull it out of the way with the truck," Nate said, looking at Jay. "Yeah, we can do that. First, let's go find something that works," Jay said, getting out.

They walked around the motor homes. "They all just look too new," Jay said. "What about a travel trailer? You said the truck could pull one?" Nate asked. "Yeah, it's just so dangerous to ride in one going down the highway," he said looking at Nate. "I guess it may be our only option, there is a lot of us going back, and the two trucks can't hold everyone," Jay said contemplating the travel trailer idea.

"There are some nice ones here, brand new," Jay said. "Man, look at that one. It's huge! What do you think? Think the truck can tow it?" Jay asked as they walked towards one. "Well, it's not like it's gonna be too loaded down, just a few people. We will still stuff everyone we can in the cabs of the trucks," Nate commented as Jay tried the door. To his surprise, it was unlocked. They stepped inside. Not only was it big, but it was also fancy.

The trailer had a huge TV over a fireplace, a sofa that folded out to a bed, and two recliners. A large kitchen. In the hallway, there were 2 bunks on each side. With curtains that gave each bunk privacy. Jay opened the bedroom door, a nice king-size bed with a wall of drawers. On the way out of the bedroom, Nate opened the bathroom door. It, too, was a nice size.

"What do you think?" Nate asked Jay. "Let's go move the tree out of the way and get this baby hooked up before anyone comes." Jay replied as they headed out the door.

They moved the tree, hooked up the trailer and drove it out on to the highway. "It pulls like a dream," Jay thought as they made their way to Jordan's house.

Day 7 D'Ann

The baby was crying. As D'Ann walked into the bedroom picked him up and gave him to Estelle to feed. "He was up several times last night, but he is latching on really well," she said. "My nipples are already sore," she said, smiling down at him. "Can I get you anything?" I asked. "A bottle of water would be great," she replied. I walked into the kitchen and grabbed some water as I looked out the window. The Gulf surrounded the house. "Oh Lord," I said. "What is it, Aunt D?" Nick asked as he came out of his bedroom, rubbing his eyes. "We are surrounded by water," I replied. "Look," as I pointed out the window. "The sun is shining though," I said. I took the bottle to Estelle. "I don't know if we are gonna be able to get out of here today to get you to the hospital and have you and the baby checked out. Water is surrounding us. I wonder if I could see how far back it goes, if it got to the truck," I said as I headed to the front door.

I couldn't see the truck, but I could tell the water hadn't made it up quite that far. "Good, the truck should be fine," I said as Nick came out the door. "I'm going to open the shutter so we can see out," he said, walking around the side of the house.

I told Estelle the truck was fine. We just needed the water to recede. "I think it recedes pretty fast," she said. I looked at the baby nursing at her breast. "I never heard what you named him," I said. "Well, before Ron left, we were still undecided between the three names. Ron jr. Which I don't really care for. Ricky Luis, but not Richard. Then my favorite, Grayson Luis," she said. "I like Grayson as well. That would be my vote," I said. "I like Ricky," Nick said. "Nick and Rick," he laughed as we joined him. "I guess I don't have to be in any hurry to decide," she said, looking down at him.

"We need to get packing, Nick. Can you help Stacie get packed? Clothes, shoes and toys," I said as Nick nodded his head and left the room. "What can I do to get you packed? It may be a long, long time before you come back here, if ever," I said. "I know it's hard to think like that, but it is the reality of the situation now," I said. "You haven't seen all the destruction and desperate people out there. It's only gonna get worse. I'm really surprised it hasn't hit out here yet. People are running out of food and water. They are desperate." I continued.

I went to her closet and took out her suitcase. "You're not gonna need dress clothes, you just need comfortable and warm, it's gonna get cold soon," I said. "Just grab what you think I will need," she said. "The dresser over there has all the baby stuff in it. I would like to take all his stuff," she said. "No problem. We can take that playpen bed still in the box also," I commented.

I ran around the house, throwing everything I thought she and the kids would need into trash bags, and set them by the front door. Every 15 minutes, I stopped to look out at the water. Estelle was right. It was receding fast. "We might be able to leave this afternoon, by the looks of the water. We just need it to recede past the stairs, so we don't have to walk in the water. If it does that, it should be off the road also," I said.

A few hours had gone by, and the Gulf had finally receded back past the stairs so we could get out. "I'm going to go get the truck, I won't be able to pull in the drive since it is sand but at least it will be close, and we can load it. Nick, can you start bringing all this stuff down the stairs? I'm sorry I won't be able to help much. My knees just can't go up and down the stairs," I said. "I Can help," Stacie said.

I went to go get the truck. Nick and Stacie carried the bags down the stairs. While Estelle got the baby ready and herself. Last night we gave her a sponge bath, but she still felt icky.

We got the truck loaded and took another look around the house. Nick carried the baby down the steps as I helped Estelle down the steps. She wasn't moving too fast; she was hurting because of the small tear of her coochie.

"Let's go," I said. We had placed all towels and blankets we had on the wet truck seat, and all got in the truck. Estelle hadn't gotten a car seat yet, so she held the baby in her arms. It wouldn't have fit anyway with all of us in the only set in the truck.

The highway, for the most part, was clear. In some places, sand was covering the low-lying areas where water had covered it. The closer we got to town, the more tree limbs and power lines down we saw.

I drove over to the local hospital. I had no idea if it was even open. The emergency room had lots of cars around it, but I figured they had been there since it started. I pulled up to the doors. They were open. "Stay here, let me check it out first," I said, walking in the doors. A few minutes later I came back out, "Okay Nick, stay here with Stacie. There is a doctor on duty and a few nurses. They said they will check your mom out and the baby," I told Nick. I helped Estelle out of the truck, a nurse came out with a wheelchair for Estelle. I handed the baby to her, and we went inside.

They took the two of them through the doors and told me to wait. I looked around the room. There were a few people in the waiting to be seen. Some had cuts and bruises, others were just waiting for someone. There were lights on, so I figured they had generators.

I walked back out to the truck. Nick had gotten out and was standing by the door. "They took them back to examine them. They should let us know in a little bit if we can leave or they need to stay."

Stacie was getting antsy, so I let her out of the truck. "Stay right here where I can see you," I said. About a half an hour went by. "I'm going to go check on her, watch your sister," I said, looking at Nick.

The nurse came out of the door. "She is fine. You did a fantastic job. We put some antibiotics on the tear and gave her some pills to take to keep her from getting any infections. The baby is excellent." "We were filling out the birth certificate information. Of course, at this point we don't know what is going to happen with that, but at least there will be a record of Grayson's birth on file," she said. "Aww, Grayson, she decided," I said with a big smile. "She should be out in a little bit. We are just getting some vitamins and supplements together and a whole lot of diapers, since there are no stores. They should last her several months," the nurse said. "Thank you!" I replied.

I waited about 30 minutes, and they wheeled her and Grayson out to the truck. I put the big bag of supplies in the back of the truck. Another nurse came running out with a huge trash bag full of diapers, from newborn to 6 months. "Again, thank you so much," I said, putting the bag in the back as Nick helped his mom into the truck.

We drove out of the parking lot and down the street. I drove slowly avoiding the tree limb and debris and not wanting to jerk the baby around too much. We drove down Broadway and over the Causeway. As always, I looked out over the water, knowing it could be a long time before I ever saw it again.

Day 7 Jay

They pulled into Jordan's driveway just about dusk. The kids piled out, tired and grumpy. Jordan, Ashlyn, and Dre came running out to meet the truck. "Man, we were worried about you guys," Jordan said. "Mom hasn't come back either,' he said. "She's not here?" Jay asked with concern in his voice. "No, haven't seen her at all," Jordon replied. "Good to see you, man," Dre shook Jay's hand and pull him in to a hug.

Everyone hugged and said their hellos and walked inside. Jay sat outside on a lawn chair that faced the road. It was getting dark, and he knew D'Ann had been gone way too long. "She's fine, you know she is," Nate said, sitting in the lawn chair next to Jay. Jay said nothing, he just looked out towards the road. Megan and Gail came out of the house. "Are we sleeping in the trailer tonight? I gotta get these kids to bed," Megan said. "Yeah, there are four bunks in the hallway. You can put Lynn in the bedroom," Jay replied as they all went to the trailer.

Jordan, Ashlyn and Dre came out and set down in lawn chairs next to Jay and Nate. "Everything okay here last night?" Nate asked. "Yeah, it was really windy, and it rained all night, but no damage, just a few tree limbs," Jordan said. "We lost all three dogs yesterday and today, so if we can bring the other two, then we will be ready to go," he continued. "We will load up the trailer and truck tomorrow after a good night's sleep," Jay said. "Hopefully D'Ann will be here by then," he said. As Jay and Jordan were putting the chairs next to the house, they saw one headlight coming up the road. Jay froze and watched as they turned into the drive. "Mom!" Jordan yelled as he ran out to the road to meet the truck. "D'Ann!" Jay said, following Jordan.

I jumped out of the truck and ran to Jay and almost jumped into his arms. "I was so worried about you. I knew you were on the gulf when the storm hit," Jay said. "Come here," as I grabbed Jay's hand and pulled him to the truck. Estelle opened the door. "Meet your new nephew," I said. "This is Grayson, Grayson, this is your Uncle Jay," I said. Stacie started squealing, "Uncle Jay, Uncle Jay," she said, trying to crawl over Nick to get to him. "Stinky," Jay said as she jumped into his arms. "Hey nephew," Jay said, giving him a fist bump.

"Let's get you guys into the house," Ashlyn said as she and Nate came out the front door. "You're a grandpa again," Estelle said as she showed Grayson to Nate. "You guys will not believe this, but D'Ann, delivered him," Estelle said. "What? You did?" Jay said in disbelief. "Yup, with my own two hands," I said with a big smile on my face. "I was scared at first because I thought I saw a bear," I said, giggling. "Shut up!" Estelle said as she gave that look.

We all walked into the house and got ready for the night. Jay and I let Megan, Gail and the kids have the trailer, as the rest of us slept in the family rooms in the kennel. Jordan and Ashlyn gave up their king-size bed to Estelle and her baby. A good night's sleep was what we all needed at this point.

CHAPTER EIGHT

Drones

Day 8

Jordan and Ashlyn were up early, banging around in the kennels. Get things ready for the two dogs they would bring with us. The dogs were old, one was blind and the other one couldn't walk very well. They had been litter mates, so Jordan said they would probably pass close to each other. But even though one was blind, she still was very active. Jordan said they were mutts, but they looked like some sort of lab mix.

Jay and I got up and walked outside. It was a beautiful morning. The sun had just come up and there were no clouds in the sky. The air was warm, but we could tell fall was coming.

Jay went in the house, made himself a cup of coffee and we sat at the picnic table, just watching the birds fly around. I looked at Jay as he looked at me. "What is that noise?" I asked. It was a low humming noise that seemed to get louder. "If I didn't know any better, I would say it was an airplane," he replied, looking at the sky. "No, that can't be. How would they fly the thing unless it was like an antique? Can those still fly?" I asked. Jay just shrugged his shoulders. The noise was getting louder. We both stood up and looked towards where the gulf would be.

Just then, as we were looking towards the sky, the sun caught the reflection on something in the sky. "What is that?" Jay pointed. "Wholly shit," Jay said as hundreds of drones flew right over the top of us. "What the wholly hell," he continued as we watched them disappear towards Houston.

We both stood there looking at each other. "I don't know. How could they fly?" I asked, standing there dumbfounded. It looked like a flock of birds flying. Hundreds and hundreds of them were flying over. We stood there, shocked. Suddenly, one lone drone flew right down in front of us. A flash of light came out of it and then flew away. Jay and I stood in shock as we watched the drones fly off towards Houston. "What the hell was that?" I asked, looking at Jay with horror on my face. We sat down not saying a word, all kinds of thoughts going through our heads.

Sitting there, suddenly, we heard a vehicle coming up the road. It pulled into the drive. It was an old jeep, with no top. Jordan and Ashlyn came out of the kennel and waved at the man in the jeep. "That's our neighbor. He checks on us from time to time," Jordan said as we followed him out to the driveway.

"Hi George," Jordan said. George had a serious look on his face, not the friendly look he always greeted Jordan and Ashlyn with. "What wrong?" Ashlyn asked. "Did you just see what I saw?" he asked. "No, what was it?" Jordan asked. "Hundreds and hundreds of drones," Jay responded. "You saw them then? I thought I was seeing things," George replied. "I got on my radio and asked if anyone knew what was going on," he said. "James from in town said the military is getting ready to close all major highways. No one is allowed in or out. Something was happening, but he didn't know exactly what. He said he would get back to me as soon as he could. "I just wanted to let you know. I know you were leaving and headed north, but you probably should wait till I have some more answers. I have got to get back to the radio in case he calls," George said as he jumped in his jeep and sped out of the driveway.

The four of us just stood there looking at each other, not saying a word. "Good morning," Nate said, coming out of the kennel office. All four of us looked at him at the same time. Nate stopped in his tracks. Looked at each of us one by one. "Everything okay?" he asked. No one answered him. I turned and sat down at the table as the others followed my lead. "What is wrong?" Nate said a little louder. Jay looked up at his dad. "We just saw several hundred drones fly over. And the neighbor just told us he heard on his ham radio that the US military has shut down all major highways. No one can come in or out of town," Jay said, looking at his dad. "He will let us know what's going on as soon as he hears. What do you make of this?" Jay asked. "Jay!" I said, getting his attention. "Remember what that soldier told us on our way from Las Vegas?" I said. Jay looked at me. "Do you think we are being invaded?" he asked. "I told you what Jake's grandpa said," I replied. "Who is Jake? And what did his grandpa say?" Jordan asked.

I told them the story of Jake and his grandparents. We all sat there in shock. "What should we do?" Ashlyn said, breaking the silence. "I don't know," Jay said. "I guess wait here to see what George finds out." Ashlyn got up from the table. "We have plenty of food and water to last us several days here," she said. "I say we hunker down here until we know something," she continued. "I guess we will have to. I don't think we have a choice right now," Nate said. "I'm going to go check on Estelle and the baby, and take Jax out to potty," I said, getting up from the table.

The house was quiet. I softly knocked on the bedroom door. "Come in," Estelle said. I peeked in the door. She was feeding the baby. "You doing, okay? You need anything?" I asked. "I need a shower," she said. "I think Jordan has something rigged up in the kennels. Let me go ask him. It might not be hot water though," I said. "I don't care, I just feel icky and dirty," she replied.

I shut the door and walked to the back door. "Jax, Waffles, let's go potty," as they both jumped off the sofa and ran out the door. "Jordan," I yelled across the yard. Jordan got up from the table and walked towards me. "Yeah?" he said. "You guys got a way to take showers in the kennel?" I asked. "Yeah, we are on well water, and we hooked the pump to a generator. In the dog's bathroom, there is a shower. We have a hot water heater attached to the propane, so there should be hot water," he said. "Oh, man, that would be great. I'm sure all of us need showers," I said. Ashlyn had walked up during the conversation. "Let me go clean it, there is dog hair everywhere," she giggled and walked to the office.

We stood and watched Jax and Waffles running and playing. "He looks like he is going to be a good dog," Jordan said. "Yeah, I like him," I said as I smiled and walked back into the house.

Estelle handed me the baby while she got her stuff together and went to the kennels to take a shower. I sat down in the rocker-recliner in the living room and rocked the baby.

I heard the troop from the trailer coming in the front door. "Shhh," I said as the twins came in arguing. "A baby!" Tally said, coming over to get a closer look. "This is your cousin, Grayson," I told her as the other came over to look. "Wow, Estelle had her baby?" Megan asked. "Yeah, and I delivered him. You would have been so proud of me, Dr. Gail," I said, smiling at Gail. "He looks good," she said. "Where is my sister?" Megan asked. "Taking a shower out in the kennels. If you all need to take one, you can take one out there. The is even hot water," I replied.

"We're hungry," the twins said. "There is food in the pantry over there. Help yourself," I said to Megan. "Can I hold the baby?" Gail asked. "Of course," I said, handing him to her and getting out of the chair so she could sit down. Gail rocked him and cooed at him. I could see that Lynn was getting jealous, so I walked over and asked, "Lynn, you want to go see the dogs outside?" as I held out my hand. She shook her head and took my hand as we walked outside.

I left Lynn with Grandpa Jay and went back inside. "We need to have a meeting with everyone," I said, looking at Megan and Gail. "When you are done feeding the kids, come outside to the table," I said, looking at Megan. "When Estelle gets done, come outside," I said to Gail.

Nick and Dre had joined everyone sitting at the table. "I told Megan and Gail to come outside so we can talk about what is going on," I said as I sat down at the table. Estelle came out of the office looking happy and clean. "Gail has the baby, but we need to talk to everyone. So put the baby down and come back out. It won't take but a second," I said to Estelle as she walked towards the house.

We all sat watching the dogs play while we waited for the others to come out of the house. The twins came running out of the house, letting the screen door bang. "Hey you two, be quiet. Estelle just put the baby down," Megan yelled, following the twins out the door. We waited a few more minutes, and then Estelle and Gail came out.

"Everyone take a seat," I said. I looked at Jay. "Do you want to tell them what is going on, or you want me to?" He nodded his head towards me to indicate I could tell them. "Okay, well, a couple of hours ago, Jay and I saw several hundred drones fly over the top of us. One came down and a flash of light came out of it. I think it took our picture." I said, as they all looked at me wide eyed. "Then George, Jordan, and Ashlyn's neighbor came over and told us he had heard on his ham radio that the military has put up roadblocks on all the major highways. They are not letting anyone in or out of towns. We are to shelter in place," I continued. "What's that mean?" Megan asked. "Well, we don't exactly know. George said he would let us know if he hears anything else. What it does mean is that we will be staying here a little longer than we thought, till we know what is going on," I replied.

"On my way down here, I helped a kid get to his grandparents in Bay Town. His grandpa was somewhat of a prepper. He had built a bunker under his house and was prepared for something like what happened almost 4 weeks ago. He also had a radio and said that what happened was an attack, and that we could see more things happen. I don't want to scare you guys, but it could get a lot worse," I said. "What does all this mean?" Gail asked. "We just don't know, honey," Jay replied. "But for now, we are gonna stay here until we know we can travel and get to the deer lease," Jay continued. "Why do we need to get to the deer lease? Why can't we just stay here?" Nick asked. "Because at the deer lease, we can hunt for meat, and Barb has a garden growing. There is fish in the river out back. Here, we will eventually run out of food," Jay said. "Why can't we just go to the store and buy some, like always?" Stacie asked. "There are no more stores. We are too close to the city here. It's not safe. People from the city will be looking for food also and some of them will not be nice," Jay said, looking at Stacie. She looked confused but didn't say any more. "We will need to conserve what we have to get through the next day or two. Until we get a better idea of what is happening outside of here, we need to keep our eyes open," Jay said.

Everyone shook their heads in agreement. "I need some coffee," Nate said, getting up from his chair. Nate and Estelle walked into the house. Jordan and Ashlyn got up, "we need to go check on the girls," Jordan said as they walked to the kennel.

The afternoon drug on. With no TV, no radio, and nothing to do but sit around. The four little ones; Tally, Jonny, Stacie and Lynn whined about no TV and how bored they were. Celia sat under a tree reading a book. While Nick and Dre played some basketball on Jordan's little basketball court, actually the driveway with a basketball rim. Nate and Jay went into the office, "to take naps," I figured, since they didn't come right back out. Gale, Megan and I just sat at the table talking about what had been going on in each other's lives since the last time we talked.

Megan and I went in the house to start dinner, while Gale tried to engage the kids in a game of hide and seek. Nick and Dre came in the back door. "Can we take showers?" Nick asked. "Yeah, Jordan and Ashlyn are out in the kennels. They can show you where," I said. Before Nick and Dre could get out the back door, Gale came busting in the door. "Megan! I can't find Jonny. We were playing hide and seek, and he went to the other side of the house. I yelled at him to come back, but he didn't. When I went around the side of the house, he was gone. I don't know if he went into the woods on the other side of the house or what," Gale cried frantically. "I'm sure he didn't go far," Megan said.

"Nick you and Dre go around and look in the woods over on the other side, me and Gale will go see if somehow he snuck in the kennels, there are a lot of places he could hide in there," I said as we all walked out the back door. Megan stayed with the other kids.

Jordan and Ashlyn were coming out of the kennels by the time we got to them. "Did you see Jonny in there?" I asked. Jordan and Ashlyn looked at each other, shrugged their shoulders, "No," they both said. "He's missing. Can you go search the kennels and make sure he didn't sneak in there?" I asked. "Sure," as they turned and walked back towards the kennels. "Let's go look on the outside of the kennels, around back," I said, walking towards the back of the property.

We walked the entire property and didn't see any sign of him. Then made our way back to the house and met Jordan and Ashlyn coming from the kennels. "We looked everywhere inside. We didn't see him," Ashlyn said. "Yeah, we walked the entire property and didn't see him," Gale responded. The four of us walked back to the house. Walking in the back door, Dre and Nick were standing there talking to Megan. "Nothing," we said. "He's gotta be here somewhere," Megan said, now sounding worried.

"I'm going to go ask his sister if he said anything," Megan said, walking into the living room. "Tally, Stacie, did Jonny say where he was going to go hide?" Megan asked. "No, he didn't say," Tally responded to her mom. "Oh, that kid, I'm gonna tan his hide when I get ahold of him," Megan said, heading out the back door. "JONNY, JONNY!" Megan yelled as she walked around the house.

Jay and Nate were coming out of the kennels when they heard Megan yelling. "What's going on?" Jay said. "Jonny has run off. We have been looking for him for an hour," Megan replied. "Did you check the kennels?" Nate asked. "Yes, and the woods," she replied in a shaky, worried voice. "Let me walk out to the woods and see if I can find him," Jay said. "I'll go this way, and see if he entered the woods over here," Nate said.

Jay walked to the edge of the woods just east of the house. There was a trail that went deep into the woods. It was getting dark, so he went back up to the house and grabbed a flashlight. "You want me to go with you?" I asked. He shrugged his shoulder in agreement.

We walked into the woods and followed the trail. The denseness of the trees made it even darker. We could see a little, but Jay turned on the flashlight anyway to light it up. Jonny was only 8yrs old, and very strong headed. He was a very tough little boy. Getting scrapes and cuts. He was definitely a boy.

We kept walking on the trail looking from side to side and would stop to call out his name and listen to see if we could hear him. We searched the ground to see if there were any footprints, but the leaves had been falling all day, which covered up any footprints.

Back at the house, Megan was still yelling for Jonny outside. Everyone searched the grounds, kennel and inside the house several times. Dre and Nick even walked out to the road and up and down it several times, yelling for him, but he never answered.

Jay and I walked the trail for what seemed like an hour. Eventually, we came to a small stream. The sky was almost dark, and there was a chill in the air. We walked along the banks of the stream, shining flashlights from side to side. "I don't think he's out here," I said, get frustrated and worried. "Yeah, let's head back," Jay said. We yelled for Jonny as we walked back down the trail.

We finally got back to the house. Walked in and everyone stopped what they were doing and looked at us. "Nothing," Jay said. Megan started crying. "He's going to be scared out there in the dark," she cried. Gail walked over to Jay and me as we stood just inside the door. "You don't think someone took him, do you?" she whispered so Megan wouldn't hear her. I looked at Jay. "Maybe we should get in the truck and drive down the road a way," I said.

Jay and I walked back out the front door, got in the truck. Jay started it and came back out of the driveway. Just as we were pulling out onto the highway, a little head popped up in the back seat. "Where are we going?" a little voice came. Jay slammed on the brakes, "What the Hell," as we both turned around and saw Jonny sitting there. We could tell by his hair and sleepy eyes he had been asleep in the back seat.

Jay turned around and pulled back into the driveway. "Boy, you are in big trouble. We have been looking for you for hours," Jay said furiously. Jonny didn't say a word, he just had an evil grin on his face. "I think he knew we were looking for him," I said, looking at him with a mean look on my face. "We were playing hide and seek, and nobody found me," he said as his grin got bigger.

I opened the front door to the house and walked in first. Jonny followed me and then Jay. "JONNY!" Megan yelled and ran to him. "Where the hell have you been?" she said. "I was playing hide and seek with Aunt Gale. She didn't find me," he grinned.

Megan hugged him and scolded him at the same time. But we were all relieved he was okay. "There is dinner on the stove, we kept it warm for you," Megan said, reaching for plates and handing them to Jay and I. "Looks good, I'm starved," Jay said.

After dinner, we all sat in the living room playing games with the kids, till it was time to go to bed.

CHAPTER NINE

Leaving Galveston

Day 9

Stretching in bed, I could feel I was alone. I looked down and Jax was still in his bed. I laid there staring at the ceiling wondering what the day would have in store for us. The kids were running and yelling in the hallway. Sounded like they were playing hide and go seek. "Dang, I wonder what time it is," I said. I laid there a few more minutes and got up.

Outside, clouds covered the sun. It seemed like it was going to be a cloudy, gloomy day. I didn't see anyone outside, so I walked to the house. Gail was in the rocking chair rocking the baby. While Estelle was washing dishes in the sink.

"Hello," I said. "Anything going on?" I asked. "Dad, Jay and Jordan drove over to the neighbors to see if he heard any news yet," Megan replied. "Looks like it might rain," Estelle said, peeking out the kitchen window. I sat down at the table and opened a granola bar. The front door swung open fast as we all jumped. "Oh, sorry, Jay and Pawpaw are back," Nick said excitedly. I got up and headed to the door. I held the screen door open so the three of them could walk in. "Anything?" I asked as Jay and Nate sat down on the sofa. Jordan walked over and grabbed three water bottles and handed one to Jay and Nate.

"Well, I think we need to find a route to the deer lease without major highways and get out of here." Jay said. "The military trying to get organized so they can block the roads and he heard several bands of militia or anti-government groups are raiding the farmhouses around town, pretty much all over. He said they don't like the military stopping people from traveling where they want." Jay said. "Well, I kind of understand that" I said. Jay gave me a look. "The militia are killing people if they don't conform and join their militia," he continued. "I think it would be best we packed everything we can into the trailer and the bed of the trucks."

"Where are Dre and Ashlyn?" Jordan asked. "Ashlyn was in the kennels looking after those two dogs. And I think Dre was playing games with the kids, keeping them busy," Megan said. "Okay, I'll go let them know what's going on," Jordan said, going out the back door. "Let's get all we can and pack," Jay said as he got up.

Everyone got to work. Taking the food out of the pantry and cupboards and hauling it to the trailer. Even the kids helped carry things to the trailer. Jordan and Ashlyn gathered all the dog food, medications and supplies from the kennels, put it all in boxes, and took it to the trailer.

By the end of the day, we had the trailer full, only leaving enough room for everyone to have a place to sit. The beds of the two trucks were loaded down, and they had put a tarp over all the stuff.

Gale and I looked at the map and figured out the route we needed to take to get out of there and avoid any major highways.

"Okay, I think we are done. First sunlight we need to be on the road," Jay said as he sat down in a lawn chair. "I'm exhausted," he said. We all sat around watching the little ones play with Waffles and Jax while Gale and Ashlyn made dinner.

After dinner, we sat around talking and joking about old times. Even the little ones listen in on our stories. Jay got up from his chair and headed to the door. "I got first watch. I will be right outside," he said. I hollered for Jax and went outside to see Jay. "Jax wants to stay with you," I said, smiling. "I'm headed to the trailer and finish planning our route. Jordan had some old city maps. Hopefully, we can get out on the side roads. I said as I walked to the trailer.

Jay slammed the trailer door open as he ran in. "D'Ann, hurry, come outside look at this," he said as I jumped from fright and got up from the table. "What?" He pointed to the east, towards the gulf. Hundreds of tiny red lights dotted the sky. "Drones again?" I asked. "I think so," he replied. "This is getting so scary we need to get out of here. I almost have our route figured out, but we still might have to travel on some major highways. There is just no way around it to get north. We need to get out before they close the bridge on 146 at Baytown," I said.

We watched the sky as the little red dots seemed to drift to the north. "Who do you think is controlling them?" I asked. "I have no idea," Jay replied with concern in his voice. "Maybe we should leave now," I said, looking at Jay.

He looked up at the sky again. "I don't know, maybe so," he replied. "Maybe we should figure out where everyone is gonna ride before we get them out here," I said. "How safe do you think riding in the trailer will be?" I asked. "We won't be going very fast, so if I take it easy driving, I think it should be fine. Maybe the kids in the trucks and adults in the trailer," he said. "Hey, a thought, does my truck have a hitch on it? Can it pull a trailer? Maybe we should grab another one and take it with us," I said.

Jay sat down at the picnic table. I could tell he was thinking about it. "I guess we go that way, anyway? Huh?" he asked. "Yeah, 517 to Dickinson," I replied. "Do you think you can drive and pull one? Or should I have my dad drive it?" he asked. "Shoot, I can do it. I pulled our 5th wheel from Colorado to Las Vegas," I replied, feeling kind of insulted.

Jay got up. "Let's go get everyone so they can get ready, and let's get out of here," he said as we walked to the kennels.

I first went to the room where Jordan and Ashlyn were with the 2 dogs and Waffles. I knocked softly, trying not to startle them. "Jordan," I whispered, opening the door. "Yeah," he replied. "You guys get up and get the dogs in the trailer. " I said as he looked through the darkness at my flashlight. "Ashlyn," he said. "I'm up, I heard," she replied. They got the dogs in to the trailer. Everyone else put their stuff in the trucks and trailer. As Jay and Nate, with Nick and Dre's help, found plywood and boarded up the windows on the house. Jordan and Ashlyn locked up the kennel and took one last look around. With tears in their eyes, they locked the door and walked to the trailer.

Jordan and Ashlyn rode in the trailer's bedroom with the 2 dogs and Waffles. Nate, Dre, and Nick rode in front, sitting at the dinette table and on the sofa. While Estelle, the baby, and Stacie rode in the truck with me. Megan and Gale and the 4 kids rode in the truck with Jay.

It was after midnight when we pulled out onto the road. We drove slowly while Jay got the feel of the trailer with it so packed down. We headed down highway 517 towards Dickinson. When we got to the RV dealership, Jay turned in to the driveway. I followed him and backed the truck up to a slightly smaller travel trailer. Jay had it hooked up in a few minutes and we were back on the road again.

Our route was going to take us through Dickinson and then east all the way to highway 146. Hoping we can get over the Baytown bridge before the military shuts it down. This late at night it was very dark, the only light we could see was the refinery fires still burning along the bay.

As we rolled into Dickinson, the Red Cross tent still had people sitting around it. It looked like they turned it in to a shelter. The streets seemed to be quiet as we drove through town. We didn't even see any military shutting down the road. "Maybe we will make it all the way without running into military roadblocks," I said to Estelle, which was feeding the baby and dozing off. Stacie had her head on my lap and was stretched out. I smiled as I looked down at her innocent face.

Jay was behind me as I pulled the empty trailer through town. It was sure easier to pull than that big 5th wheel we had. I reminisced in my head about the time I pulled the 5th wheel from Colorado to Las Vegas, when I saw flashing lights up ahead. "Dammit, I thought we would get through town before the military blocked the road. I pulled to the side of the road as Jay pulled up behind me.

He jumped out of his truck and ran up to my open window. "See that way up there? What do you think? Should we take the back roads and try to get around it? Or just keep going and take our chances?" I asked. Jay stood there thinking for the longest time. "Do you know of a road that will go around and still come out to 146?" he asked. "I'm sure that's 146 where the lights are. Even if we find a road to bypass it, who's to say there isn't another one?" I replied.

We looked ahead in silence. Then Jay's dad came around the side of the trailer. "What's going on?" he asked. "Lights up ahead, don't know whether we should find a way around it, or just take our chances," Jay replied. "What do you think?" I asked Nate.

"We can turn off on 3436 and go up to 646," I said, looking at the city map I pulled out of the side of the door. "I guess we can do that. We might end up in the same situation when we get to 646 and 146," Jay replied. "I say we take the chance and take the back roads and see what it looks like," I said. "Okay, let's do it. " Jay said as he and Nate walked back to his truck.

I only had to go a few blocks before the turnoff to 3436 was there. It took us through a residential area, but the houses were few and far between. It was too dark to see what condition the homes were in. We approached 646. I pulled out on the highway and looked east to see if I could tell there were any lights down in that direction.

I waited for a couple more minutes for Jay to catch up with me and then turned east on to 646. Still looking and searching the area, I still could see no lights. "I wonder if the lights were something else and not military back there, because there isn't anyone at this intersection," I said to myself.

We pulled out on to 146 headed north, next town Kemah. We took it nice and slow, mainly because of pulling the trailers, but also to search up ahead for any lights or movement.

We made it through all the towns between there and the bridge. It was really late, and we were getting sleepy. I pulled over and asked Jay if he thought we could stop at Jake's and his Grandparent and spend the night in their driveway. It seemed like a safe and secure neighborhood. Jay wanted to keep driving but knew falling asleep at the wheel would be disastrous. So, he agreed we would stop. He followed me to the house. I got out and told him to wait there. I went to the door and knocked. Grandpa had cameras all over so he could see me if he was awake. But no one came. I went back to the truck where Jay was. "Maybe we should just cat nap right here for a couple hours, then in the morning we can go. I think we will be safe here," I said. "Okay, lock your door, and just sleep sitting behind the wheel in case we have to take off quickly," he said as he walked back to his truck to do the same.

CHAPTER TEN

Taken

Day 10

A knock on the window startled me awake. During my sleep I had slumped over and was laying against the window. I popped my head up quickly to see Jake standing by my window. I opened the door and gave him a hug. "What are you doing here?" he asked. "We just needed a safe place to sleep a couple of hours. We got all our family and are heading back to the deer lease," I said. "Is everything okay here?" I asked. He looked down at his feet. "No," he answered. "What's wrong?" I asked. He looked up at me with tears in his eyes. "Grandpa had a heart attack or a stroke, I don't know which, but me and grandma couldn't help him. He passed away 2 nights ago. I buried him in the backyard. But me and grandma don't know how to work on all the stuff he did. The water stopped working yesterday," he said with tears in his eyes.

Jay looked up from behind the wheel and came over to us. "Jay, this is Jake, the boy I told you about," I said. "His grandpa just died." Jake motioned us to come into the house. "I'm gonna stay out here and keep an eye on things. We really need to get going," he said. "I can't leave them here to fend for themselves, Jay. They don't know how to do any of the thing's grandpa did." I said, looking at Jay. "Plus, we could go get all of their supplies and he had a ham radio that would be very helpful if we can figure out how to work it." I continued. "Go see what they want to do. They will have to ride in the trailer, though," he said.

I walked to catch up with Jake and told him I hope they will come with us. "I'll ask grandma, but she is so distraught after grandpa died, I don't really think she knows what's going on," he said. We walked down the stairs and into the living room. Grandma was sitting in her rocking chair, just rocking and staring straight ahead. I walked up to her and gently put my hand on her arm. She looked up at me. "Grandma, are you okay?" I asked. "Oh honey, I'm fine. I'm just waiting on Grandpa to get home," she replied. I looked up at Jake and shook my head. "Get your stuff together and grab some clothes and stuff for Grandma. I'm going to get the guys and we are going to grab the supplies you have left and the radio. Do you know how to work it?" I asked. "Grandpa was teaching me. I have the basics," he replied. "Good, we are going to take it also," I said as I went up the stairs.

I asked Jay to come take a look at Grandpa's set up. I showed him the water system and all the plants Grandpa had planted. "It's like a greenhouse in here," Jay said. I took him into the storage room and all the rows and rows of food. "Oh, wait, you haven't seen the best part yet. Come here and look at this," I said, taking him to the 3 big deep freezers. I opened the lid, and we just stood and stared at all the frozen meats. "I don't know if we can take all this. We are still hours from the deer lease. It won't stay frozen," Jay said. "We can pack as much as we can into both trailers, fridges and freezers. There are a couple coolers over there, we can at least try. "Oh, and let's cage up those chickens in the backyard and take them for fresh eggs," I added.

We walked back into the kitchen; the fridge was still stocked with all kinds of items. I'm going to use this stuff and make a big breakfast before we hit the road, and maybe some sandwiches for later. Jay rolled his eyes. I knew he wanted to get on the road, but everyone was hungry, and I didn't want the food to go to waste.

Jay walked up the stairs and told everyone to come down for breakfast and to help carry as much as we could fit into the vehicles and trailers. They carried boxes and boxes of food, plants and other supplies up the stairs, until the smaller trailer was almost full. Jay and Jake unplugged the radio and took all the parts to it out to the trailer. While Jordan and Ashlyn tried to round up the chickens. They had found wire cages in the garage. Waffles and Jax were very interested in the chickens, and kept barking at them, so Jordan put the cage in the bathroom so the dogs couldn't get to them.

We all sat down in Grandma's living room and dining room and ate a huge breakfast. Grandma was still confused and didn't seem to know what was going on around her. Megan and Gail packed up Grandma's things, they took down all the pictures of Grandma and Grandpa and put them in a box.

Estelle and Ashlyn put all the blankets, sheets and pillows in trash bags as the kids ran them upstairs and out to the trailer. We took a few looks around the house and gathered up anything we thought we could use and took it out to the trailer.

Jay and Jake helped grandma to the big trailer and made her comfortable in one of the lower bunks. "I'm going to go lock up the house and then we will be on our way," Jay said to Jake as he sat with Grandma while the rest of us finished. "Let's get going, see if we can get over this bridge," Jay said as we took off towards the Baytown bridge.

At the top of the bridge, we could see out into the gulf. "Are those war ships?" I asked Estelle as she looked out over the gulf. "I don't know. They kinda look like it," she replied. "I don't remember those ships there when I came this way," I said.

We were making good time. The roads were empty and beside a few older cars and trucks on the road; it was quiet. Pulling into Dayton, we noticed another Red Cross tent set up with lots of people around it. I passed it and several blocks down the road; I pulled over as Jay pulled in behind me. I jumped out and met him halfway. "I think we should go talk to the red cross and see what is going on," I said. "I don't know," Jay sounded leery. "We need to know if they know about the drones and what the military is doing," I said. "Fine, I will wake my dad and we will walk back there and find out," he said in his grumpy I don't want to do it voice.

I waited at the truck, watching Jax and Waffles while Jordan and Ashlyn took the two elderly dogs out to potty. Everyone else was stretching and standing around. The kids were running around playing tag.

Jay and Nate came back with concerned looks on their faces. "We need to go now!" he yelled. "What is it?" I asked. "they said the military is shutting down this highway. We got to go before we get stuck here." Jay said.

We drove a little faster out of town and on the highway. We now had an urgency to get to the deer lease, so we only stopped in case someone really had to stop. As we went through towns, it seemed like more and more towns had the Red Cross and had shelters set up.

It was late afternoon when we got to the outskirts of Livingston. We rounded the corner of the highway and up ahead was a roadblock. "Shit, Shit, Shit," I yelled. It startled Estelle, and the baby started crying. "A roadblock ahead and it looks like military. There is no place we can go," I said, stopping as quickly as I could hauling the trailer. Jay stopped suddenly as well. I met him halfway again. "What do we do?" I asked, my voice shaking. "I don't think there is anything we can do. We must go that way," Jay replied. "Let's see what they have to say, I guess," he said as he went back to his truck.

There were jeeps and a couple of other big trucks sitting alongside the road. A couple of soldiers stood in the middle of the highway, holding up their hands for us to stop. "Ma'am, please turn off the truck. Is it just you 4?" he asked. "Yes, but that's my husband behind us," I said. "Step out of the truck, please. Ma'am, you and the children can stay put," the soldier said to Estelle.

I got out and walked to the back of the truck with the soldier. "Sir, can you step out of the truck?" he said as he looked in the truck and saw Megan, Gail and the 4 kids. "Is anyone else with you?" he asked. Knowing they would most likely look in the trailer anyway, he didn't want to lie. "My father and a few more family members are in the trailer. We didn't have room in the truck. I know they shouldn't be riding back there, but we are trying to get home," Jay said. The soldier radioed to another soldier to come and have the people exit the trailer. "How about your trailer, anyone in it?" he asked, looking at me. "No, it's empty," I said as another soldier opened the door. "Why did you even ask if you were gonna look, anyway?" I thought to myself.

Nate, Dre, Nate, Jake, Jordan and Ashlyn came out of the trailer. "My grandma is asleep in there. She's not feeling well," Jake said. I could hear the dogs start barking as one soldier entered the trailer. "Let me go get the dog he might bite," Ashlyn said as she looked at the soldier for permission. He waved at her, indicating to go ahead.

"What is this all about?" Jay asked as we all stood there waiting for an answer. At about that time, 5 more soldiers came over to where we were. "The United States Government with the cooperation of the military has put into law, that any man over the age of 18 and under the age of 50, will be drafted on the spot and taken to a secure location, to train to fight in case of an imminent invasion," the soldier said. "WHAT?" I said. "What does that mean?" The soldier looked at me and then at everyone else. "It means these men right here will be going with us," he replied. "NO, you can't do that," I screamed as the soldiers one by one grabbed the men's arms. "Jake is only 16 years old, and Nate is 65 you can't take them," I screamed. "Where are you going to take them?" as I ran to Jay. He ripped his arm out of the soldier's hands and held me. "No, they can't do this," I cried.

"D'Ann, D'Ann, listen to me," Jay whispered. "Get everyone home. Dad can drive my truck, get to the deer lease. We will get there as soon as we can," he said in my ear. "No, NO!" I begged. Ashlyn and Jordan were in an embrace, crying. "Can I at least tell my mom goodbye? She is in the truck with my new baby brother?" Nick asked. A soldier escorted him to the truck. As I watched Estelle start crying and holding Nick. I went over to Jordan and held him. "You stay close to Jay, you hear me?" I whispered in his ear. Jordan was not a fighter. He didn't have a mean bone in his body. I walked up to Dre, "don't worry Dre, Jay will get you guys out of this. Stay close to Jay," I said as I hugged him. Nate was hugging Jay with tears in his eyes. I went back to Jay and gave him one last hug. "Don't worry, we will be home before you know it," he said. "Take care of my son," I pleaded as the soldiers grabbed their arms and escorted them into a nearby tent.

I couldn't control my sobs. Ashlyn and I held each other as we cried. "Come on, we need to get out of here." Nate said, "I can't leave them here," I cried. "Come on, you must. Jay will figure out a way for them to get home," Nate said, tugging me toward the truck.

Everyone got back in the trucks and trailer as we drove off. I was crying so hard I could hardly see the road. "Are you able to drive, okay?" Estelle asked through her sobs. "Yeah, I'm okay. We got to be strong," I said, wiping my tears and focusing on the road. "Let's get to the deer lease and see what Doug and Sean have to say," I said.

It was getting dark out, but once we got through Lufkin and Nacogdoches, it was clear all the way up to Henderson. Pulling into Henderson, the roadblock was gone. I continued to drive through town to highway 79. That would take us to the deer lease. As we passed by Walmart. We could see that they had placed spotlights and they set a Red Cross tent up. "Wow, they got the Red Cross here," I said as we approached. "There sure are a lot of men over there, and I don't see any military," I said, slowing the truck down. "What are you going to do?" Estelle asked. "I'm going to tell them what just happened to us and if they don't wanna be drafted, they better hide," I replied as she looked at me like I was crazy.

I pulled the truck and trailer into the parking lot as Nate followed me. We parked several rows away. "I'll be right back, then we will get out of here," I said as I jumped out of the truck. Nate got out of the other truck. "What are you doing?" he yelled at me. "I'll be right back in just a minute. Stay here," I demanded.

I walked up to several guys that looked to be in their mid-30s, standing around joking and laughing. "Hey," I said as I walked right up to them. They all stopped talking and joking and looked right at me like I was a crazy woman. I'm sure my eyes were puffy from crying and my nose and face were red. "Have you guys seen the military around here?" I asked. They looked at each other and shook their heads no. "Well, me and my family just came here from Livingston. The military are on their way up here. They took my husband and all the men in my party that were 18 to 50 years old. Said it was a mandatory draft. I suggest if you don't want to be drafted, you guys go hide. I am completely serious," I said as another woman with a couple of kids overheard me and walked over to me. "She's right, they took my husband just a couple hours ago right outside of Jacksonville," she said, starting to cry. "Why, why would they do that?" one man asked. "I don't know, but when we were down in Galveston getting my family, we saw hundreds and hundreds of drones fly over. Don't know where they came from and don't know where they were going. Don't even know if they were us or foreign," I continued. "Believe me or not, but I'm just wanted to warn you," I said as I looked around and had caught the attention of everyone around.

I headed back to the truck and nodded at Nate to go. Several families took off running and some jumping on their ATVs and older vehicles.

Nate and I drove out of the drive and headed towards the house. Just before we got to the turnoff to the deer lease, we could see several miles ahead towards the direction of Jacksonville, strobe lights like the ones on the military jeeps. "Oh my God, they're coming," I said as I turned down the county road to the deer lease. I remembered I still had the key to the lock on the gate. I jumped out, unlocked it and drove the truck and trailer through. Then watched as Nate drove his truck and trailer through. I locked the gate back up and followed Nate to the compound.

Nate pulled the trailer straight in to spot number 2 as I pulled my trailer in to spot number 1. I jumped out of the truck as I saw Doug, Sean, Barb and Andie sitting at the picnic table. I ran as fast as my crippled legs could carry me to them. Barb got up and ran towards me. We embraced in a hug.

Doug and Sean were waiting for Jay to come out of the truck or the trailer as they saw the rest of the family exit.

"Doug, you and Sean have to hide, NOW!" I screamed. "What are you talking about?" Doug said as Nate arrived at the table. Nate and Doug embraced. "Where is Jay?" Doug said. "Where's Dre?" Sean also asked. "That's why you guys must hide. The military is coming. They took Jay, Dre, Nick and Jordan. They are drafting anyone between the ages of 18 and 50 to train. And you can't refuse, or you will go to a concentration like a camp. We saw the military down the road for several miles. They are making a sweep. We need you guys here. You must go hide." I said franticly. Doug looked at Nate, "It's true," Nate agreed.

"Grab some water and stuff and go get in the underground bunker. We will cover it so it can't be seen." Barb said. Shaking his head like he just could not believe it, Doug walked to the house with Sean.

"Is everyone okay?" I asked as Megan, Gale, Estelle and the kids all walked up. The kids were tired and grumpy, so I walked with Nate back to the trailers and hooked them up to the solar electric. "Let's just get the perishable stuff in to the freezers in the solar house. We can get the rest of the stuff tomorrow," I said.

Nate and I took a couple of boxes and bags and put the meat in the freezer. Then walked back to the house where Megan and Gail and the kids were all sitting. "Why don't you all go to bed? Hopefully, things will be better in the morning," I said. Megan and Gail took the kids and went to the big trailer. Estelle and the baby headed to my trailer. "Jake, is Grandma still asleep? Yeah, I gave her some sleeping pills. She will be out all night. She's on the sofa. I will sleep on the floor next to her," he said. "Okay, I will introduce you and show you around tomorrow," I said as he walked back to the trailer.

Ashlyn and Jake moved the two old dogs to the living room and made them a bed on the floor so Megan and Gail could sleep in the big bed. She changed the sheets on the bed and covered the older dogs up so they would stay warm. Jake laid down beside the sofa and next to the dogs. They seemed to relax as Jake pet them.

After getting the dogs settled, and taking the chickens to the chicken coop, Ashlyn came out and sat down at the table. "We are going to have to keep watch," I said to Ashlyn and Andie. Barb and Nate came from around the house. "They are all tucked in. No one will know they are there." Barb said. I looked at Nate. "What should we do now?" I asked. "I guess we wait to see if they show up?" Nate replied. "Okay, we need coffee," he said, walking into the house. "And a diet coke," I yelled back at him. We stayed vigil throughout the night talking about what the guys must be going through. Trying to figure out what we do next. With no sign of any military, at least tonight.

Day 10 Jay

They escorted the four guys to a large fenced off area with guards posted all around. There were cargo trucks and jeeps parked in a row. With several military style tents. The soldiers took them to one of the larger tents. When they walked in, they saw cots in rows. Several other men of various ages were sitting on their cots talking. Jay and the guys found 4 cots next to each other and sat down on them. Jay sat across from a man about his own age. "Do you know what is going on? Have they said anything to you?" Jay asked the man. Several of the other men standing and sitting around heard Jay's question, so they all huddled around in a circle to listen and talk about their experiences.

After about 30 minutes of guessing and trying to figure out what was going on. The tent doors opened and what looked like a captain stepped in with several other soldiers.

"Listen up," he yelled over the talking. All the men became quiet and turned to face the soldiers. "Tomorrow, we will transport you to the training facility at 06:00 hours. There are MRE's in the back. Eat and be ready to leave at 6am," he said, then turned, and they all walked out the door.

"This is fucked up," Jay said. He gathered Nick, Jordan, and Dre close. "We gotta get out of here. I'm not doing this shit," he said. "Just do what they say for now, keep your heads down and I will figure out a way out of here. The important thing is we all have to stick together. Don't let them separate us," he said. They got up with the other men and walked to the back of the tent. They saw fruit and protein bars on one table and MRE on another. "Yuck," Jordan said as he picked up an MRE. They walked back to their cots to eat their food. "So, what do you think?" he asked the others. "I don't know, but this is messed up. I don't wanna be here. I got a family to protect. Who the hell are we fighting anyway?" one man said as they all agreed. "Something just doesn't seem right about those soldiers," one of the other men said.

He had no idea what time it was. He just knew the sun had gone down several hours ago. "Get some sleep everyone, we are gonna need it," he said to the guys. He laid down on his cot and tried to figure out what to do next.

CHAPTER ELEVEN

Separated

Day 11 Jay

"Everyone up, go get your breakfast and meet in the area over by the trucks by 6:30am," a voice came yelling in the tent. Jay and all the men scrambled to get up. No need to get dressed. They never undressed. They all went into the tent for breakfast. At least this time there were eggs, probably powdered, and coffee.

They all ate some eggs and fruit and drank coffee. As soon as they were done, they headed over to the trucks. The trucks were the kind you see in the movies that were always loaded down with people.

Nick and Dre were the young ones. They had hardly said two words since they took them. Jay could tell they were scared, terrified. He walked over to where they were standing. "It's gonna be okay," he said as he put his hand on Dre's shoulder, then Nicks. Once all the men were gathered around, the captain came over to where they were standing. "We are transporting you to our training facility a few miles north of here. Load up in the truck," he commanded. There were close to 20 men all together. It was a bit crowded, but they all huddled together. They had to all stand due to not enough room to sit.

The truck took off out the gate. Jay knew the area well and watched every move the truck made. Several miles down the road, he could tell they were heading into the Davy Crockett National Forest. The truck drove down forest roads with trees all around. If a person wasn't careful or didn't know these woods, they could easily get lost.

Jay knew these woods very well. He and his dad used to go hunting in this area before Doug inherited his grandpa's deer lease. He knew there was an old church camp down this road and bet that was where they were taking them. The forest was very overgrown since the last time he had been here, when he was younger. The truck pulled up to a large fenced in area. A couple of soldiers opened the large gates and let the truck drive in. Jay looked around and noticed there was now a fence around the area was the "church yard" with razor wire along the top. A soldier was standing guard along the fence about every 15 to 20 feet apart. The soldiers all carried ARs with them. Jay looked them over. The man last night was right. Something didn't seem right about these soldiers.

The truck pulled next to an enormous hall, where they most likely held the church services during camp. The buildings were old but seemed in decent shape.

"Everyone out and go inside. Take a seat," one soldier yelled. The men piled out of the truck and walked into the hall. Sitting in several rows up front were about 30 other men. "Damn, they must have gathered men up from all around," Jay whispered. The new men all sat down behind the men already in the hall. Once everyone was sitting, the captain and several other soldiers walked to the front to address them all.

"We are going to split you men up into age groups," he said. Jay looked at the other 3 guys. "It's okay," he mouthed as he saw the terrified looks on all three of their faces.

"18-30 will go with Sargent Lundy," as the Sargent stepped away from the other soldiers and walked towards a doorway. Nick and Dre stood up, took one last horrified look at Jay, and followed the other 15 men out the door. "31 to 40-year-olds go with Sargent Walter," he said as Jordan and 20 others got up and followed the soldier out the door, we all came in. "41 to 50 years stay here, and Officer Hext will be in to assist you," the captain said.

Jay and about 15 other men stayed seated. The Officer ordered them to follow them out the back door. The soldiers held the door open as the 16 men walked out the door. As they walked out, they noticed they had just walked into a 50 x 50-foot cage made of chain link. The cage had a chain link ceiling and one door on the opposite end that was chained shut. The second the last guy was through the door, the door slammed shut. "What the fuck?" several of the men said, running back to the door, which had no handle on it to get back into the building. "What is going on?" Everyone kept yelling. Jay looked around. They were trapped in a cage. Men started yelling and screaming. They were rattling the walls of the cage, but no one came. They couldn't see around the building to see if the other men had suffered the same fate. "Fuck," Jay thought as D'Ann's words came to him, "Take care of my kid," were her last words to him. Now, they were separated, and God knows what was going on.

After several hours of yelling and screaming and rattling the sides of the cage. Most of the men calmed down and sat down in the dirt. The men were still talking and carrying on really loud. "Hey," Jay yelled, "quiet, quiet, Shhh, let's see if we can hear the others," he said. The men looked at Jay but did as he asked. Off in the distance, they could hear some of the other group cussing and yelling up a storm. "It doesn't sound like they are too far from us," a guy said. "My sons are in those other groups," another one commented.

"We need to keep our cool if we want to get out of this alive," an older man, probably close to 50 years old, Jay thought. "I knew those were not soldiers," he continued. "Who do you think they are?" Jay asked him. "I don't know, but I heard a little before they took us on the ham radio. This is not good," he continued.

Just then, the door swung open. A soldier pointing his rifle at the men yelled, "Get on your feet and get to the far side," as they scrambled to get up. He stood between Jay and the door. Then they watched as they actually pushed 10 more men into the cage. The soldier walked backwards out the door, never taking his eyes off the men. "What the hell is this?" one of the new guys said. "Welcome to jail," Jay replied. Jay walked over to the far corner and sat down in the dirt. He was tired from the little sleep the night before and his head felt like it was going to explode. He had to figure out a plan to get them out of this as he drifted off to sleep.

Day 11 D'Ann

D'Ann, Ashlyn and Andie had stayed up all night. Nate had finally gone off to bed shortly before daybreak. Barb came out to where we were sitting. "Did you guys see anything?" Barb asked. "Nope. Maybe we should take the ATV's out to the highway and see if we see anything." I said. "Yeah, maybe we should do that before we let the two men out of the bunker," she replied.

We got up and walked towards the barn where the ATVs were housed. Barb got on one and I on another and rode out of the barn and towards the gate. She unlocked the gate as we rode on to the county road towards the highway. We slowed down when we got close. Looking both ways, we rode out to the middle of the highway and looked in both directions. We didn't see anything for miles. "I guess they went on by," I said. "I guess we can let them out," Barb said. I shook my head in agreement as we rode back towards the house.

Once we parked the ATVs back in the barn, I helped her move the stuff off the top of the bunker and opened the door. Doug and Sean were still asleep on their cots. "Hey guys, I think it's safe for you guys to come out," Barb yelled down from the top of the stairs. "Okay, we'll be up in a minute," Sean yelled back.

We walked back to the house and started breakfast. Little by little, everyone woke up and gathered around the picnic tables. The door swung open to the house. Casey and all three dogs came running in. "D'Ann!" she yelled, running up to me, giving me a big hug. The dogs started dancing around, all excited to see me. "You made it home," she said, still hugging me. "Where's Jay?" she asked, looking around. "Well, that is a story we need to tell everyone together, so I will let you know during breakfast. You want to go get my mom up? She is doing, okay?" I asked her. "Yeah, she's great. Her and Gracie are up, I will go get her," she said as she and the dogs ran out the door. Finished up a breakfast casserole and took it out to the table. Everyone had come out of the cabins and trailers. Jake helped his grandma sit down at one of the tables. "How are you feeling, Grandma?" I asked as she sat down, "Are you hungry?" I continued. Grandma nodded her head as I poured her a cup of coffee. I turned around as I saw my mom come around the corner. I went to her, and we hugged. "Glad you're back. Who are all of these people?" she asked as I walked with her to a table.

"Can I have everyone's attention?" I said, as everyone sat down. "Before we eat, I want to tell you all what is going on, then I want to say a pray for the safe return of Jay, Jordan, Nick and Dre. I know some of you don't know everyone, so I will go around and introduce you. Starting over there, is Jay's sister and Nate's daughter, Estelle, and new baby boy Grayson. That's her daughter, Stacie. Nick is her eldest, which is one that was taken. Jay's other sister, Megan, and her 3 kids, Jonnie, Tally, and Celia. Over here is Gale. She is Jay's daughter and that little one is Lynn, Gales' daughter. That is Nate, Jay, Estelle and Megan's dad. Over here at this table is my mom Kay, my daughter-in-law Ashlyn, and the newest member of our family, Casey." As I walked around the tables and stopped in front of Jake. "This is Jake and his grandma, Leona. Jake lost his parents. He helped me on my way down to Galveston. I took him to his grandparents' house. On our way back from Galveston we stopped at their house and unfortunately grandpa passed away. I couldn't leave grandma and Jake to starve, so here they are. Jake, I hope you and Grandma will be happy here and make this your new home. This is Sean, a great friend we brought from Las Vegas, his wife Andie, and Sean's mom Vickie. Dre, that you all met is Sean's brother. And finally, Doug, Barb and their two daughters, Abby and Ally. This is their place." I said as I walked back to the front of the area.

"Now, on our way here, Jay, Jordan, Nick, and Dre were taken from us. The military stopped us outside of Livingston and said the Government issued a draft of all 18-50-year-old men had to stay and fight. I don't know who they are fighting. I don't know how long they will be fighting. But Jay assured me he would take care of the other 3 and get back here as soon as he could. This is all I know. But if we could bow our heads in silence, say your own little prayer that they will come back to us safe and sound." I said as I bowed my head.

After about 2 minutes I looked up and said "Amen." I passed around the 3 large casseroles as everyone ate in silence. I sat down by Barb at the table. "Doug, what needs to be done around here? We have some kids that can help and more adults that can help do something. If they sit around, they will get bored. Let's figure out some chores and stuff for them to do." I said as Doug looked around at the kids and the 5 teenagers. "I see the fence is almost done. You guys got that done fast," I said. "We brought a lot of food, the back of the trucks are full, and the trailers are full, so maybe Andie, Ashlyn, and Vickie can organize the food and make lists of what we got. Maybe my mom can help keep an eye on Grandma, and Jake can help you with whatever you need done." I said.

"We are going to need to construct some more cabins, with this many people here," Doug said as Nate and Sean sat down at our table. "We have the wood already to make about 10 more. That was our plan before all this happened," Doug said. "Let's get started on them today," Nate said. "I think tonight we need to go hunting. "Get us some more meat," Doug said. "I would love to go hunting," Sean spoke up excitedly. "I've never been before," Doug smiled. "Okay, whoever wants to go, we will head out right before dusk."

I stood up before everyone left. "Can I have your attention again? Can everyone help bring all the supplies from the back of the trucks and trailers and put it all on the tables here? Andie, Ashlyn and Vickie, can you make a list of everything we have and organize it, while Barb and I will make an area in the bunker for everything," I said. "Thanks everyone, let's get going."

"Megan! Gail!" I yelled. "We need to come up with some chores for the little kids to do, so they don't get bored. "Yeah, we can do that Gail said. "I can help when the baby is asleep," Estelle said as they walked towards the trailer.

Kay sat down with Grandma and introduced herself. "I'm Kay, I'm D'Ann's mom," she said. "I'm Leona," she said. They sat and talked as I walked off to help Barb.

It took Doug and the guys all day to put together a couple more cabins. They were pretty crude to start with, a ceiling, floor and 4 walls. "I think we might need to go to town and find some more supplies to build more," Doug said. "Maybe me and Jake should go since the military might be there. Let's make a list and you guys can go first thing in the morning." Doug said.

Everyone worked on getting all the supplies out of the trucks and the trailers. While the girls cataloged the supplies, the teenagers carried it down into the bunker. Doug and Nate grabbed the radio and took it into the house. Jake helped them set it up in the living room. He showed them how to use it. They sat and listened for any talking, but all they heard was static.

When it got close to dusk, we watched the guys grab their guns and ATVs and headed out to go hunting. While the rest of us sat around a bonfire and talked about old times.

The men got back about an hour later with a large wild hog. They hung it up in the tree to let it bleed out overnight. Then tomorrow they would cut it up and place the meat in the smokehouse to smoke for a few days.

After a full, exhausting day, Sean decided he would take watch while the rest of us went to bed. "What are we going to do to get the guys back?" I asked them before I walked off. "I just don't know. We must trust Jay will get them out of there," Nate replied. "I just hate that we can't do anything to help them," I said, with tears streaming down my cheeks. "All we can do right now is pray," Nate said. I shook my head in agreement and started walking towards the trailer. See you in the morning," I said. "Good night," Nate replied as he walked to the big trailer.

CHAPTER TWELVE

Not who they seem

DAY 12 D'Ann

The sound of a baby crying woke me up. I sat up in bed with Jax by my side. The other 3 dogs had spent the night with Casey. Estelle was on the couch feeding the baby as I walked out of the bedroom. I looked at her as she had tears going down her cheeks. "How are we going to get the guys back?" she cried. "I don't know, but you know your brother he will let nothing happen to them, I promise," I said, trying to comfort her. "I'm going to go talk to Doug and Sean and see what they think," I said as I walked out the door.

Sean had just finished watching when Nate said he would keep an eye out this morning until he and Jake went to town. I grabbed a diet coke out of the house refrigerator and said down beside Nate on the porch swing. "What are we going to do to get the guys back?" I asked the 3 men. "I think we need to trust that Jay will get them all out of there and back here. He knows the area between here and Livingston well. We used to hunt a lot in that area. We have to have faith. You cannot go running off to save him. Promise me you will not!" Doug said. I looked down at the dirt. "Promise me, D'Ann," Doug said again with a seriousness in his voice. "Okay, Okay, I won't go after them," I said with tears in my eyes. "Doug is right. You can't go after them. It is way too dangerous," Sean agreed. "Okay, I promise," I said as I got up and went into the house to help Barb with breakfast.

Barb had come in the back door with a basket full of eggs and the last of the wild hog bacon that had been curing in the smokehouse from the pig they had shot last week. "Good morning," she said. "Morning! Any talking on the radio yet?" I asked. "No, haven't heard anything. I see it on your face you're planning something, aren't you?" she asked. "No, I promised I wouldn't go after them," I replied.

As Barb started cooking, the back door came flying open. "D'Ann, come, please my grandma is not well," Jake yelled. I got up from the table as Barb turned off the stove and we ran out the back door to the large trailer. Gale was sitting on the floor, wiping Grandma's head with a wet cloth as she lay on the sofa. She was tossing and turning and speaking incoherently. "Grandma, are you in pain?" I asked. But she didn't respond. She just kept tossing and turning and mumbling. "I think I have some medication that will calm her down," I said as I ran out the door to the other trailer. We got her to sit up and take a drink of water and take the pill. Gale and I stayed with her while Barb went back to finish breakfast. She settled down and fell asleep. "I think she will be out for a while," Gale said. "I'll stay with her for a while," Ashlyn said. "I'll bring you some breakfast," I said, going out the door to the house. Jake followed me to the house and went to the front to sit with Nate.

Everyone was up and around. They started congregating around the picnic tables. Jake ate his breakfast first and then headed to the trailer to let Ashlyn take a break and eat.

"What needs done today?" I asked Barb. "I was going to start the fall garden over on the other side of the house, if someone wants to help." She said. Megan and Gale both spoke up and said they and the kids would love to help.

Casey and the twins said they would go down by the fence line to gather up the last of the apples and peaches from the trees.

Vickie helped Kay back to her cabin, as Andie and I let all 5 dogs out to play. Jax was the biggest dog and was not the playing type. Him and my mom's dog, Gracie, just sat watching the 3 little dogs run around chasing each other.

I sat on the grass as my little ones came and loved on me. The sound of buzzing caught my attention. I stood up from the ground and looked at the sky. At first, I didn't see anything, but the buzzing got louder. Off towards the west, the sun hit the reflection of drones in the sky. They seemed to be pretty far away. But I could still tell what they were. At the same time, Doug and Sean, after putting up the last wall of a new cabin, stopped in their tracks hearing the buzzing. They looked to the west as well. "What the hell is that?" Doug said as I walked up to them. "Those are the same type of drones we saw when we were at Jordan's house," I replied. "That's crazy. What are they doing around here?" Sean asked. "I don't know," I replied as we continued to watch the drones fly to the south.

Day 12 Jay

At daybreak, the sound of automatic gunfire and men screaming woke Jay and the other men up. They stood up but stayed quiet so they could try to figure out what was going on. Suddenly, they saw 3 men running to the east of their cage towards the fence line. They all stood there and watched as the men tried to scale the fence. Suddenly gun fire erupted, and the 3 men fell to the ground lifeless. "Oh my God," one of the men yelled next to Jay. Jay stood there with the other men in total shock. No one said a word. After several long minutes, they all sat back down in the dirt, trying to comprehend what they had just witnessed.

After about 30 minutes, the door to the building opened and Officer Hext and two soldiers walked out with their ARs pointed at the men. The men all stood up and crowed together in the far corner, not know what to expect, especially after what they had just seen.

Behind the soldiers two more soldiers walked in with a box full of MREs and bottled water. They sat the boxes on the ground and walked back into the building followed by the soldiers with guns. They heard the door lock as the soldiers shut the door.

Slowly the men walked over to the box, and each grabbed a water and a meal. Still as quiet as can be, no one said a word as they ate their meal and drank their water.

A couple of the men were getting very agitated. Pacing up and down the fence, cussing and yelling out occasionally. Jay sat and watched the 2 men getting worked up. Another man approached them, "Man, come on, settle down, you don't know what they will do to us," the man said. One of the agitated men pushed the man to the ground, "Shut the fuck up," he said, and started yelling louder and louder.

After about 15 minutes of the 2 men yelling and cussing, the door opened as 2 soldiers with ARs came through. All the other men scrambled to their feet and back to the far corner of the cage. "Fuck you guys, you can't hold us here for no reason," one of the agitated men said. The other one piped in and agreed. The soldier pointed his gun at the man. "Shoot me motherfucker, I dare you," the man said as the gun went off and the man fell to the ground. Blood pouring out into the dirt. The other agitated man didn't say a word, just watched as his buddy fell to the ground. Another shot rang out and the 2nd man fell to the ground. The soldier looked at the other men hunched in the corner. "Anyone else have a complaint?" he asked. Jay and the men just looked at the soldier. "You four right there," he said as he pointed to Jay and 3 men standing beside Jay. "Pick them up and follow us." Jay and the 3 men hurried to pick them up and drag them out. Jay grabbed the first man under his arms as a guy picked up his feet. The other two did the same with the 2nd man.

Officer Hext held the door open for them as the other soldier kept his gun pointed at the other men in the corner. "Follow me," a soldier said as they walked through the building and out the front doors. Jay looked around to get an idea of what was going on and see if he could see the other men.

They carried the men over to a truck and were told to load the dead men in the back of it. Then the soldier told the 4 men to get in the back of the truck with the dead men. Jay started to shake, not knowing what was going to happen to them. Officer Hext jumped in the back with them and held his gun on them the whole time. They drove over to the fence where the other three dead men lay. The soldier instructed them to load up them up in the truck also and to get back in.

The truck then drove out the gate onto a dirt road. Jay noticed they had driven several miles deep into the forest. He said a prayer, thinking this might be where he dies. Then the truck came to a stop.

The smell of death and decay overwhelmed them. One soldier yelled and told them to get out. The four men jumped down from the truck. They each looked at each other, thinking this is where they would die. The soldier that was driving jumped out of the truck and over to the side. The soldiers instructed the four of them to grab a body and carry it over to a big hole that had been dug out and throw the bodies in.

Jay and one of the men carried the first body to the hole. Getting to the edge of the hole, they could see and smell the multiple bodies in the bottom of the hole. Jay gagged as he dropped the body to the ground. The soldier came over and kicked the body, so it went over the edge and into the hole.

Jay went back, and they grabbed the next man and did the same, gagging and coughing the whole time. When they had placed all 5 bodies in the hole, the Office Hext told them to get back in the truck.

Jay noticed him and the other men had blood all over them. Trying to be polite and not get shot, Jay asked Office Hext, "Will there be any way to wash up when we get back?" he said, showing the Officer all the blood on his hands and arms. Officer Hext didn't respond. He just kept looking at Jay.

Jay didn't say another word the entire way. When the truck got back to the compound, it stopped in front of the building they had come out of. Two soldiers on the ground told them to get out and follow them. Officer Hext yelled to the other soldier, "Let them go use the bathhouse to clean up." As the soldier looked at them up and down. "Follow me," he replied.

Jay and the 3 men followed the soldier down a path and another soldier walked behind them. Jay looked around and studied the area as they went down the hill to the bathhouse. He saw several cages like the one he was in, with several men in them. They watched as Jay and the 3 men were escorted by two soldiers and disappeared down the trail and into the bathhouse. One soldier followed them in while the other one stood guard outside the door.

Jay walked over to the sink; a trickle of water came out. But it was enough to get the blood off his hands and arms. He took off his t-shirt and rinsed it out the best he could and put the wet shirt back on.

The air was chilling, being the beginning of fall and a wet shirt on his skin, but at least he felt cleaner. After all the men had done their best getting the blood off, the soldiers escorted them back to their building and into the cage.

Jay and the three others didn't say a word until they knew the soldiers were gone. "What happened? What did you see out there?" a man asked. Jay and the 3 men explained what had happened and what they saw. "A hole with a bunch of decaying bodies?" a man asked. Jay shook his head.

Jay walked over and sat down in the corner. One of the other three men walked over and sat beside him. "Man, that was so fucked up, we gotta figure a way out of here. What do they want with us?" he asked Jay. "Maybe to just get the men out of the way so they can take over the country and our women," another one of the men said, sitting down on the other side of Jay. Jay didn't respond. He just kept staring at the dirt. "I'm Sam," his body carrying partner said. Jay finally looked up at him. "Jay," he replied. "I'm David," the other one said. "Michael," the 3rd one replied. "What are we going to do?" David asked. Jay again didn't respond. "I got two boys in one of those cages. They are probably so scared. They are only 19 and 20," Sam said. Jay finally looked up again. "I have my stepson, nephew, and a good friend out there as well. I promised my wife I would look after them," Jay said, still staring out at the fence.

They sat in silence, each one trying to think of a way out of there without getting killed. Shouts and screams were heard in the distance, then gunshots, then silence. Jay and the others just looked at each other. Several of the other men huddled in the opposite corner from Jay and the 3 guys that helped with the bodies. Jay kept glancing over at the group huddled. They were whispering, but he could make out what they were talking about. He just hoped they weren't planning on doing anything stupid that would get them all killed.

The sun was heading down behind the trees. His stomach was growling, and his mouth and throat were dry. He realized they had not given them anything to eat or drink since that morning. "Are they going to starve us?" he said under his breath. "I know I'm so thirsty," Sam said as Jay looked at him, thinking he had not said it out loud.

The men started getting restless again. They were hungry and thirsty. Every 15 minutes, soldiers walked around the cage on patrol. As the soldier made his rounds, one man from the huddle ask the soldier if they were going to get anything to eat or drink. Jay noticed it was Office Hext. Jay said nothing, but his eyes met the soldier's eyes. "I'll see what I can do," Officer Hext said, still staring at Jay.

Ten minutes later, the door opened. Officer Hext walked in with his gun pointed, and behind him was another soldier with another box of food and water. Several of the men from the huddle got to the box first, some taking more than one water and food. There was just enough to go around for each man to have one of each. But when the men took over one, some didn't get any. Yelling and a fight broke out between the men that took more than their share and the men that didn't get any.

"Stop it, stop it," Jay yelled, "you're going to get us all killed," David and Sam helped Jay break up the fight. "Here, take what's left of my water," Jay said as he handed a half of a bottle of water to one of the men that didn't get any. When Jay did that, one of the men that took more than his share handed one of the other men that didn't get any the extra he had taken. "I'm sorry, I shouldn't have done that," he said.

Jay, David, Sam, and Michael sat back down in their corner, but this time, several of the other men from the huddle joined them. Sam handed Jay his bottle of water. "Here, take a drink, I'll share." Jay took the bottle, took a drink, and handed it back.

"Do you see that lock on the gate?" Michael whispered to the other 3. "I think if I can get something, I can pick the lock," he said. "Don't ask me what I used to do before here," he laughed quietly between them. "If I can pick the lock, we might be able to get out of here," he continued. "But what about the guard and the fence? How are we going to get around that?" David asked. "I can't leave without my boys," Sam said. "Same," Jay replied. "We'll figure it out, let's sleep on it and see what we can come up with," Jay said.

Even though the sun had just gone down, Jay was feeling exhausted. He leaned his head back on the chain-link fence and closed his eyes.

Thoughts of Las Vegas went through his head. How simple life was just two months ago. Working at the dispensary, getting a promotion that he would never get to experience now. Going out to eat at the many restaurants Vegas offered. Gambling in the casinos. The stuff he knew was gone forever now.

Now he was sitting on the dirt in a cage with several other men, wondering what was going to happen next, hungry and thirsty, and missing D'Ann.

Day 12 D'Ann

We watched the drones disappear to the south. Nate walked up to where we were standing, watching them. "What are you guys doing?" as he looked at the sky where we were looking. "Drones again," I said, "Like the ones we saw at Jordan's." We all stood there looking at the sky a little longer.

"Are you going to town?" Doug asked Nate. "Yeah, do you have a list of things you want me to find?" Nate asked. "Why don't we go look at some farmhouses for supplies instead of risking going to town?" I asked. "I guess we could," Nate replied. "You know what? There is a small community just down the next county road about 10 miles. Lots of farmhouses along that road," Doug said. "Why don't me and Sean take one truck, and you and Jake take the other, and let's go see what we can find," Doug said to Nate. "I'm going also," I said, looking at Doug and Nate. "I want to find some more supplies, maybe some blankets and pillows stuff like that," I said. Doug looked at Nate and shrugged his shoulders. "I'm fine with that," Nate said. "I'll go get Jake and we will be ready to go," I said. "I'll meet you at the trucks," I continued as I walked towards the trailer.

I knocked lightly on the door of the trailer, not wanting to disturb grandma. Ashlyn came to the door and opened it. "Jake in here, we are going to go look for supplies," I whispered, looking at grandma sitting on the sofa. "How is she doing?" I asked. "A lot better," Ashlyn replied. Jake walked out of the bedroom. "You ready to go?" I asked. "Yeah," he replied. "I'll stay with her," Ashlyn said. Jake and I walked out and to the trucks.

Sean and Doug grabbed their rifles and jumped into the big truck as Nate, Jake and I jumped in the other truck. Sean opened the gate as we all drove through.

The first farmhouse we came to looked empty. The house was boarded up. Slowly driving into the driveway in case it wasn't empty. "Stay here. Let me go with Doug and check it out," I said as I jumped out with my gun in my hand.

It had been almost a month now since the event happened. If people didn't have supplies, they had surely died. Doug and I approached the front door. The handle was locked. He pointed for me to go around the north side of the house. As I walked around, I notice a window that was not boarded up. I slowly peeked inside. It was a bedroom. The bed was still made; the room was tidy, and I could tell dust had accumulated on the dresser. I tried to lift the window to open it, but it didn't budge. I walked around the back side and met Doug near the back door. He tried the screen door, and then the handle on the old wooden door locked. There were a couple of flowerpots with dead plants in them on the small porch. "In the movies, there is always a hidden key under the pots or the rug," I said, whispering to Doug with a grin on my face. He rolled his eyes at me and kicked one planter off the porch. We both started laughing when we saw a key laying in the dirt left over by the plant.

He picked it up and put it in the keyhole. The door opened. We cautiously walked in. It opened to the farmhouse kitchen. The kitchen was clean, no dishes in the sink, but a slight musty odor. We walked into the living room. We could tell it was an older couple by the looks of the décor. The farmhouse was a two-story small home. I searched all the rooms downstairs as Doug went upstairs. "It's all clear," he yelled down. I went to the front door and waved to the others to come in.

There were three bedrooms upstairs and one downstairs. We grabbed the blankets, pillows and sheets off the beds. I found the linen closet and grabbed several more blankets and sheets. Jake and Sean carried them out to the trucks. "Do you think we can get these mattresses for the new cabins?" I asked. Doug and Sean got to work carrying the mattresses down the stairs and out to the trucks.

We searched the kitchen for any leftover canned goods, not finding much. We grabbed everything we thought we would need. The guys went to the barn in the back to look for materials to build more cabins, while I looked around the house some more. I grabbed shampoos and soaps out of the bathrooms, and cleaning supplies from under the sinks. On the wall in the kitchen, I noticed a white board hanging next to the fridge. On the shelf was a marker. I opened the marker and wrote on the board: "I'm sorry we entered your home. We needed your supplies to keep our family safe and warm for the winter to come. Thank you, and God bless you wherever you are."

I grabbed the trash bags I had filled with supplies and walked out to the truck. The guys had driven the big truck to the barn and were putting all kinds of boards and tools in the truck. "I think the truck is full, let's go home and empty it, then we can try the next home," Doug said as we all piled back in the trucks.

When we got back to the lease, Megan, Gale and Andie helped carry all the supplies to the newly built cabins. They took the shampoos and soaps to the bathhouse. "Are you guys going back for more?" Megan asked. "I think so," I replied. "If you find some puzzles or board games, grab them for the kids, even any schoolbooks or coloring books, stuff like that." She added. "Okay, no problem, I'll look," I replied.

After unloading the trucks, we grabbed some lunch Barb made for us and headed back out to the next place we could find. Down the same road were several homes. All the homes seemed to be vacant, some with vehicles parked in their drives, some not. I saw a home that had some bicycles laying in the yard. "Oh, there," I pointed to Nate. "Let's see if this home is empty. I think they had kids. We can get the bikes for the kids to ride," I said as he pulled into the drive.

The house was more modern than most of the farmhouses in this area. It looked a lot newer with newer cars in the drive. We parked at the end of the drive and walked up to the house. I knocked on the door, tried the door handle. It was unlocked, so I opened the door. I knew that smell well. It was not near as strong as the last time I smelled the smell of death. But I knew what we would find. I looked at Sean and he shook his head. "Jake, why don't you stand guard out here in case someone drives by," I said, not wanting Jake to see what we were about to see in this house.

Doug, Nate, Sean and I walked in. Right away we noticed a woman and a man lying on the living room floor. They both had gunshot wounds to their heads. A gun was still in the man's hand. "Looks like murder suicide," I said. "There must be kids here," Doug said as he walked towards the bedrooms.

The first bedroom we came to, the door was closed. We slowly opened it. In the bed was a small blond headed child. The child looked like he was asleep, but as we got closer, we too could see a bullet wound in the child's head. I put my hands over my mouth. The site was too much. I walked out of the room. Doug and Sean continued down the hallway to the next room. The door was slightly ajar. Doug, pushed it open all the way and again laying on the bed was an older child, with a clear bullet wound as well. They walked out and to the last room. Opened the door but was relieved to not see anybody. This room must be the parents' room.

We checked the rest of the house and met back in the kitchen area. "We should bury these people," Sean said. Nate and Doug shook their heads in agreement. "Let's go see if we can find some shovels in the garage or that shed out back," Doug said as the three of them walked out the back door.

I grabbed a trash bag and stuffed it full of all the DVDs, music CDS, and board games I could find. They had bookshelves of books, even children's books. I grabbed as many as I could fit in the bag and still be able to carry it. I drug it to the front door, "Jake will you take this and put it in the truck, then grab those two bikes and put them in the truck?" I asked.

I went back in, got all the blankets and pillows that were not in the bedrooms the children were in. After the guys had removed the children from their rooms. I went in and gathered schoolbooks and anything I thought the kids would need.

It took over an hour for the guys to bury the family. It was getting late in the day, so after getting everything we could, we headed back home.

The day had been long. Everyone pitched in to do what they could to empty the trucks of supplies. Kay and Vickie, with the help of Megan and Gail, made the new cabins as comfortable as they could. So, they could move into them. Grandma and Jake moved into one of the cabins. As Stacie begged her mom Estelle to "go camping" as she put it, with Lynn in Gail and Lynn's cabin. Estelle and Grayson stayed in the smaller trailer with me, as Megan and her 3 kids stayed in the bigger trailer.

After we ate dinner, Doug and Sean built a bonfire out of some of the scrap lumber. Everyone but the kids sat around the fire. The twins and Casey had taken the little ones inside and made a theater in their bedroom, as they watched DVDs on their television.

Eventually everyone said good night and headed to their cabins. "Who's going to take watch tonight?" I asked, hoping someone would cause I was exhausted. "I can," Nate said. "I will help grandma to bed, and I can help," Jake said. As we all agreed and headed to our own beds. "Good night yawl," I said as I headed to my trailer.

CHAPTER THRITEEN

The river

Day 13 Jay

Jay woke up to the sound of the door opening and a soldier yelling for everyone to get up. The men, being the older ones, all struggled to get up off the hard ground after sleeping in odd positions. Three soldiers with their guns pointed at the men, motioned them all towards the door. "Single file, line up!" one of the soldiers said. They all followed the soldier out the door, through the building, and out the front door. In the yard, they saw the other men in the same lineup. Jay looked over at all the men and finally saw Jordan. He searched but did not see Dre or Nick. A pit in the middle of his stomach started to growl. Sam was directly behind Jay. "I don't see my sons," he whispered to Jay. "I don't think the younger group is here," Jay whispered back.

The soldiers split the group up. Three of the older men that were not as fit as the others were separated and take off by another group of soldiers. Then two men were taken off by another soldier.

"The rest of you in the trucks," as the soldiers herded everyone towards the back of two trucks. Jay didn't say anything, he just did what he was told. Once all the men were loaded, the trucks drove out the gates and into the forest, the same direction he they had gone the day before with the dead bodies. He recognized the area. As the truck stopped next to the big hole that contained several bodies.

The soldiers indicated for the men to get out and grab a shovel. They walked over to the hole and were instructed to cover up the hole with the dirt that was piled up. The other truck had stopped a few yards on up. The younger group of men jumped out of their trucks with shovels and began digging. "Look," Jay whispered to Sam, "they are digging more holes, means more are going to die." As Sam and Jay glanced over at the men digging.

It had taken several hours when both sets of men were done. They loaded back up in the trucks and headed back to the compound. Jay searched the area as they went through the gates, taking mental notes on how many guards were and where they were. The buildings and the other cages. Near the other end of the compound, he could see a group of men that were constructing more cages. "Those must be the young ones," Jay whispered to Sam. Sam looked in the direction Jay was indicating. "I think it is. I think I see Adam," Sam said with a little excitement in his voice.

The truck stopped in front of a large building. As the soldier escorted them in, they instructed them to pick up the food and bottles of water that were laid out on tables. The three men that were taken earlier were cooking the food in the kitchen area. And the other two men were setting up tables and chairs for the men to sit at.

There was plenty of food and water for the men to eat. They took what they wanted and sat down at a table, staying in their group. There were about 10 soldiers posted throughout the building. Once they were done, they were instructed to clean their area and follow the soldiers back out. As they were walking out, the middle-aged men were walking in to get their food. Jay and Jordan's eyes met. Jay could still see the fear in Jordan's eyes. Jay mouthed to Jordan, "Soon," as Jordan shook his head that he understood.

They were then herded back into their cage. Jay, Sam, David and Michael went to their corner. "So, let's compare notes. What did everyone see? Is there a way out of here?" Jay asked. Michael reached into his back pocket and produced a knife. "Where the hell did you get that?" Jay asked Michael. Michael just grinned. "Never mind, I don't want to know," Jay said. "I think I can get the lock off the gate," Michael said. "When it gets dark tonight and everyone has gone to sleep, let try it." Sam said. They all nodded in agreement.

The men sat around hatching out a plan. "Once we get out of this cage, we have to somehow make it to the other cages to get our kids,"

Sam said. "There are guards everywhere. How are we going to do that?" David asked. "Very quietly," Sam replied.

The men noticed some others in the cage were listening in on their conversations. "Let's stop talking about this, we got ears," Jay said as they all looked around at the other men watching them. Jay sat back against the fence and watched the sun go down behind the trees.

The air had a chill in it when the sun went down. It was definitely fall in east Texas. The leaves of the trees were changing colors, "if it wasn't for their situation, it would be quite beautiful," Jay thought.

Sam scooted closer to Jay. "I think those men heard what we had planned," he whispered to Jay. "Yeah, I think so," Jay replied. "They could get us all killed," Sam said. "Maybe we should wait one more day, see what they have us do tomorrow, and get a better look at the grounds," Jay whispered. Sam shrugged his shoulders. "Tell Michael not to do it tonight," Jay said. Sam was sitting between Jay and Michael. Sam turned his head to Michael. "Jay thinks we should wait one more night so we can get a better look around tomorrow," Sam whispered to Michael. Michael shook his head no. "I'm not staying another day in this place. I'm doing it tonight," he whispered back. Jay heard what Michael had said. "It's too dangerous. You're going to get us all killed," Jay said, leaning forward glaring at Michael. Michael sat back and put his head against the fence and shut his eyes. "Fuck," Jay whispered to himself.

Jay leaned back and shut his eyes. It was several hours later when he heard the rustling of the lock on the gate. Jay opened his eyes and saw Michael messing with the lock. Every 15 minutes, he would sit down and pretend he was asleep as the night guard walked around the fence. Then, when he was gone, he would get up and try again. A couple of the other men that had been watching and listening to them earlier noticed Michael. They got up to help him. Just before the next guard was due to walk by Michael unlocked the lock. He left it hanging there to look like it was still locked, as they sat down and pretended to be asleep again.

The guard never noticed. Michael got up, took the lock off, and quietly slid the chain out of the gate. He opened the gate and 5 of the other men followed him out the gate. Jay nudged Sam awake as they watched the men go out the gate. Sam started to get up. "Wait!" Jay said. At about that time, a guard came around the corner of the building. The six guys took off running. Shots rang out as the soldier chased the men, yelling for them to stop. Jay, Sam and David stayed right where they were, as well as 10 of the other men still in the cage.

More shots rang out, echoing through the trees. Two soldiers ran to the gate and pointed their guns directly at the men still in the cage. Jay put his hands up but stayed sitting on the ground. The other men did the same. "Don't move, unless you want to end up like your friends," the soldier yelled. They all sat silently. A soldier ran over to the gate and secured it with another chain and lock. Once it was locked, the soldiers ran off to where the escapee was lying on the ground. Jay looked at Sam. "Dammit, he ruined everything, if he just would have waited," Sam said. "We will figure this out," Jay replied. Jay notices flashes of lights in the south night sky. "It's going to storm," he said. "We are going to get rained on," David commented.

As the guard made his round, Jay got up and walked to the fence. He noticed it was Officer Hext. "Sir, look, we obeyed and didn't try to get out when the others did. Please have mercy on us. There is a storm coming, and it's getting cold out. Can we at least have a tarp or something to cover us up to protect us from the chilly rain?" Jay begged. Officer Hext looked at him with what Jay thought was compassion in his eyes. Then walked up to Jay and stood just a foot away from him. "I will see what I can do," Officer Hext whispered as he walked away. Jay was shocked. "Thank you," he said.

The storm was getting closer; the thunder was getting louder. After about 30 minutes, the door opened, and they threw two large tarps in the cage and then the door shut and locked again. David got up and grabbed one as the other group of men got the other one. They huddled up underneath just as the rain started coming down.

It took Jay a long time to go back to sleep. The thunder sounded like gun shots that kept ringing in his ears. Jay shivered as the cool air and rain chilled him to his core.

Day 13 D'Ann

I got up out of bed and let Jax out to go potty. I noticed that the men were all standing on the porch with their guns, as Jake was running to his cabin. I walked over to the house. "What's going on? Any news from the Radio?" I asked. "Jakes grandma is gone," Sean said with panic in his voice. "What? How could she be gone? Did you check the bathhouse?" I asked. "We've been everywhere," Nate replied. "We need to check the forest, she probably just wandered off," I said. "I'm going to go get Megan and Gale up to help search," Nate said as he walked towards the cabins. "I'll get the twins and Casey up. They can help," Doug said.

About 15 minutes later, we all met at the picnic tables. "Sean, Nate and I will head out on the trails on the ATV's," Doug said. "Abby, Ally and Casey, come with me. We will take the trail out back towards the river. She could have walked out of the open area of the fence that's not completed. Megan, Gale and Andie walk the driveway," I said.

We all took off in our assigned directions. Jax followed us along the trail. It was quite a way from the compound to the river. But the walk was beautiful, the leaves were changing colors, and the forest was still and quiet. I could hear only the birds in the trees.

It took us about 45 minutes to walk to the river. But we weren't walking at a quick pace. We searched the sides of the trail thoroughly. As soon as we got to the river, Jax started barking. "Stop!" I yelled as the girls stopped in their tracks. "Stay here. Let me see what he is barking at," I said as I drew my gun. Jax ran alongside the river bank out of my sight. "Jax, come here," I yelled. I rounded the corner and saw Jax standing over a man. The man was on the ground. It looked like he had been camping in the area. He had a tent and had a small fire going. "Jax," I yelled. Pointing my gun at the man. "What are you doing here? This is private property?" I asked. Noticing he had a fishing pole in the water and a fry pan next to the fire. "I'm just trying to survive," the man said. I grabbed Jax' collar and allowed the man to sit up. He looked to be in his late 30s. The twins and Casey came around the corner of the bend. "Larry?" Abbie yelled. "That's Larry. He lives down the hill. What are you doing out here?" she asked. "Trying to survive, they are rounding men up in towns and all around.

I got away before they saw me. I've been hiding out here for a few days," he said as he got up off the ground and stood up.

"Have you seen anyone else out here?" I asked. "No, no one," he said. "Only thing I've seen, and it's really weird, but a bunch of drones flew over," he continued. "I hid in the tree line when I saw them. I didn't know what they were looking for," he said. "Okay, well, we won't make you leave. Just keep your eyes open for anything suspicious and will you let us know up at the house?" I asked. "Yes, of course. Thank you for letting me stay," he said. "No problem," I replied as we walked back to the trail.

Jax started barking again as we headed back upstream. He ran past the trail and upstream further. "Jax, hold on," I yelled as we got to the trail. "you guys stay here. Let me see what he's barking at this time," I said as I tried to catch up to him. Around another bend in the stream, I saw it. I stopped in my tracks. "No, no!" I ran to where Jax was barking. Laying half in the water and half out was Grandma. I pulled her out of the water. I could tell by the purple color and the coldness of her skin that she was gone. "Oh, Grandma," I said. "I'm so sorry, you go be with Grandpa now. I laid her in the grass alongside the stream. I knew I had to go get the men.

Jax and I walked back to where the girls were standing, throwing rocks into the stream. "Can you guys hurry back to the house and let them know?" as I looked down with tears. "I found Grandma, she's passed away," I said. I looked at Casey, hoping it wouldn't bring back terrible memories for her. She teared up and reached out to hug me. "Abby and I will run back, you stay here with Aunt D'Ann," Ally said to Casey as they both turned and ran up the trail.

Casey and I sat down on some boulders and threw a rock into the water. "I feel back for Jake. He lost his parents and now his grandparents," Casey said. "You can really help him cope, since you went through a similar thing." I looked at her. "I will, I will help him through it," she said, picking up another rock and throwing it in the stream.

Almost an hour passed when we heard the motors of ATVs coming up the trail. I stood up and saw Doug and Sean. I pointed over toward Grandma. Doug grabbed a tarp off the ATV as they went over to her. I stayed by the ATVs with Casey and Jax. Several minutes later, they came back carrying her wrapped in the tarp. They put her on the back of Doug's ATV. Sean looked at us. "Do one of you wanna ride back?" Sean asked. "No, I would rather walk. Beside I have Jax," I said. "I'll walk with D'Ann," Casey replied. "Oh Doug, one of your neighbors is camping out down the stream," as I pointed in his direction. "A man named Larry. He said the military was rounding up men, and he got away and is hiding here. I told him it was okay since you all know him. He said he would let us know if he sees anything out here. I hope that was, okay?" I asked. "Yeah, I'll go talk to him," Doug said as he walked down the stream.

Several minutes later, he came back. "It's all good," Doug said. "Let's get Grandma back. "See you two at the house," Doug said.

The ATVs took off toward the house as Casey, Jax and I walked the trail. We took our time taking in the beauty and solitude of the forest. It took us over an hour to get back to the house. By the time we got back, Doug and Sean had already dug a grave for Grandma on the other side of the yard and were covering her up. Jake stood over the grave sobbing. "Casey, go to him," I said as she jogged off towards Jake.

Kay, Vickie and Andie had given Barb a break from cooking and had fixed a nice big lunch. We all sat and ate and planned a memorial for Grandma. After lunch, Jake had asked Doug if he could have a couple of pieces of wood to make a cross for Grandma. Nate and Jake went out to the shop and constructed a beautiful cross. Nate engraved "Grandma" into the wood. No one could remember her real name. Everyone called her grandma. "Jake, what is Grandma's real name? I had forgotten?" I asked. "It was Leona," he said. "Kenneth and Leona were my grandparents."

We all gathered around her grave that evening, everyone saying a couple of words and ending in a prayer. After that, we all sat down to eat dinner that Kay, Vickie, and Andie prepared. As it got later in the day, we could see a storm was building in the south. "Looks like we are in for a bad one," Doug said, looking off to the south as the sun was starting to go behind the trees. "Maybe you guys in the trailers should stay in the house tonight, or there is one more cabin, but no bed," Doug said. "I'll get the blankets and pillows from our trailer and me and the kids can stay in the cabin. They won't mind sleeping on the floor. We will have a camp out," Megan said as the kids yelled with excitement. Celia rolled her eyes. "You can stay in our room if you want," Abbie said to Celia. "Please," she responded with a smile.

Everyone helped clean up the dinner and then moved the chairs and lawn furniture to the shed so it would blow away. The men closed the doors in the sheds and made sure everything else was battened down. I walked my mom to her cabin and decided that Jax and I would stay in her cabin with her and Gracie. Casey took the 3 little dogs and stayed with the twins and Celia.

The rain drops started falling as the lightning lit up the sky and the thunder crashed around us. Mom and I sat in her cabin talking about our family in Kansas, hoping they were safe.

My mom had 2 sisters, June and Sherry, and one bother Tommy. They had all lived in Kansas most all their lives. June was the oldest. She had married Edgar, and they had 3 kids, Rae, Kristin, and Jeb. My mom was next with 3 kids, me being the oldest, Mike, and then Jace. Sherry had 3 kids Scarlett, Genevieve and Braxton. Then there was Tommy, also with 3 kids, Darlene, Tami, and Ricky.

Growing up, me and my cousins Rae and Kristin grew up more like sisters. The other cousins were a lot younger than us and grew up more with our children. But we were a very close-knit family. But as with most families, when my grandma passed away everyone started having their own families. We all grew apart. Some moved away, and some just were busy with life.

We talked late into the night, reminiscing about all the times we had when I was young. We wondered if the families all survived and thought maybe when Jace got back, we would go to Kansas and see if everyone was okay. The storm seemed to get stronger as the night went on. "I guess we better get to sleep. I got a lot to do tomorrow," I said. Jax and I made a bed on the floor with left over blankets and pillow, and before too long, all of us were snoring.

CHAPTER FOURTEEN

The Escape

Day 14 Jay

The morning came early. The dirty beds they had been sleeping on were now a muddying mess. All the men were shivering as they crawled out from under their tarps. The soldiers came to the door and told the men to get up and line up. The soldiers escorted them to the big building where they ate last night. This time, the men had cooked a hot breakfast with oatmeal and coffee. Jay and his cage mates walked in. Jay saw Officer Hext and nodded towards him. Officer Hext looked around to see if any of the other soldiers noticed and nodded back. Jay noticed Jordan's group come in the door as well. He smiled at Jordan and nodded to him. Jordan smiled back. What used to be a group of 21 was now a coup of 10. "Damn, where did the others go," Sam whispered to Jay. Jordan and his group got their food and coffee and sat at the tables on the other side of the room. 2 guards walked around each group.

Just as Jay and his group were finishing up. The youngest group walked in the door. "Oh, my God! There are Junior and Adam," Sam said, looking at his sons. They were wet and shivering. They saw their dad and wanted to run to him. But Sam held his hand out to indicate stay where they were. He mouthed to them "keep your head down," as they both shook their heads in agreement.

Jay saw Dre and Nick right behind them. Jay gave them the same look and gesture. They also shook their heads in agreement. Jay and Sam walked out the door. "At least they are still alive," Sam whispered to Jay. Jay looked around the compound. Tree limbs were down all over the place. Some gigantic trees had fallen on the fence surrounding the compound, knocking it over. The guards escorted the men to the bathhouse. "Shower, there are clean and dry clothes you can put on," one soldier yelled. "Nothing like taking a shower with 13 men, kinda reminds me of jail," Jay said.

After the men had changed into their new clothes, which happened to be jumpsuits like they have in jail, but only a dark green instead of bright orange. They were taken back to the building where their cage was attached. Jay noticed walking back that several of the soldiers were arguing standing next to a gigantic tree that had fallen on one of the trucks smashing the cab. The soldier in front didn't open the door to the cage. Officer Hext walked in the door behind them. "There are cots over there set them up and you can stay inside for now. There is another storm coming. We will be back to split you up in a cleanup detail after the next storm passes." He looked at Jay and winked, turned around and walked out the door with the other soldiers. Jay stood there, not knowing what that was all about.

The men grabbed the cots and set them up. There was not enough to go around. So, Jay, Sam and David got 2 blankets each to make a bed on the floor. They took their blankets and pillow and headed to the far corner of the room away from most of the other men.

"Did you see the gigantic tree on the fence behind the buildings?" Jay asked Sam and David. "Yeah, it will take them days to get it off," David said. "Right, and that is where we will escape. If the others are inside those cabins, it will be a lot easier to get them out," Sam said.

Jay and the men sat and listened to the thunder getting closer. The cabin was dark with no sunlight coming in through the only two windows. Jay got up and walked over to the windows to see where the guards were standing. To his surprise, he didn't see any guard immediately outside their cabin. The rain was pouring down now, thunder and lightning everywhere as small hail pounded the ground. Jay walked to the door and turned the handle. To his surprise, it wasn't locked. He cracked it to look around to see if he could see the soldiers. As his hand went around to the front of the doorknob, he felt a key stuck in the lock. He quickly pulled it out and stuck it in his pocket.

He shut the door and turned around. Every man in the room was looking at him. "I don't know if this is a trap or what, but I don't see any guards out there. Before you all make a run for it and get shot down, let me and a couple of guys go out and see where they are. The storm is terrible out there, but I think we can do it.

Sam got up quickly and ran over to Jay. "I'll go," he said without hesitation. Another man from the group of 10 came over also. "I used to be a cop. I know how to get around undetected," he said. "Okay, the rest of you, stay here and stay quiet. "We will be back," Jay said as he and the other 2 snuck out the door. Even though it was afternoon, the storm made it seem like it was early evening, as dark as it was.

The first place Sam and Jay wanted to go was the other cabins to get Sam's kids, Dre and Nike. Then over to Jordan's cabin. Jay went first, he crouched down and as soon as a bolt of lightning hit and the thunder started, he hurried over to the truck with the tree on it. One by one, the other two did the same thing. Standing up and peeking around the truck, he scoured the area as good as he could through the rain. He didn't see any movement or the guards. There was a tree standing between him and the next building. If he can get to the tree, then he should be able to get behind the next building.

All three of them made it to the building. They peeked in the windows and saw the same setup as their own building. Men on cots sitting around talking, but no guards. Jay studied in the room. He didn't see Jordan or Dre and Nick. Sam also looked and didn't see his two sons. "Let's not open this door yet, till we find our families," Jay said to Sam. "We don't need men running all around this place getting the guard's attention," Jay said.

Jay peeked around that cabin. The mess hall was in plain view. The big double doors were open, and he could see the guards were inside. "I can't tell how many are in there," Jay said. Sam traded places with Jay and looked as well. "I don't think they are all in there. Some are missing," Sam said. "They could be over in that barn close to the gates," the cop said. "Let's get to the next cabin. Once we open the doors, the men are going to come running out. We will only have a few seconds to get to the other buildings to get them out," Jay said.

"Okay, you ready? Once we open the doors and get to our families, we need to run to the fence that is down. If you head north, you will hit a stream. Stay close to it, follow it north and it will take you to the next town. But be careful. We don't know if there are more military groups doing the same thing," Jay said.

The next clap of thunder happened, and Jay, Sam, and the cop took off running to the next cabin. They peeked in the windows and saw Dre, Nick, Junior and Adam all sitting on cots. There were only 6 other men with them. Jay tried the key in the lock. It opened, and he walked through the door, followed by Sam. Dre and Nick ran to Jay as Sam's sons ran to him. "Come on, everyone, we must go. Stay low and follow us, and be quiet," Jay commanded. They all followed Jay, one by one, crouching down and running to the next cabin. Again, Jay peeked in the window. He saw Jordan laying on a cot. Searching the room, he only saw 4 other men. He unlocked the door and went in. Jordan jumped out of his cot and ran over to Jay. "Come on, we gotta go. Head to the fence that is down by that tree and run he said to the other men. One of the young guys came forward. "My dad is in the other cabin," he said. Jay handed him the key. "Go get him, but be careful," Jay said.

Sam and his sons, along with several other men, ran for the fence. Two men followed the other kid to help get their families out of the other cabins. Jay brought up the rear of the group, escaping over the tree that had crushed the fence when he heard a shot ring out and shouting. "Go, go," Jay said as he pushed some of the men over the tree. All the men scattered. Some went south, some going east, while Sam and Jay ran north with their families.

Between the claps of thunder, they could hear gun gunshots. The bullets struck the trees as they ran. Nick and Dre, of course, being younger, ran faster than the rest. Adam and Junior were right behind them. Jordan, Jay, and Sam behind them.

Another couple more shots rang out, one hitting the tree right in front of Jay. Then, out of the corner of his eye, he saw Sam falling to the ground. Jay stopped to help Sam up. Blood appeared on the side of Sam's thigh. Junior turned around and saw Jay trying to help his dad get up. He ran back to help Jay get Sam. "He's been shot in the leg," Jay yelled to Junior. "It's just a nick," Sam said, getting up. Several more shots rang out. They knew the soldiers were chasing them and closing in. "You and your dad go that way and get in those bushes, get some pressure on that leg. We will keep leading them this way. Met us at the river about 2 miles north. Just keep heading that way," as Jay pointed to the north. Junior helped Sam into the bushes about 10 yards away. They lay down so the soldiers wouldn't see them as Junior ripped part of his shirt and placed it on the wound.

Jay took off running and caught up to Jordan, Dre, Nick and Adam. "Where's my dad and Junior?" Adam asked franticly. "They are hiding in the bushes, you got nicked by a bullet and can't outrun the soldiers. Go, run, we got to get more distance between us and the soldiers. "We will meet your dad and brother at the river," Jay said as they all took off running again.

Running through the trees as the rain poured down. The ground was muddying, leaving footprints for the soldiers to easily track them. Stopping to catch their breath, "We need to split up. The soldiers are tracking us with our footprints. Dre, you and Nick go that way, try to step on branches and bushes, don't leave any footprints. Keep heading to the river. Go up stream and find a place to hide. We will meet you there. Let's go this way, try not to leave any footprints," Jay said to everyone as they tried to step on branches, weeds and bushes. Jay, Jordan, and Adam ran as fast as they could, dodging trees and big rocks. Eventually getting to a very hilly and rocky area. Jay saw a huge tree that had fallen and taken a couple more trees with it. "There, let's get under those trees and wait them out," Jay said as they gently walked, leaving no trace to the trees. Then slid in the mud under the tree and waited. The three of them huddled together for warmth. They were all exhausted. Too scared to move, they laid there for hours in the rain and thunder and listened for movement, eventually fading off to sleep.

Day 14 D'Ann

The storm had passed, and morning came. I stepped outside of my mom's cabin and looked to the south. Dark clouds were still visible.

"Another storm is coming," I said to Jax and Gracie as they went potty. The ground and grass were wet. "Come on, get back inside," I yelled at the dogs and opened the door.

The air was brisk as I walked down the path to the house. Nate and Doug were sitting on the porch, drinking coffee. "Everybody survive the night?" I asked as I walked up to the porch. "Yeah, just a couple of tree limbs down. Not too bad. We were able to catch a lot of rain in the rain collections system. So, we should be good with water for a while." Doug said. "Looks like more rain is coming though," I said, pointing to the south. "I'm really getting worried about Jay and the boys. I thought they would be home by now," I said. Nate looked at me and shook his head. "I am too," he said. "There hasn't been any talking on the radio?" I asked. "There was some the other day, but there is so much static we couldn't make it out. I think we need to get an antenna. Maybe we will pick something up then," Doug said. "Maybe we should drive to town and see what is going on, ask around," I said. "Okay, let's do it," he commented. "Okay, let me go change my clothes and I'll be ready to go," I replied.

Nate and I jumped into the truck. "Be careful," Doug said as we drove out of the driveway. "We don't have a lot of gas, but I think we have enough to get there and get back," Nate said as we drove to town.

We got to the edge of town and noticed the roadblock, but it wasn't the military. It looked like the same people that were there the first time I drove close to town. They stopped us in the middle of the road. "Where you folks going?" the man asked. "We are looking for information," Nate said. "What kind of information are you looking for?" he asked.

"About 3 days ago, we were stopped outside of Livingston on our way here. We live just right outside of town, on the Strong property." Nate said. "Yes, I knew the old man that used to live there. He was quite the character," the man said. "Well, like I was saying. We got stopped outside of Livingston by a military roadblock. They took my son, her husband, my grandson and step grandson and a friend. Said the government passed a law that any man between the ages of 18 and 50 was to go with them," Nate said.

The old man looked at Nate and then at me. He turned and yelled to a man standing by the barricades, "Fred, come here." Fred walked over to where we were parked. "Yes sir," Fred said. "Tell them about that military group that came through here a couple days ago, taking the younger men," the old man said to Fred. "Them there wasn't no military," Fred said. "At least not United States Military. Don't know who they were but they are not in the military. Oh, they acted like it and looked like it, but I'm a retire marine and I can promise you they weren't military."

Nate looked at me. I got goosebumps on my arms. "They set-up camp right outside of towns, telling everyone they had to go with them. But the very next day, the National Guard came through looking for the fellers. They said they had drones flying over the area looking for these militia groups, so they could capture them. I heard the militia are killing all the men they capture if they don't conform to their military," Fred continued. "WHAT?" I screamed, "that can't be true," I said. "Well, that is what the soldiers from the National Guard told us," Fred said. "We need to go to Livingston and find them," I said to Nate. "No, they wouldn't be there now. They take them somewhere else, so they don't get caught," Fred said.

I started to cry, "Oh my God! What are we going to do?" I cried. "Look, the National Guard has set up a post in the Wal-Mart parking lot, go talk to them. Fred walked back and moved the barricades out of the way so we could drive in.

We sped away and pulled into the Wal-Mart parking lot. They set several tents up near the entrance to the store. There was a Red Cross tent, and a medical tent set up. A soldier from the National Guard stood outside a large tent to the west of the Red Cross tent. We parked in the lot and walked up to the Guards. "We must talk to someone about the military taking our men," I said. "Wait here," the guard said as he turned and walked into the tent. A few minutes later, he came back and opened the flap in the tent. "Go in. The captain will be right with you. Take a seat over there," as he pointed to a row of chairs.

Nate and I walked over and sat down. A few minutes had gone by when a National Guard soldier came and asked us to follow him. We followed him to the back of the tent. Behind the room divider was a desk and 2 chairs. "Have a seat," The Captain said. The captain sat down behind the desk and beside him were two more guards. "So, tell us exactly what happened," the captain said.

I explained what had happened. The captain looked at the other two guards, then back at me. "I'm sorry to tell you, those were not military. We have found that some military militia groups with unknown leaders have spread out all over the country and are executing men if they don't join their militia. They want to take over the country and with little resistance. Some of our own militaries have joined their groups," the captain said. "Executing them?" I cried. "From what we have learned is they are using them to build an army. If the men don't comply then they are getting executed," he replied. "Oh my God," I cried. I put my head in my hands and broke down. Nate put his hand on my shoulder to comfort me. "What can we do?" Nate asked.

"We have a few soldiers that have infiltrated their militia and are feeding us information on their operations. We already shut down several of their operations and rescued several men. That is about all I can tell you as of now. Tell me where you were when your men were taken," he asked.

I couldn't talk. The thought of my husband and son being executed still rang in my ears. Nate explained where they were taken. "We are sweeping the area in that direction but haven't made it to the Livingston area. We hope to be there by the end of the week," the captain said. "By the end of the week? They could be dead by then," I cried, looking at the captain dead in his eyes. "I'm sorry, ma'am, we just don't have the resources to go any faster." He apologized.

I got up from the chair and walked away. "Thank you, sir," Nate said and ran after me. I cried all the way to the truck. "We have to go to Livingston," I said, climbing into the truck. "I don't think that is a very good idea, D'Ann," Nate said. "I just can't sit here and let my child and husband die," I cried. "I understand, but we need to let the National Guard do their jobs. We could get killed ourselves if we go looking for them," Nate replied.

I sat in the truck and sobbed. Nate tried to comfort me the best he could. But he, too, was worried about the guys. "I'll be right back.

You going to be, okay?" he asked. I shook my head okay as he got back out of the truck. Through my tears, I watched him walk back into the National Guard tent.

I sat staring out the window, watching people go in and out of the other tents. Some people were carrying boxes full of all kinds of items. Some were full of clothing and blankets. Then, a few minutes later, I watched those same people carry boxes of food and supplies.

Nate finally walked back to the truck and got in. "What were you doing?" I asked. "I told the captain where he could find us in case there was any news. I gave him a description of the guys. He said he would send someone out if they had news." Nate said, putting his hand on my knee. I shook my head in acknowledgement. "I've been watching people come and go from that tent over there in front of the store. It looks like they are exchanging goods, let's go see what is going on in there," I said looking at Nate. "Okay, let's go see," he replied as we hopped out of the truck and walked towards the tent.

We walked inside the tent. The walkway extended into the Wal-Mart store. There were tables set up in long rows. On the tables were goods like clothing, blankets, pillows, all kinds of linens. Continuing to walk, we saw tables with soaps and shampoos, first aid items, medications. We stopped at one table and asked the person standing behind the table. "So, what is this?" The lady standing behind the table replied, "It is an exchange program. You bring what you have and exchange it for things you need." I looked at Nate, "that sounds like a great thing to do. Can anybody do it?" I asked. "Yeah, just bring in your items. They will set you up a table. If you don't need what someone brings in, you don't have to exchange with them. They can go over there," as she pointed towards where the pharmacy would have been. "They can take their items and get a voucher. The voucher can be used at any table. If you accept a voucher, then you can use it at any table also," she explained. "Okay, thank you," I said.

We looked towards the back of the store and saw more tables with canned goods and vegetables. We continued to walk around the store. There were more items in the auto department for vehicles, even saw gasoline cans full of gas and diesel for exchange. "Maybe we should go get some stuff and exchange it for some diesel since we are running low at the house," I said. "Look over there, some wood and fencing," Nate said, pointing towards the garden center area. "This is such a good idea," I replied as we walked back towards the front of the store.

We got back in the truck and drove back to the house. Doug and Barb were waiting on the front porch. Vickie and Sean had seen us drive in and ran to the front of the house. We sat down on the porch and told them about what the National Guard had said and about the exchange program. "So, they are going to go look for the guys?" Doug asked. "They said they would," Nate replied. Vickie started crying. Sean tried to comfort his mom. "I'm going to take her back to her cabin," Sean said, helping his mom up. "I need to go tell Ashlyn and Estelle about what they told us," I said, but I didn't get up. I just stared towards the gate.

"The exchange program sounds great," Barb said. "We have tons of canned items we can take and some fresh vegetables that will spoil if someone doesn't eat them. I guess I planted too much," she said. I didn't respond. "It will be okay; they will get home. You know Jay won't give up," she continued. Again, I didn't respond. I just kept staring at the gate, hoping Jay and Jordan would walk through it. When I finally snapped out of it, I saw Estelle and the baby walking from the trailer towards us. "I guess I need to tell her," I said as I got up and met her halfway. She broke down and cried. I took the baby from her and held him. His soft skin was against my face as tears slid down my cheeks. I helped her back to the trailer and into the bunk. "Why don't you take it easy? I'll take the baby for a while and give you a break," I said. She didn't respond. She just curled up into a ball and cried.

I took Grayson and walked back to the house. I sat in the swing and rocked baby Grayson till he was fast asleep. Ashlyn walked around the side of the house. I looked up at her and could tell she had been crying. "Sean told me, "she said as she sat beside me on the swing. "We just must keep praying they come home to us. Jay will keep Jordan safe," I said. "I know," Ashlyn agreed.

The sky was turning dark with storm clouds again. "Looks like we are in for another round," Doug said as he helped Barb carry out a big pot of stew for dinner. Slowly, everyone gathered at the tables. We bowed our heads and prayed for the return of our men. We had just finished eating when the first raindrops started falling. I walked my mom back to her cabin. But I didn't feel like talking or being around anyone, so I went to Casey's cabin, told her I was taking the three little dogs, and asked her to watch Jax. The dogs and I went back to the trailer by ourselves. We crawled into bed, all three dogs crawled under the covers as I pulled the covers over my head and cried.

CHAPTER FIFTEEN

Forgot Dad

DAY 15 Jay

Jay jerked awake. It was still dark out. The rain had stopped. He felt around in the dark and could feel the other boys were they lying beside him. He lay there and listened to the forest and the surrounding sounds. Off in the distance, he heard the water rushing into the river.

He slid out from under the tree, not trying to disturb the others. He was going to get a look around as good as he could through the dark. The sky was getting lighter to the east as he made it to the river. He kneeled behind some bushes and try to see if he could make out anyone along the river. The rain the last 2 nights had made the river full and almost out of its banks. He sat there for several minutes listening to any sounds, but the water was running too fast and was too loud.

After several minutes, he wandered back towards the direction he came, towards the boys under the tree. Walking slowly and as quiet as he could. He heard a twig snap off to his left. He stopped in his tracks and knelt to the ground. He heard footsteps coming towards him. He got to his belly and crawled into the weeds, trying not to make any noise. The footsteps were so close he could have reached out and touched their feet. "I don't know which way to go," he heard a voice whispering. He knew that voice. "Nick?" Jay whispered. "Jay?" Nick replied. Jay got up and crawled out of the weeds. "Jay!" Nick said as he hugged Jay. "Man, are we glad to see you? I think we have been walking in circles," Nick cried. "Come on, let's go get the others and head to the river," Jay said as they walked through the mud to where Jay had left Jordan and Adam.

The sun was almost up as the 5 of them walked to the river. They approached the river with caution as they looked for Sam and Junior. "You guys stay here, stay out of sight. I'm going to go downstream and see if they are there," Jay said as he walked through the high weeds along the river. He walked about a mile when he came to an area that was surrounded by cliffs. "They wouldn't have come this way," he thought. He started back towards where he had left the guys.

The sun was shining almost overhead now, and it felt warm on his wet clothing. It took him about an hour to get back to where the guys were sitting. "I didn't see them; they must not have made it this far. Sam might not have been able to walk that much," Jay said, trying not to alarm Adam, but Jay knew it could be because they were captured again. "We need to get out of the open. Let's start walking upstream and see if we can find some shelter." Jay said. "Then I will go look for them," he assured Adam.

They seemed to have walked for hours when they finally came upon a pasture with a farmhouse a few hundred feet away. They stayed in the tree line and made their way closer, hidden in case someone was in the house. "Stay here. I'm going to get a closer look," Jay said to the boys. There was an old tractor between him and a barn. He crouched down and ran to the tractor. Looking around the tractor to watch for any movement in the barn. When he thought it was safe, he continued to the barn. The barn door was open, and he could tell as of the storm last night there were no footprints in the mud, in or out of the barn. He snuck in the side and looked around. It hadn't looked like anyone had been in the barn for some time.

He went to the side barn door that faced the farmhouse. Between the barn and the house was a drive that was covered in rainwater. "Ugh, this is going to be a muddy mess," he said, looking at all the mud. He searched the area and saw a grassy area to the west of the house. "If I sneak around that way, I can stay in the grass and get to the back door," he said to himself.

He watched the house for a few more minutes. Then he made a run for it. Running in the grass that was still a little slippery from the rain, but at least not as muddy as it would have been going through the drive. He made it to the corner of the house. He stood and listened for any sounds. Then crouched and snuck up to the window of what looked to be the kitchen. He slowly peaked in the window. He saw no movement. The kitchen was disheveled, like someone had ransacked it. He investigated the living area as far as he could through the curtains. He could tell the chair and a table with a lamp on it had been thrown in the middle of the room.

He continued to the back door, wiping the mud that had accumulated on his shoes. He turned the knob and opened the door. Looked over where the boys were and motioned them to stay and give him a minute. He walked in the door, tracking the floor with mud. He walked into the living room. Everything was flipped over the furniture laying on its side. He went room by room to see if anyone was there. Each room was in a total mess. Mattresses tossed around clothing from the dress thrown all over the floor.

Once he knew the house was clear, he went to the back door, whistled, and motioned for the boys to come. He pointed towards the barn to indicate take the same route he did.

The boys got to the house; Jay met them at the door. "Take off your muddy shoes," he told them, like they were little kids. Jay told each person to go to a different room and look thoroughly through it. They found clothing that would fit them and changed out of their muddy clothes. Jay and Jordan had the same size feet and found shoes that fit. But Dre's and Nick's feet were too big, and Adam's feet too small. They would have to clean the mud off their shoes and let them dry.

In the back closest on the top shelf, Jay found a shotgun with several boxes of shells. "They must have missed this one," he said with a big smile, bringing it to the living room.

"Let's see if we can find some food," he said as they looked around the kitchen. Everything had been tossed out of the kitchen cabinets and they found no food. "I wonder if they have a cellar?" Jordan asked as he slipped his muddy shoes back on and went outside.

He walked around the side of the house and saw 2 wooden doors on the ground. He opened them and there were steps leading down under the house, but at the bottom of the steps was water. "It looks like it flooded," he said, not wanting to go down to look. Jordan hated spiders and snakes and knew that was a breeding ground for them.

Looking over to the side of the house, he saw a small greenhouse. "Maybe there are some vegetables still," he said as he started walking towards it. Opening the door, he saw several plants. They were all dried up and dead. He looked around and didn't find anything that was edible. He walked back out of the door and saw a garden a little way back. He saw several plants but wasn't sure what they were. He walked over and pulled one plant up out of the ground. It was a potato. Small but in decent shape. He pulled several more out of the ground, carrots as well.

Standing up, he heard a noise. He looked to the back side of the barn and noticed some chickens. He put the potatoes down on the ground and walked towards the chickens. There was a small chicken coop next to the barn. He had an idea. He ran back to the pile of potatoes and picked them up, and then ran to the house. "Jay," he yelled, all out of breath. "I found some potatoes and carrots," he said, throwing them in the sink. "I also saw some chickens. There were eggs laying all around." Jordan said. "Who knows how long the eggs have been there? We would be safer catching us a chicken and cook him," Jay said. As they all looked at the stove. "Propane let's see if it will light," Jay said as he walked over to the stove.

On the back of the stove was a box of matches. Jay stuck it on the box, turned on the burning and stuck the match in it. The flames came to life. "Yay," they all said at once. "Here's a big pot," as Dre, picked up a pot from the floor and handed it to Jay. "But who's gonna kill the chicken and take the feathers off?" he asked, looking at Jay. Jay looked at Jordan. "Don't look at me. I don't kill animals, I heal them," Jordan said with a smile. Jay then looked at Nick. "Nope, Nope," Nick said with his hands up. "I'll do it," Adam spoke up. "I used to watch my grandma do it when we visited them on the farm," he said.

Adam and Dre went out to catch one of the chickens. "Since you're already muddy, can you go see if there is a well outside for water?" Jay asked Jordan. Jordan shook his head, grabbed the pot, and went back out the door.

After about an hour, Adam brought a dead naked chicken into the house. Nick and Jordan starred at the naked chicken with no head. Jay grabbed the chicken and gutted it, put it in the pot of water Jordan had found and put it on the stove. Nick had found a knife on the floor and cut up the potatoes and carrots after washing them in a bucket of water and put them in with the chicken.

While the dinner was cooking, they picked up the furniture and put it back in its place. Searched the house for any more guns and ammo, only finding one shotgun and a couple boxes of shells. Jordan took the bucket back out to get more water so they could boil it and have it for drinking. As he was standing there, he heard a noise coming from the tree line. He slowly put the bucket down and ran to the house.

"Jay, Jay," he yelled. Jay got up from the couch and ran to the back door. "What?" he replied. "I heard a noise. I think someone is in the tree line," Jordan said, all out of breath. Jay hurried back to the sofa and grabbed the shotgun, loaded it with two shells, and went to the window that faced the tree line. The house was dark inside with no lights and the sun was shining in from the west, hitting the windows, so the sun reflected on us. Nick and Dre went to the back door, shut it and looked out the kitchen window. Jordan and Adam watched the front of the house. Jay sat there for several minutes, looking for any movement at all.

The sun was going down behind the trees, casting shadows across the yard. Then he saw two shadows coming out from the trees, one running and one limping over to the tractor. "I think it's' Sam and Junior," Jay said, as he walked to the back door. He opened the door and waited. He then saw the two figures run for the barn. "Sam!" Jay yelled.

Sam and Junior walked out of the barn door. "Jay, is that you?" Sam yelled. "Yeah, come on up to the house," Jay yelled, holding the door open. Junior helped Sam into the house. "Dad!" Adam yelled, running to his dad and brother, wrapping his arms around them. "Help me get him to the sofa," Junior said. "We need to get that wound cleaned up and some clean bandages," Jay said. "Go get the water," Jay said to Jordan as he ran out the door to get the bucket, he had left out there. Jay cleaned Sam's wound and dressed it. Then gave Sam and Junior some clean dry clothes.

The chicken soup was nice and hot. They all sat around the living room not saying a word, just slurping down the chicken soup. After dinner, they moved mattresses and blankets into the living room, so they could all sleep in the same room. They had found several candles and lit them around the room. Jay kept the gun close as they all talked about their families and made plans for what to do next. "I'm going to keep taking watch tonight," Jay said. "I can help," Jordan said. "I'll wake you in a couple of hours to take over watch," Jay said. "Okay, everyone else, get some sleep. We need to get going in the morning," Jay said.

Day 15 D'Ann

The dogs started stirring, showing they wanted to go out and go potty. I reluctantly got out of bed and opened the door for them to go out. I waited for Brooklyn to stand at the door and bark so I could let them back in. They came running back in and stood at the kitchen cupboard where they knew their snacks would be. But this was a different RV; I had no treats. I walked right past them. They just looked at me like "What the heck, lady? You forgot something." I laughed at them and told them to get in bed. They all jumped on the bed except for Brooklyn. She was too fat. I had to bend down and pick her up and put her on the bed. We got back under the covers as I thought about Jay and the life we had in Las Vegas. I thought about Nadia and Benny and if they made it to their family and if they were still safe. Wondering if someday I would see them drive in the drive.

I heard a small knock on the door, but I didn't want to get out of bed to answer it. I covered my head again with the blanket. "DAnn?" a small voice came down the hallway. Casey tip toed to the bedroom. The dogs were excited to see her and crawled out from under the blanket. "DAnn, you awake?" I took the blanket off my head. "Yeah," I said, looking up at her. "Are you okay? I'm worried about you," she said. "The best thing you can do for me is look after my mom and dogs like you have been. It helps me tremendously," I said. "I know it's early, but do you want breakfast or anything I can get you?" she asked. I thought for a moment, "Is there any diet coke left in the house?" I asked. "I could use a diet coke," I replied. "I'll go check," she said as she walked down the hallway and out the door.

Several minutes later, she came back with a cold diet coke. "Thank you," I said as she handed it to me. "If you could take Lil Man and Tator, Brooklyn will stay with me. I think I'm just going to go back to sleep. I have a horrible headache," I lied. "Oh, Okay. I'll make sure no one bothers you," she said as she walked back down the hallway. "Come on Lil' Man, Tator, let's go, let mama sleep," she said to the dogs as they jumped down and followed her out the door. Just like I suspected, Brooklyn didn't move. She stayed with me, as I put the blanket over my head again, not wanting to deal with the day and eventually falling back asleep.

I woke up to the sound of kids yelling and screaming outside. I sat up and looked out the window. The bigger kids were chasing the smaller kids' play tag. I stretched and looked at Brooklyn. "I guess we better get up," I said. I got up, changed my clothes and we went out the door. The weather was warm. The sun is shining. I knew winter was coming, but I loved these warm days before it got bitterly cold. It snowed sometimes in this part of Texas. It never lasted long before it melted away. But I hoped those days were still a few weeks away.

I walked up the path to my mom's cabin. She was sitting in the rocking chair on the porch. Last year when we built the cabins, we made a side trip and went to Cracker Barrel and picked up 10 wooden rocking chairs for the porches of the cabins.

"Hello, watcha doin?" I asked. "You see it? This is what I'm doing," she replied. I sat down in the rocking chair next to her. We both just stared out into the yard. "Do you think you could take me back to my house to get a few things? We were in such a hurry to get out and get here. I forgot your dad?" she asked, breaking the silence. I looked at her as she looked at me for an answer. "It's only a couple hour drive," she said. I giggled a little. "You forgot Dad!" I said, shocked but amused. She shrugged her shoulders like she didn't know what to say. I sat a few more moments without saying anything, trying to think of a reason why we couldn't do it. "I guess we could do that.

I don't see why not. I'll check with Nate to see if he can go with us just in case we need a man," I said. "I think we must go to town and get more diesel, though. Let me go check. Be right back," I said, getting up out of the chair.

I walked to the barn where I heard the men talking. Nate, Doug, and Sean were working on the ATVs. "Hello, Nate. Can I talk to you for a second?" I asked. Nate looked up and walked towards me. We walked outside. I turned and looked at him. "My mom needs to go back to her house to get a few things. One thing in particular is my dad," I said with a smile on my face. "She forgot your dad?" he asked with a puzzled look on his face. I shook my head and smiled. "Will you go with us? I think we need a man with us just in case," I asked.

We walked back into the barn. Nate walked over to the cans of diesel. 3 were full. "This is diesel for the trucks, right?" Nate asked Doug. "Yeah, what's up?" Doug asked. "We need to borrow the truck for a while," Nate said. "I'll make sure we get more diesel before we come back," I added. "Yeah, go ahead," Doug replied, not asking any questions.

Nate and I carried the three cans to the truck and filled it up. We placed the cans in the back so we could get more. "If we leave now, we could be back before dark," I said. "I'm ready. Go get your mom. I'll pull around to the driveway," he said.

I walked to my mom's cabin. "You ready? If we leave now, we can make it back before dark," I said. She walked over and grabbed her purse. "I don't think you need that," I said again with a smile on my face. "True, guess I'm just used to carrying it everywhere I go," she replied. She fished around in her purse and pulled out her keys, then put her purse under her bed, pet Gracie on the head and told her to be good. "I'll go tell Casey to let her out to potty," I said as I walked over to where Casey and the kids were playing.

"Casey, can you let Gracie out to potty later? We will be back in just a little bit," I asked. "Can I go with you? I've been stuck here for weeks. She looked at the children and said she needed a break. "I can let Gracie out and the other dogs," Ashlyn said, sitting nearby with the older dogs laying in the grass. "Are you sure?" I asked. "We should be back before dark," I said. "No problem," Ashlyn replied.

"You ready? I asked Casey. We walked towards the truck; she was so excited about getting out. We climbed into the back seat. "Casey's going with us for labor work," I said, smiling at Casey. "You mean I have to work?" she asked, laughing.

I opened the big gate as Nate drove through. We got to the highway, noticed a couple of older vehicles driving towards Henderson. We pulled out and headed towards Tyler. To get to my mom's house on Lake Fork, we would have to drive through Tyler. It would be interesting to see what was going on in Tyler now. It had been 30 days since the event happened. The people that were prepared for such an event would have survived, but millions of people would not. They would have starved to death or died from a lack of water. Some would have met a much worse fate. The militia and gangs would have killed many.

The National Guard and other branches of the military were now in place in the cities, securing them. Except for the militias that were posing as military and taking our men. But from what we were told, the National Guard was closing in on them.

On the highway, we passed several vehicles, even many ATVs and motorcycles. The closer we got to town, we saw a few bicycles, even saw a couple people on horseback. "People must have figured out how to get things running," I said to break the silence. "They probably had too, to get to town to keep from starving," Nate replied. "That's probably true," I agreed.

We got to the loop that went around Tyler. "We should still be on alert. Keep our eyes open," Nate said. We drove past stores that had windows broken out. Some looked like the owner may have cleaned it up, but nothing could be seen in the stores. The loop took us through a couple of neighborhoods. The scene brought me back to Las Vegas. Some houses were boarded up, some with just windows broken out. A couple looked like people were still living there. They had makeshift bars on the windows and had put a fence with razor wire on the top around their yards. The tops of the windows were boarded up, but looked like holes to peek out of, or to put a gun out.

We finally got to highway 69 that took us north out of town and towards Lindale and Mineola. We stayed alert as we traveled down the highway. Once we got to Mineola, we turned off on highway 37, towards Quitman.

Quitman was a small town, but the closet town to my parents' and brother's house. They didn't have a Wal-Mart, just a grocery store and a few smaller mom and pop stores. As we pulled up to the intersection of highway 37 and 154, both my mom and I looked out the right side of the window, just like we did every time we came to this intersection.

Highways 154 and 37 made a T, 37 went north and south and 154 dead ended at 37 and then went west. At the T, a carpet store had once been in the building. The windows had been boarded up. With parking in the front of the store.

Almost 14 years ago, my dad had parked his car, walked up to the sidewalk, and stood in front of his car looking in the carpet store window. Before my dad knew what hit him, literally, an 18-wheeler ran the red light hit the back of his car. The car hit my dad and threw him into the plate-glass window. His face hit a pole inside the store. They rushed him to the hospital. He survived the injuries, only to pass away 5 years later from cancer. Now we were going to rescue him from the house. Hopefully, he would still be there, right where my mom left him.

Driving down the county road, my brother's house was just a ½ mile out of the way. "Can you take the next right? I wanna check Jace's house," my mom asked Nate. He turned drove to his driveway. The place where Jace and Peggy had built their house was my dad's old shop area. It had a huge garage and a couple of outbuildings. He had put a 6ft tall chain-link fence with two big gates around the 1-acre property.

The gates were securely locked with a heavy-duty padlock and chain. We stopped in front of the gates. We looked around. The house was still secure. But it didn't look like Jace had been there for a long time, either. The grass was overgrown, and their driveway, which they had not put rocks on before the event, was still mud with no tracks.

Nate backed out and turned around to head to my mom's house, which was only 5 more miles down the county road. The area where my parents lived was on a dead-end cul-de-sac with nice big expensive homes. My mom knew most all her neighbors. "I wonder if they left or if they are okay. They could fish for food and there are plenty of deer," she said as we passed by. "Maybe we can check on them?" she asked. "Let's get everything you need, get it loaded, and then we can check on them." I said.

Nate pulled into her driveway. The house looked intact, there were no broken windows, and the front door was still locked. We entered the house besides dust and a couple spider webs. It looks just like she left it. She walked into her sunroom and came out with a round container, which I knew was my dad. "I can't believe you forgot him," I said as she handed him to me. I took him out to the truck and set him on the seat. "Dad, I'm so glad you don't have to live through the hell we are living through now," I said. Casey came out with her arms full of clothing. "She said we might be able to trade these," as she put them in the back seat.

We walked back to the house together, just as Nate was walking out with a box full of shampoos, soaps, and toiletries. "Let's get the pillows and blankets," I said. My mom was boxing up her pictures and memorabilia that she and my dad had gotten on their many travels.

We walked around the house looking for anything that could be of use at the deer lease. Nate took the last box out of the truck and put it in the bed of the truck. Before he turned around, he heard a gun cock. "Turn around," he heard a man's voice say.

Nate slowly turned around with his hands up. "What are you doing in that house?" he asked. "We are here with Kay getting some of her stuff," Nate said, not taking his eyes off the gun. "Kay's here?" the man asked. "Kay?" the man yelled. My mom came out of the house. "Dean? I'm so glad to see you are okay," my mom said, walking over to Dean and giving him a hug. Dean put the gun down. "Is Charlene, okay?" Kay asked. "Yeah, she is up at the house," he replied. "You need to go see her," he added. "Go ahead, we are about done," Nate said as he walked back to the house.

I walked with my mom and Dean to his house next door. "Are Keith and Beth, okay?" Kay asked. They were the neighbors that lived directly across the street from Dean and Charlene. "Yeah, their son came and got them."

"Our daughter and grandkids made it here," Dean said as we walked through the door. "Charlene, we have company," Dean yelled. Charlene walked around the corner from their kitchen. "Kay!" Charlene yelled as she hugged Kay. "D'Ann, it's so good to see you made it here from Las Vegas. We were worried," Charlene said. "Here, sit down," she added. "We can't stay long. We wanna get back before dark," I said. We sat and told them everything that was going on, from our trip here from Vegas to the trip down to Galveston, and even about the men and what we were told about the military.

"Wow!" Dean said. "We've run off a few people, but for the most part, people haven't come down here. We fish every day, and remember the deer we weren't supposed to feed or kill? Well, we have a generator and keep a good supply of venison in the freezer," Dean said with an evil grin on his face. "That's great. I'm glad you guys are doing okay," Kay said. "I got that old car that you gave us when Gene died, going. We go to town occasionally. There is a Red Cross tent in the grocery store parking lot. They set up some kind of exchange program," Dean said. "They did that also in the town close to us. Do you have a pen and paper? I'm going to write you instructions on how to get to our place if things get terrible," I said.

"Well mom, we better get going if we're going to make it back before dark," I said getting up. "Thank you so much for looking after my house. Hopefully, we will be back in it soon," Kay said. "I hope so. We miss you," Charlene said as she gave Kay a hug. "Be safe," I said as I hugged them, and we walked out the door.

The truck was loaded. Kay locked the front door, and we all climbed into the truck. Driving back to Quitman, I asked if we might stop at the exchange and see if we could get the cans filled with diesel. Everyone agreed, pulling into the parking lot. We saw the Red Cross tent hooked to the grocery store. Off to the side was the National Guard. "I wanna go talk to them," pointing towards the Guard Tent. "I'll catch up with you in a second," I said as I walked toward the tent.

A soldier was standing outside the doorway. "Can I help you, ma'am?" he asked. "I just have a question. The National Guards told me about the militia groups that were taking men. My husband, son and nephew are the ones that were taken. Can you tell me if you guys are still looking for them? My family was taken over by Livingston, so I'm sure it's not in your area, but do you have any information you can give me?" I asked, with tears in my eyes. "Let's go talk to my captain," he said as I followed him inside.

He explained to the captain what I had told him. "I'm sorry. I wish I could tell you something good. We are mostly clearing out the groups down in this area. We haven't got any information on the militia groups up there. Your best bet is to go back to the ones you talked to before. They may have more information," the captain said. "Thank you, I will," I replied.

I walked out of the tent and saw Nate carrying two of the cans into the tent. I caught up to him as we walked to an area that went out to a garden center area. My mom and Casey were there and handed the man filling gas cans up a couple of vouchers. "Where did you get those?" I asked as I walked up. "Your mom traded some of her clothing and shoes," Casey said. "I still have a couple left. Do you wanna go shopping?" my mom asked with a smile on her face.

While Nate filled up the cans with diesel, my mom, Casey and I walked around looking at everything. "Oh, my goodness," I said, seeing cases of Diet Coke and other sodas. "Let's go see how much they want," my mom said. We walked up and asked the man standing there. "Where did all this come from?" I asked. "We got it from the coca cola plant outside of Tyler," he said. My mom handed him a voucher. He looked at it and said you can get 3 cases. "Wow!" I replied. Casey helped me carry 2 cases of Diet Coke and a Case of Mountain Dew to the truck. "I better stay out here and keep an eye on stuff, go ahead and see if my mom needs any help," I said to Casey as she went back inside.

Nate carried the two cans out to the truck; he poured one into the truck and put the other in the bed of the truck. "It's getting late, we better get going," he said. "If you stay here and keep an eye on the truck, I will go get my mom and Casey," I said.

I went inside as my mom and Casey were heading out, each with a sack of junk food. "Okay," I said, shaking my head yes and smiling. We all jumped in the truck and headed out of the drive. "Who wants a Twinkie?" my mom said, opening a box of twinkies. We all said yes at the same time. It had been a long time since we had junk food. "The box said that they had expired a couple weeks ago, but they still feel soft," she said. "I don't care. Give me one," I said, smiling. I took the first bite; it was like heaven. Casey and I smiled as we gobbled them down.

We finished the entire box by the time we got to the Mineola. The sun had just set behind the trees. The sky had turned into an orange and purple glow. We weren't seeing as many vehicles on the road now. "Hey, look up ahead," Nate said, getting all of our attention. Halfway between Mineola and Lindale, the military was setting up another roadblock. "That is an odd place to put a roadblock," I said. I slid my gun under the stuff sitting on the seat between Casey and me.

Nate stopped the truck at the barricade. The soldier said the same thing the soldier said when they took the guys. "Can I see your driver's license?" the soldier asked. "Why, why do you need to see my driver's license? Nate asked. "We need to prove you are over 50 years old," the soldier said. Nate looked back at me. I looked out the front windshield and saw there was no soldier standing in front of us. "GO!" I whispered to Nate. "Hang on, everyone," I yelled as Nate stepped on the gas. The truck busted through the wooden barricade as we sped off. I looked out the back window, expecting a gunshot or a soldier to run and jump in their jeep and come after us. But the soldier just stood there looking at us to drive off.

Nate didn't let off the gas till we got to Lindale. Squealing around the corner, turning into the grocery store where we saw the National guard. He drove right up to the tent. Several soldiers came running out of the tent with their guns in hand. "Sir, Sir, what the hell are you doing? Get out of the truck," the soldier said with his gun pointed at Nate.

"I'm sorry, I'm sorry, we had to get here. There is a militia group set up just 5 miles north. They stopped us and said the same thing about the group that took our men. They are just setting it up," Nate explained, all out of breath. Several of the soldiers had heard what he was saying and ran into the tent. About 5 minutes later we saw 2 large jeep and a big truck speed out from behind the tent.

"How many men did you see?" he asked. Nate turned to look at me again. About 5 weren't there?" he asked. "I think that is what I saw. We busted through their barricades to get to you," I said. "We will take care of it," the soldier replied. "But next time don't come barreling at us like that, you just about got shot," he said.

"I'm sorry," Nate replied. We sat there trying to collect ourselves. Mom and Casey really didn't understand what was going on. They just sat there, terrified. I explained to them those were not real military. They are a militia group that are taking the men, forcing them to join their group or they are being killed. I explained they were trying to take over the United States. "We don't know if the government is responsible for them or what," I said.

Once we composed ourselves, Nate drove out of the drive and towards Tyler. "After that, you got any more junk food in your bag. I think I need some," I said as we all let out nervous laughs.

We made our way around the loop back to highway 110, which would take us to 79 and then back to the deer lease. As we got to Highway 110, we spotted a Red Cross tent in the Wal-Mart parking lot, just like all the others. There was also a National Guard and Army Tent next to it. The Red Cross looked like they were closing up for the evening, as we drove by. "I sure hope they got those guys, so no one else falls for their crap," I said.

The night was black now as we drove home. I leaned my head back on the window, closed my eyes, and thought about Jay. Wondering what he was doing now, hoping he was safe and warm. Even though it was still warm during the days, the nights were getting chilly.

We got to the lease early evening. Took the items my mom wanted to her cabin and put the other things she brought for trading in the storage shed. I helped her put her things away and sat my dad on the little dresser we had gotten from one of the farmhouses. "After the day we've had, I think I'm going to go curl up with a book. Good night, I'll see you in the morning," I said as I walked towards the trailer. When I got to the front of the house, I noticed Nate sitting on the porch talking with Doug, Sean, Barb, and Andie. I walked over to them and sat down in a chair. "How are you doing?" Andie asked.

"Not good. I must keep busy, so I don't break down completely. I want to go to town tomorrow and see if the National Guard has any news on the guys," I said. "I want to go with you," Sean said. "Okay, I'll see you in the morning. Good night," I replied.

CHAPTER SIXTEEN

Jordan

DAY 16 Jay

Right before dawn, Jay whispered to Jordan he was going outside to walk around the house. "I'll come with you," Jordan replied. They slipped out the back door. The sky was still black, but a sliver of sunlight shone on the horizon. As they rounded the side of the house, they saw a light coming from the forest. Jay stopped at the corner of the house. Jordan stopped right behind him, almost running in to him. "What is it?" Jordan whispered. "I think I saw a flashlight over near those trees," Jay replied, pointing to the forest. "Follow me," Jay said.

He ran towards the barn, around the back side, and entered the forest so they could come up to the other side. Not having a light, it was difficult to maneuver around the trees and bushes. They had to go very slow not to make any noise. They no longer saw the light, but they could make out voices. "I'm going to get a little closer to see if I can hear what they are saying. Stay here," Jay said.

Jay crept low to the ground to get as close as he could, but not too close that they would hear him. He was a few yards from Jordan but could not see him. Jay lay there for a few minutes, trying to listen to the voices. He still couldn't make out what they were saying, but it sounded like there were at least 4 or 5 different people talking.

The one word he heard them say was Sargent. Jay knew right away it was the militia group. He backed out, crawling slowly and quietly till he reached where he had left Jordan. "We need to get back to the house and get everyone out of there. Those are soldiers, and with their guns, we are outnumbered. "Shit," Jordan whispered.

Jay and Jordan hurried their fastest to get to the house without being seen or heard. They flew in the back door, Jay screaming for them all to get up. They had to get out of there, NOW! He had found a backpack in one of the bedrooms and quickly filled a couple of jars up with the water they had boiled the night before for drinking.

"Can you walk?" Jay asked Sam. "I can walk just not too fast," he replied. "Everyone ready?" Jay asked. "Let's go out the back door, see if we can get to the road and away from here before they know we are gone," Jay said as they all went out the back door. Junior and Dre got on either side of Sam and helped him through the mud.

They got to the barn and stood there for a few minutes. When they thought it was clean, they ran to the tree line, followed it to the road, crossed the ditch on to the road. "You guys keep going. I'm going to stay back a little and make sure they don't follow us," Jay said.

The men walked as fast as they could till, they got down the road at least a mile. Then they went to the tree line and hid till Jay caught up with them. They did this for over 5 miles. As soon as Jay caught up, they would take off while Jay stayed and watched.

The sun was up now. Jay knew it would be easy to spot them, so the next time he caught up with them, he suggested they stay in the trees, try to walk along the road but in the trees so if someone came down the road they wouldn't be seen.

They had gotten approximately 10 miles from the farmhouse. Sam's leg was really hurting him now. The blood had seeped through the makeshift bandages on his leg. "We need to stop for a little while," Junior said. "He needs to rest, and we need to re-bandage his leg," he continued. "Okay, let's go a little deeper in the woods and rest," Jay said.

They found a small clearing, and helped Sam lay down. Jay took the bandages off. The wound looked worse, and it was starting to smell. "I think it's getting infected. We need to get you to a town that has a medical facility," Jay said. He got in his bag and pulled out the shirts he had ripped up to make bandages. He wrapped his leg as best he could. "I think you should wait here for a while, and I will go scout to see if I can find another house or shelter," Jay said. "I should go with you," Jordan said. "No, I need you to be the lookout. I will leave the gun for you," Jay said.

Jay took Dre, Jordan, and Nick to the side. "If anything should happen and I don't make it back before dark, just keep following the road to the north, it will eventually come to Highway 7, there are a couple small towns once you get there, find a vehicle and get Sam to a doctor, and then get to the deer lease. "If I find a vehicle, I will come back for you," Jay said. "But my mom said stay together," Jordan said, looking at Jay. Jay nodded his head in acknowledgement. "I know, but we have to find transportation, or Sam is going to die," Jay said.

Jordan looked at Sam, nodded his head. "Okay," he said. "I promise I will be careful, and I will be back. We just need a car," he said, getting up. He sat the backpack on the ground, took one jar of water out, took a big, long drink, closed the lid and set it down in the grass. "See you soon," Jay said as he walked out of the clearing and back into the woods.

Day 16 D'Ann

I opened my eyes to the sunlight streaming in through the curtains. I rolled over and felt a body lying next to me. JAY! I thought. I turned back over and saw Casey lying next to me. My hopes were dashed. I got out of bed and got clean clothes out of the closet and snuck out, trying not to wake her up. I walked down the path to the shower house. It didn't look like anyone else was up. The shower was not too hot, but at least it wasn't freezing. It didn't matter, it still felt good to just stand in the running water.

I got dressed and walked up to the house. I sat on the porch swing and took in the quietness of the morning. I could smell coffee brewing in the old fashion percolator. Ten minutes later, the house door opened. Barb walked out with a cup of coffee and a cold can of Diet Coke.

I smiled as I took it from her. "Thanks," I said. "How are you holding up?" she asked. "Not good. I want to go see what the National Guard has to say, if there is any news today," I said.

We sat in silence and stared out at the trees and the drive. The wind was picking up, and the clouds were starting to build to the north. "I think it's going to rain," Barb said, breaking the silence. "Under any other circumstances, I would love all this rain, after being in the desert so long and no rain. But I'm just worried they are out in the elements: cold, scared, or hurt," I said. "Just keep praying. That's all we can do," Barb replied.

"When Sean and Nate get up, we are going to run to town. Do you need anything? They have that exchanged place set up," I asked. "If you don't mind, I might go with you," she replied. "Sure, we can go shopping," I said with a smile.

Barb got up and went into the house as I sat and watched the birds flying around. I looked towards the trailer and saw the three little dogs running towards me as fast as they could. Tator jumped up in my lap, all excited to see me. I picked Brooklyn up and loved on her, as much as she would let me. Then, from around the corner of the house, Jax and Gracie came running. "Got all my dogs," I said as Jax came up to me and put his big old head in my lap. Brooklyn did not like that. She snapped at Jax. I sat her on the ground, and she ran off to bother Gracie.

Ashlyn walked out from the corner of the house with the 2 older dogs. They didn't look quite as energetic as before. "Good morning, how are the girls?" I asked Ashlyn when she sat next to me on the swing. "I think it's getting closer, maybe a week or so. I wish Jordan was here. He knows more than I do about these things. I'm just trying to keep them comfortable," she added. "I know. That's the best you can do right now. I'm going to town today to see if there is any information about the guys. I'll let you know what I find out," I said.

We sat and watched the dogs play until we saw the kids come running out of the trailer. "I'm gonna take the old gals back. They get really nervous around the little kids," she said, getting up out of the swing. "Okay, I'll let you know what I find out," I replied.

Barb came out with some milk and cereal and sat it on the table for the kids. They had no clue that the milk was powdered milk to them. It all tasted the same. "You want some milk?" Barb asked me.

"Ewe no thanks," I replied, smiling. She laughed and went back into the house.

It was midmorning when Sean and Nate finally appeared. My stomach was in knots waiting for them to finally get up so we could go, but I didn't want to seem like a bitch and hit them first thing with "Let's go," so I didn't say anything, while they ate cereal with the kids.

After taking their bowls in the house, they walked out. "Are you ready to go?" Nate asked. I looked at him, and he smiled. "How long you been up and ready?" he asked. "Oh, a few hours," I said with a smile. We both laughed, "Okay, I'll get ready, Sean, you ready?" Nate yelled as Sean was walking to his cabin. "Yip, let me tell Andie I'm going, and I'll be right back," Sean replied. "Barb wants to go as well. I'll go tell her we are ready," I said, getting up out of the swing and walking into the house.

We all met at the truck, Nate and Sean sat in the front, and Barb and I sat in the back seat. When we got to the gate, I jumped out and unlocked it. Nobody said a word on our way to town. We watched as we passed a few people on ATVs riding along in the ditches. You could see the trails the ATVs were making all the way to town. For some people, it was their only way to get to town to get supplies.

We pulled into town; the roadblock was gone, and it seemed like there was more activity on the streets. Driving into the parking lot, there were several ATVs parked alongside old cars and trucks. "Looks like the place is getting busier," I said as we got out of the truck. "Let's go see if there is any information. Then we will take those vegetables in and trade them."

We got to the National Guard tent. The same soldiers were standing guard as the last time we were here. They recognized us as we recognized them. "Good morning," one of the soldiers said as he opened the flap to the tent. "Good morning," we all said as we walked in.

We all sat down in the chairs that were lined up against the wall. The soldier sitting at the desk nodded her head and said she would let the captain know we were here. She got up and walked behind a partition. A few minutes later she came out, "You can go in now," she said. "I'll wait here," Barb said.

The three of us walked over to the captain's desk. "Good morning, we just wanted to see if there was any news yet on the militia by Livingston," I asked. "Have a seat," he replied. There were only two chairs, so I and Nate sat down while Sean stood behind me.

"The latest news we have from one of our operatives we have infiltrating their group is that several of the men broke out of the facility after the storm the other night. The militia group is searching for them. But we have captured several of the militia soldiers and have shipped them to a secure facility. We are trying to get information out of them. For your particular men, we don't know names of who escaped and who was recaptured by them. But they are still holding up at the old church camp. We are close to gathering enough guards here and at the outpost near Livingston to take them down. That's about all I can tell you. But there were a lot more men that escaped than were recaptured. We have sent out rescue teams to get those men out of there. So hopefully your men are among those," he added. "When do you think you will have more information?" I asked. "They are sending in the rescue teams as we speak. I hope to have more information soon," he added.

"If our men are the ones rescued, can you send someone to let us know? We are just right outside of town," I asked. "We will see what we can do," the captain replied. "Otherwise, we will check with you tomorrow if that's okay?" I asked. "Sure, no problem, thank you for coming in," he said as he stood up, indicating we could leave.

We walked out of the tent and told Barb what he had said. I was excited yet fearful not to know which one Jay and the boys were, escapees or recaptured. But at least now we had hope.

Barb and I took the vegetables in and exchanged them for vouchers. We gave Nate 2 vouchers to get more diesel for the truck, and the other vouchers we stocked up on spices and planting seeds for the garden.

We got back to the deer lease and explained to everyone what the captain told us. Everyone was present, so we formed a circle, held hands and said a prayer for the men to find their way home.

Barb and Vickie made a delicious meatloaf for dinner out of some of the frozen hamburger meat we had brought from Grandma's house. It took about all the hamburgers due to how many mouths there were to feed. But no one complained. After dinner, the teens took the small kids and did a movie night again. While the adults sat by a fire and talked about old times until late. Everyone said their goodnights and went their separate ways.

Day 16 Jay

Jay walked along the tree line parallel to the road. The sun was high in the sky, making it nice and warm on his skin. It seemed like he had walked forever till he finally saw a farmhouse up a little way further. Once he got to the edge of the driveway, he stayed in the trees and sat and watched the place for movement for quite a while. After about an hour, he snuck up to the house.

The house was a small story typical farmhouse. With a big wrap-around porch, there were 4 rocking chairs on the porch. "D'Ann would love this place," he thought. He peeked in the living room window, looking the room over, saw no movement. He tried the door handle, unlocked! He opened the door and quietly searched the house. The house didn't look abandoned. There was no dust on the furniture, and everything was in its place. The kitchen was clean with a pot of water on the stove. "Somebody still lives here," he said to himself. He looked in the cupboards and found it was full of food. He grabbed a can of tuna, opened it, and inhaled it. Opening the fridge, hoping for a cold drink, but the fridge was empty. Then he noticed on the floor in the corner a half case of water. He took 2 bottles; he drank one right away and put the other in his pocket for later.

"I better not stay long. They might be back anytime," he said. He walked back out onto the porch. Over to the left was a small barn, and from the looks of the driveway, it might double as a garage, he thought. He walked across the yard and opened the side door. No vehicle was in the garage. Only storage boxes along the back wall and a workbench on the side wall.

An idea struck him. If I wait here, when they get home, I can take their vehicle when they go into the house. Jay walked back into the house, grabbed a couple more bottles of water, a homemade loaf of bread, and another can of tuna. He decided he would wait until the owners got home and then take their vehicle. He walked out to the tree line that surrounded the house to wait.

Day 16 Jordan

Jordan and the others had decided they had rested enough, and they would try to catch up to Jay. "It's better to be all together," Jordan said. Junior and Dre traded off with Adam and Nick, helping Sam to walk. It was slow going, but they were getting there. Staying in the tree line was more difficult than walking on the road, but they knew it was safer. The sun was approaching late afternoon. They had only gone a few miles when they needed to stop and rest again.

"Looks like we need to change his bandages again," Junior said, pulling out some more shirts they had ripped. He took the old bandages off and cringed. The wound was terrible, it was oozing pus, and the redness was spreading around the hole. Junior poured some of the water they had in a jar on it to wash some of the pus away. "Dad, this looks really really bad," Junior said, looking at his dad. "I know it hurts worse too," Sam replied. Junior looked at everyone else. "I think we need to hurry and find that vehicle," he said with urgency.

Adam gave Sam a drink of water. "I'm going out to the road to see if I can see anything," Jordan said. "I'll go with you," Dre said. Out on the road, they walked a few yards to get around a bend in the road. "Look, it looks like a farmhouse about 1/4 mile away, up on that next hill," Dre said. "Yeah, I see it. Maybe we can get to that for shelter tonight," Jordan replied.

They walked back to the group. "Do you think you can make it about another quarter mile? There is a farmhouse up there. We might be able to take shelter before it gets dark." Jordan said. "We can try," Sam replied. "We don't have a choice," Junior interjected.

Day 16 Jay

Jay waited and waited. A couple hours went by. "I don't think they are coming home," he thought. "I need to get going. I can't wait any longer," he said. Just as Jay was walking around the house towards the road, he heard a vehicle driving up the road. It sounded like an old diesel truck. He had nowhere to go. The house was too far away for him to make it to the house, and the woods were too far, with a barbed wire fence. Hoping it was the homeowner, he just stayed put.

The truck pulled into the driveway and three soldiers jumped out with their guns drawn. "Fuck, Fuck," Jay yelled. There was still a lot of distance between him and the soldiers, and not as much between him and the house. "I not going back," he said to himself and took off running towards the house. Just as one soldier took aim at Jay, the fourth soldier jumped out of the truck. "STAND DOWN!" he yelled. But it was too late. Multiple shots rang out and Jay fell to the ground.

Day 16 Jordan

The guys had made it to the edge of the yard when they saw an old truck pull into the driveway. They crouched down, hoping not to be seen. They all watched as three soldiers got out of the truck. Between the soldiers and the house, they could see a man standing there. "Jay! that's Jay," Jordan whispered loudly. Jordan started to stand up when Dre pulled him back down to the ground.

They watched as, in a split second, Jay took off running towards the house. They watched a fourth soldier get out of the driver's seat and yell "Stand down," at the same time two shots rang out. They watched as Jay fell to the ground. "NO!" Jordan yelled, standing up. Again, Dre pulled him to the ground. "QUIET! You're going to get us all killed," Dre said firmly. Tears welled up in Jordan's eyes. Nick crawled over to Jordan, and they cried together.

They watched as the three soldiers put Jay's lifeless body in the back of the truck. Then all four of them got in. Sam crawled over to the edge and was watching with the others and noticed the solider driving was Office Hext from the compound. The truck peeled out of the driveway and was gone in a matter of seconds.

Junior and Adam helped their dad to get him to the house. Jordan and Nick helped each other as Dre watched to make sure they were safe.

The house was unlocked. They went in and laid Sam on the sofa. Jordan and Nick sat at the kitchen table and seemed to be in shock. "Go see if there is any alcohol or peroxide in the bathroom," Junior said to Adam. Adam came back out with a bottle of rubbing alcohol. "Dad, this is going to hurt like a motherfucker, but I gotta do it," Junior said. Adam handed his dad a wet washcloth as Sam put it in his mouth. Junior poured the alcohol directly into the hold. Sam screamed bloody murder with the washcloth in his mouth and then passed out from the pain.

The sound of the scream seemed to have brought Jordan out of his shock. He got up and walked over to the sofa. "Can I help?" Jordan asked in a shaky voice. "I need some more bandages. Can you find something that will work?" Junior asked. Jordan walked back to the bedroom and found some t-shirts, him and Nick ripped strips from the shirt as Junior bandaged his dad. Sam was still unconscious. "I don't think we can move him yet," Junior said.

Jordan and Nick rummage through the cupboards and found some canned ravioli and spaghetti enough for all of them. "Here's some instant coffee. Anyone want some?" he asked. They all agreed, while Nick boiled the water.

The sky got dark as night set in. They washed the dishes and put them away. "How are we going to get out of here? Sam is really sick," Jordan whispered to Dre and Nick. "We need to get a good night's sleep, and in the morning try to find us a ride," Dre said.

CHAPTER SEVENTEEN

Finally, Home

Day 17 Jordan

Jordan woke up to the sound of moaning. He had slept in a recliner next to the sofa. He opened his eyes and saw Sam tossing and turning on the sofa. Jordan got up and went to Sam. Sam was burning up with fever. "Junior, Junior," Jordan whispered, shaking Junior. With sleepy eyes, Junior looked up at Jordan. "Sam is running a fever; we have no choice. I'm going to have to go look for a vehicle and get us out of here, or he will die soon," Jordan said. "I'll go with you," Nick replied. "You guys need to be careful but quick," Dre said, getting up off the floor and sitting in the recliner Jordan just got out of.

Jordan and Nick walked out the door. Neither one was in that good of shape, but they decided they would jog on the road. It would be the fastest way. They had almost made it a mile when Jordan hanging his head down and holding his side. "I gotta stop for a minute," he said between breaths. They both gasped for breath. They put their arms over their heads and walked.

Another quarter of a mile, they were coming to an intersection. They could see from where they were that something was lying in the road. They slowly approached until they could make out what it was. Jordan walked slowly around the scene. The three soldiers that had shot Jay were lying dead in the middle of the intersection, all three had been shot in the head. But the truck and the 4th soldier were nowhere to be found. But what was there were the three soldiers' guns. Jordan and Nick quickly took the guns off the dead bodies. They stood up looking all four ways, but knew they needed to keep heading north. That is what Jay told them to do.

They figured they had travelled only about 5 miles from the farmhouse they left everyone else at. They walked until they got to the top of the hill. From there, they could see more of the valley. "Look, there are a few houses over there. Let's see if we can get a car," Nick said.

Even though from the top of the hill it didn't look too far, it still took them over an hour to get to the first one. They cautiously walked up the driveway. There were no cars in the drive, so they decided to look in the windows of the garage. Sneaking up to the garage, they peeked in the window. "Damn it," Jordan said. No car was in the garage. The next house was about another quarter of a mile up the road. This time there were two houses, one across from the other. One of the houses had a new SUV in the driveway. Jordan and Nick, not really knowing what an EMP did to new cars, approached the car. The doors were locked. "I wonder if they have keys in the house," Jordan said.

Sneaking around the car, they ran to the front door. Jordan knocked. Then he knocked louder. He felt the door handle. It was locked. "Come on Jordan, let's forget this one and go to the two down the road. It looks like they might have an old truck," Nick said.

Jordan and Nick ran back out to the road. They could see miles ahead and behind them, so they stayed in the road and jogged to the next farmhouse. It didn't take them long to get there. Before they got too close, they ran down the ditch and into the tree line to observe the two houses to see if anyone was around. After about fifteen minutes, they snuck up to the first house, where they saw the old truck in the driveway. Once they got close enough, they could see the truck was being worked on and pieces and parts were hanging down from it and laying all around on the ground. "Dammit," Jordan said.

"What are we going to do now, I think was should head back, and maybe tomorrow go the other directions at the intersection where those soldiers are," Jordan said. "I guess," Nick said.

The two of them started walking back up the road. It took them quite a while to get back to the intersection where the dead soldier lay.

They walked past them and didn't touch them. Nick wanted to kick their bodies for what they had done to Jay, but he just kept walking.

Eventually they reached the farmhouse they had left everyone else in. Dre met them on the porch. "We couldn't find anything. There are not that many farmhouses out there," Nick said. "How's he doing?" Jordan asked. "Not good," Adam said, coming out the door. "Let go see in the barn if we can make a stretcher, so we can get out of here," Jordan said.

Jordan, Nick and Dre walked out to the barn looking for wood that would make a strong but light stretcher to drag Sam on. They found a pile of boards, nails and some twine laying in the corner of the barn.

After putting together what they thought would be a strong stretcher, they took to the house. "Let's get our shit and get out of here," Nick said. Jordan and Nick took the stretcher inside, grabbed some blankets, and made it as soft as they could. Junior and Adam were at Sam's head and Dre and Jordan at his feet, and Nick was in the middle. They slipped Sam from the sofa to the stretcher. Junior and Adam said they would carry him first, while the others carried backpacks full of food and water and left the farmhouse.

Day 17 D'Ann

I woke up early. For the first time, I had hope, hope that the men would come home soon. I decided today we needed to really get organized. Everyone needed to have a list of chores they can be responsible for. I grabbed a notebook and pen and sat down at the dinette table.

The kids all needed to do schoolwork, even though we had no clue what the future looked like. They still needed to learn to read and write. The older kids just need to continue their learning and learn new skills on how to survive in this new world.

I got up from the table and walked down to the house. I sat at one of the picnic tables with my pen and paper. Barb saw me and came out to visit. I told her we needed to get organized. There were so many of us now, and it wasn't fair for her to do most of the cooking. We need to spread out the chores.

"I agree," she said. "How are the girls? With their studies, I figured they could help teach the little ones to read and write. There are 4 little ones and 4 teens, then Celia is in the middle. But we could have all the teens team up with a little one and be their mentor. Celia could be like the teacher's helper and help with which every kid might have trouble," I said. "Just a thought. Maybe we could go into the library and see if we can get some more books," I added. "I think it's a great idea," Barb said. "What's a great idea?" Megan asked as she and Gail came from around the house.

I explained my idea to the kids. Megan and Gail thought it was a great idea. "There are 25 of us now staying at the deer lease. At least there will be when the men got home. We need to get organized and divvy up the chores. I'm making a list, so anything you want to add, just tell me. We can do this all together, so everyone had a say in it," I said.

They all agreed, "I would like to get the medications and medical supplies all together and make a kind of clinic, with that many people there are bound to be some bumps and bruises, and with winter coming the flu," Gale said all excited. "I think that would be great," I agreed. "Let's get everyone together and explain our idea, and see what they think, maybe after breakfast," I said.

We got up from the table and all went into the house to get breakfast started. "I'm glad to see you are feeling a little more cheerful," Barb said. "I am just feeling hopeful that they are coming home," I replied.

Day 17 Jordan

The guys had decided that since they were armed with three AR rifles and a string of ammo, they would walk right out onto the road. Besides, it would be a lot easier carrying Sam than trying to carry him through the weeds and trees.

Dre carried one of the ARs and walked a few yards in front, then Junior and Adam carried their dad on the stretcher. Nick, with one of the AR's walked beside the stretcher. While Jordan walked several yards behind, most of the time turning around and walking backwards.

When Junior and Adam's arms got tired, they would switch off with the other three. Stopping about every mile to rest, drink, and eat. They seemed to be making good time. They had passed the dead soldiers with no regard for them. They didn't even acknowledge their existence because of the way they shot Jay. They passed the farmhouses that Jordan and Nick searched. Everything was still the same. No one had been there since they were there earlier.

They continued to walk another few miles when they decided to rest again. They were passing around a bottle of water when they heard the sound of humming. They looked up to the west and coming right at them were ten to twenty drones. They seemed to hover right about them and then turned around and went back the way they came.

"What the hell was that?" Junior yelled. "Drones, we saw those when we were down in Galveston," Jordan said. "We better get going," Junior said, getting up. They all got up and walked a little faster this time. Once they got to the bottom of the hill, they slowed down.

By the position of the sun, they knew it was getting to be late afternoon. They continued to walk about a half a mile when they came to a big hill. "Man, I need to rest a little before I go up that hill," Adam said. They all agreed and sat down for a break. They had drunk all the water they had except for one glass jar. They all took little sips and then put the lid back on to save it. They tried to get Sam to drink, but he was still in and out of consciousness. Dre and Jordan handed Junior and Adam the guns and picked up Sam to continue up the hill.

Just as they had taken several steps, they all stopped in their tracks. An engine. It was upon them before they could react. Over the hill, a hummer jeep came barreling down the road. They got to the side of the road and sat Sam down. "Let me have the gun," Dre said to Adam. Adam was more than happy to hand it off.

Dre, Junior and Nick stood between Sam and Jordan and the hummer. Pointing their guns at the hummer, it came to a stop right in front of them.

Two National Guard soldiers jumped out, "whoa, whoa, we are here to help you. We are not the militia that had captured you. We are with the National Guard. We can get him to a hospital and get you guys' home," the soldier said, still with his hands up.

Dre looked at the other guys, not sure if he should trust what they were saying. "How did you guys know we were out here?" Dre asked. "The drones! We are out looking for the militia group that took you guys, and we saw that one of your men was hurt," the soldier said. "We can take you to Nacogdoches and get medical attention for him," he added.

Junior looked at Dre. "I think we don't have a choice. If we don't get him to a doctor, he's going to die," he said. Dre looked at Jordan and then at Nick. "Well?" Dre asked. "Let's go, let's get out of here," Jordan said.

The soldier got out of the hummer and helped put Sam in the back, while the guys jumped in the back and the back seat. The soldiers did what they said they were going to do and drove them straight to Nacogdoches and to the National Guard Medical tent.

After assessing Sam's injury and the infections, the head doctor approached the guys that were standing outside waiting for information on Sam. "We need to transport him to Henderson. They have the hospital up and running. He needs to have surgery. We have him stabilized and need to leave at once. They can take you guys with him if you need to go," the doctor said.

"Yeah, we are from that area. That gets us closer to home anyway," Nick said. "That's my dad, so yes, we will go also," Junior said. All the guys jumped back in the hummer after they got Sam settled in the back.

It only took 30 minutes to get to Henderson Hospital. The emergency crew took Sam in right away, and away to surgery. Junior and Adam waited in the waiting room. Dre, Nick and Jordan stood outside. They could see that they had brought in several huge industrial size military grade generators to run the electricity for the hospital.

There were several National Guard and Army soldiers standing around outside the emergency room doors. Dre walked over to a bunch just standing around. "Once we find out our friend is okay, is it possible to give us a ride to where we are staying right outside of town?" he asked. "I don't see why we can't," the soldier replied. "Just let us know when you're ready," he added.

Dre walked over to Nick and Jordan. "They will give us a ride to the deer lease when we are ready. Let's go see if Junior has any information," he said.

They all walked into the waiting room just as the doctor was finishing up talking to Junior and Adam. "What did he say?" Jordan asked. "They are going to keep him for a few days and pump him full of antibiotics to fight the infection, but they think he will survive," Junior said. "That's great news," Jordan replied. "You know, I never asked where you guys live?" Jordan asked. "We have a farm outside of Kilgore, just north of here," Adam said. "When he is ready to travel, I'm sure they will take you home," Jordan said. "Yeah, they said we can stay here as long as we needed to," Adam continued.

Dre, Jordan, and Nick said their goodbyes to Junior and Adam and wished them well. Then the three of them walked out to the soldier and said they were ready. They walked to a jeep and jumped in, waving goodbye to Junior and Adam as they stood outside the hospital doors.

The soldier told them he had to stop at the outpost and get some information from the captain to take to a family out of the same direction. After a few minutes of sitting outside the Walmart parking lot, the soldier came back. "Alright, you ready to get home?" the soldier asked. "More than you know," Jordan replied with excitement.

They gave directions to the soldier as they drove down the highway to the deer lease. The gate was locked, so the jeep couldn't drive in. "You can stop here. We can walk in. We really appreciate the ride," Jordan said. "Hold on, this is the address I was supposed to deliver this message to," the soldier said, pulling out an envelope. "I need to give this message to a D'Ann Zepola, do you know her?" he asked. "That's my mom," Jordan said urgently. "Please give this message to her, it's from the captain," the soldier asked.

Jordan took the sealed envelope from the solider, thanked him again as they ran off towards the house. They all were out of breath by the time they reached the cattle guard. They flew over the gate without stopping. Yelling and screaming, "We are home!" they yelled.

I had been sitting at one of the picnic tables when I heard screaming and yelling coming from the driveway. I got up and turned towards the noise. Three figures were running towards the house. Although it wasn't dark yet it, it was difficult to make out. But their voices were recognizable. "JORDAN?" I yelled as I got up and started towards them.

We met halfway and embraced in a hug so hard we fell to the ground. "Oh my God, you're here," I said, looking around for Jay. Sean, Vicki and Andie came running around the side of the house, "DRE!" They all screamed as they ran towards each other.

As the rest of the family came out to see what all the racket was, Nick found his mom as she cried in his arms.

"JORDAN, where is Jay?" I cried. "DRE, NICK! Where is JAY! I demanded. Dre, Nick and Jordan came over to me. Jordan sobbed and couldn't get the words out. Dre stepped over and took my hands. I ripped them out of his hands and backed up, "NO, NO, NO, don't you tell me," I said, sobbing. Ashlyn held Jordan as he cried uncontrollably. Doug and Barb wrapped their arms around me as we all sobbed.

Nate fell to his knees. "NO, NO," is all he could say. As Gail realized what was going on, she dropped to the ground beside Nate as they embraced. Doug and Barb helped me to the picnic table to sit down before my knees buckled beneath me.

Barb went to the house and brought out a box of Kleenex for everyone and handed me a bottle of water. "This can't be happening. It wasn't supposed to happen like this," I cried. I rocked back and forth as Barb held me.

We all sat crying and holding each other till the sun went down. I was in shock. I couldn't move. I didn't want to move. I had cried so much in the last hour I had no more tears. I just stared out in the dark in the driveway, thinking this had to be a joke. He would walk up the drive any minute. After about an hour, we were all still sitting at the tables. I looked at Dre, "I'm ready, I think to hear what happened," I said. "I don't think you want to hear all the details; just know we watched as the militia that took us shot him several times as he was running away. He was on the ground. They picked him up and threw him in the back of the truck. But the odd thing about all this is a couple miles down the road, the three soldiers that shot him were lying dead in the middle of the road. The fourth solider and truck were nowhere to be found," Dre said. "Oh, here mom, the solider said to give this to you, it's from the captain," Jordan said as he handed me the envelope.

Through my tears, I opened the seal envelope and pulled out a handwritten note:

Dear Mrs. Zepola;
As I told you yesterday, we have operatives infiltrating the militia groups. This morning, one of our men drove in from the Livingston area. He had brought a man in that had several gun-shot wounds. As of this writing, he was in grave condition and being prepped for surgery at the Henderson Hospital. Before he went unconscious, he said his name was Jay Zepola. After looking at our log, we compared the name to the missing men, and we believe it is your husband. He is at Henderson Hospital.

Sincerely,
Captain Bradshaw

I couldn't breathe, I was hyperventilating, and then everything went dark. When I woke, I was lying on my back in the grass, everyone was standing over me and Barb had a wet cloth wiping my face. She had a concerned look on her face. "Come on D'Ann, wake up," she said. I laid there a few more moments, trying to collect myself and figure out what had just happened.

After I had passed out, Doug grabbed the letter that had fallen to the table and read it out load to the group. Nate ran to get the truck and pulled it right up beside the tables.

Barb and Doug helped me up off the ground and over to the truck. "I'm coming too," Gail demanded. "I'll watch Lynn," Megan said.

Nate took off out of the driveway. Doug had given him the key to the lock. Once we were out of the drive, Nate drove like a bat out of hell down the highway to Henderson. I jumped out of the truck, still a little woozy, and ran into the hospital. I got to the nurse's station and asked for Jay Zepola. "Have a seat over here and I will get the doctor," she said, walking away before I could, as if I could see him.

A few minutes later, the doctor walked over to us. Me, Nate and Gale all stood up, eager to hear what he had to say. "Are you the family of Jay Zepola?" he asked. "I'm his wife, this is his father, and daughter," as I pointed to them. "How is he? Can we see him?" I asked franticly. "I'm sorry, we did everything we could," the doctor said. "It's in God's hands now," he continued.

"Can I see him?" I demanded through my tears. "Only one at a time," the doctor said. I followed the doctor through the doors and to a room down the hall.

I was shaking as my hand pushed the door open. Through my tears, I walked into the room.

EPILOGUE

Six months later

Spring had come to East Texas, thunderstorms, warm weather, green grass had returned. The Deer lease had become a regular small town. The men had built a small schoolhouse at the front of the property. A couple of kids from around the area joined our 5 little ones and Celia. One of their moms had been a schoolteacher in town and was now tutoring the kids.

On the back of the Schoolhouse was a small room that Gail sat up as a medical clinic. People from all around the area brought their supplies to help stock it. Gail would treat them and even make house calls for some of the elderly that had survived the "event."

Megan, Vicki, Ally, and Abby volunteered their time in town at the Red Cross Tents. Going to town 3 times a week.

Sean and Andie had been surprised when she found out she was pregnant and Gail with my help, delivered a precious baby girl last week. Andie and Estelle spent their days taking care of their babies, making homemade baby food, and washing cloth diapers.

Jordan and Ashlyn were planning their move back to the Galveston, to reopen their dog rescue. They figured with all the people that didn't survive there would be a lot of pets that would need their help. They had gotten a cargo van to search for sick and injured animals.

Casey and Jake had become a couple and with our approval had decided to go back with Jordan and Ashlyn to help them with their dog rescue.

Nate and Dre joined a group of men that would go house to house searching for survivors in East Texas that needed help or brought to a shelter.

My mom Kay had returned to her home at Lake Fork. About 5 months ago, Jace and Collin had finally rescued Peggy from the Dallas area, and after going to the college campus, found out that all three girls had survived by staying at the campus shelter. After getting to his family, he headed to his home in Lake Fork. Since they were able to get supplies now in Quitman, he took mom back to her house. About once a month I would go to visit them to make sure they were okay.

After Jace had been home a couple months, he and mom made their way to Kansas to check on my brother, Mike and his family. They too had survived with a few of their neighbors by living off the garden, and wildlife in the area. Mom learned that several other family members did not survive.

Doug and Barb kept us all fed with the meat Doug would hunt, and the meal Barb would cook. Her garden was flourishing.

Doug came running out of the house. "Hey everyone come here, listen to the radio," he yelled. I helped Jay out of the chair he was sitting in, after six months of me helping him do physical therapy he had finally graduated from a wheelchair to a walker, and on his way to a cane.

Everyone gathered around the ham radio. There hadn't been any noise coming from the box in over six months. Now suddenly, there was a man talking.

To All American Citizens, over 8 months ago the United States electrical grid, communication grid, and transportation grid was attacked by a domestic militia terrorist group. The United States has been crippled by this for 8 months now. We have lost millions of people. It has plummeted us into the dark ages.

All branches of the United States Military have worked side by side to identify and arrest the ones responsible for this Cyberattack. They will be brought to justice and face corporal punishment.

As of this week, our many experts that have been working on this night and day, have finally found the virus that caused the cyberattack and are ridding the systems of this devastating virus.

In the coming weeks, we will be restoring the power to electrical grids that suffered no damage to their substations. In other words, as the substations come online, so will your electricity. Then we will work to restore the cell tower grid, so communication will come online. It could take several weeks to months to complete this, please be patient with your local companies.

This will not be a quick fix, there is a lot of damage out there. But we are working night and day to restore what we can. This is the first step of many. We will release more information as it becomes available. Thank you and Stay Strong America!

We all looked at each other, as loud screams of joy erupted!

www.ingramcontent.com/pod-product-compliance
Lightning Source LLC
Chambersburg PA
CBHW050735230626
47052CB00002BA/277